The Dancing Water was written by my father during the
nights in 1942 when he was fire-watching in the City of
London for the company that employed him. He drew on his
personal experiences for the sectors on advertising as he
worked for Sir Charles Higham who was the MP for Islington
and was the first man to be knighted in the advertising
profession.

The book was successfully published by John Gifford Ltd and
was followed by two further popular novels.

He was sent by Charles Higham to Hollywood and the
experiences on the Normandie and in Los Angeles are first-
hand knowledge.

Amusingly the "Bobby" child was based on me at the age of
three!

 The book is typical of its era with attitudes and prejudices
which might be unacceptable in the 21st century. It is a
wartime love story with many unexpected twists and turns.

George Pickering

Contents

CHAPTER 1

BLACK sleek streets, and pavements shining with myriads of reflected lights; lights from shops, from 'buses, from winking blinking sky-signs, monotonously jerking into being their fantastic slogans of the day-creating in the gullible British public the urge to buy.

But on this evening the gullible British public seemed in no mood to lift their eyes and attend.

London's groping, striving mass had finished yet another working day. They spewed out from the doors of huge buildings in fast-flowing streams, joining the main current hurrying and jostling on the sidewalk. Fought for coveted though crowded accommodation on the 'buses; surged irresistibly into the Underground stations, draining away like the very rain water flooding along the gutters. Some, with total disregard for life or limb, darted fitfully into the traffic stream, setting drivers cursing volubly at such reckless daring, not one whit appeased by the unspoken tribute to their skill.

Geoffrey Manners sighed contentedly as he looked around him. He loved London. Even on an evening such as this, when Winter in its last dying convulsions threw up a night of darkness and driving rain, almost as if it was the last barricade against the relentlessly approaching saviour of Spring. London was his city. In some ways other cities had perhaps more to offer, but London was at heart such a warm, friendly, and comfortable metropolis.

It was good to have that sense of "belonging"; he liked to feel himself a fragment of this huge surging colossus.

With these thoughts running through his mind he drove the low, sleek car through the heavy traffic, jockeying for the best positions.

A red, unwinking eye barred his progress; he braked, relaxing in the comfortable seat. The flashing electric signs flaunted their garish appeal before him. One in particular caught his eye and he laughed quietly. Blenkinson was a fool — putting a sign like that here. It was like sending details of maternity wear to the Bachelors' Club. And yet, he mused, in this advertising business people had been known to do even that. Of course, the sign cost an awful lot of money, and, after all, Blenkinson's brother-in-law was connected with the concern that owned the site! He sighed when he thought of all the rackets that were mixed up with advertising — given the opportunity it could render such a genuine and useful service to the community. But at the moment its usefulness was impeded by the necessity of having to drag with it the dead weight of all the rackets and nefarious practices that unscrupulous persons could devise. Advertising had a long way to go before it could live up to all the high-faluting talk of an honourable profession that its prominent men loved to gush about on the occasions of their public utterances. Still, it all depended on exactly what was meant by profession. There were all sorts of professions. The oldest for instance. It was a rotten night for "them," he thought, glancing out of the car window.

The rain was still splashing down as Piccadilly slipped away behind him. The traffic thinned a little as he directed his car towards the Embankment and his ultimate destination, "The Savoy."

He parked his car in Savoy Place, and made for the brilliantly lighted entrance. The rain still blustered about him, coming from all directions as if someone had dipped a mop into a bucket of water and was whirling the head round and round. Once inside the doors, however, and the cold and rain were but a memory. The warm, inviting, conditioned-air welcomed him, breathed the whole "willingness-to-serve" of the place.

He checked his hat and coat and walked slowly to the American bar, drawing a cigarette from a slim gold case. The bar-tender greeted him familiarly, slicked a Dry Martini before him, and dived busily back to his mysterious mixings of alcoholic potions.

Settling himself comfortably on the high stool Geoffrey sipped his drink, and relaxed into a sort of dreamy retrospective mood. He was rather early for his appointment — it would be a somewhat noisy and talkative appointment — and it was nice to be able to sit here quietly and day-dream a little.

He liked this bar — it was one of the more recent acquisitions. It had not been here on the occasions of his earlier and less frequent visits. He had been only a boy then — still at school, but his father had said "We will take you with us Geoffrey. You're almost a man now, and you must get around and see how things are done. I want you to learn how to enjoy yourself!" And so, on days of celebration or anniversary, and always on New Year's Eve, there would be an early dinner at their home in Bayswater and then a play or a musical comedy, and finally supper at the Savoy.

He felt sure that his father could have had no true conception of the awkwardness and boredom that he experienced in being trailed in his footsteps.

His father had been a big man. Athletic in his youth, he had maintained his physical fitness by swinging gigantic dumb-bells in his bedroom every morning, and then plunging himself into a cold bath. He had looked upon Geoffrey's reluctance to leave the comfort and warmth of his bed as a glaring sign of the decadence of new generation. But, in spite of the exercise, Mr. Manners, Senior, had put on weight; he was by no means fat, but his large-framed body had filled out with flesh, and it had made him bulky and given him a somewhat overpowering appearance.

Geoffrey's mother had died when he was seven years old. Even now, after a span of more than twenty years, he could remember that she had been as tiny and inoffensive as his father had been large and overpowering. He remembered best her bright blue eyes, the mass of soft curls in which she had worn her thick hair of a rather indeterminate colour, and the small soft breasts against which she had pillowed his head when he had been unhappy and she wished to comfort him, or when he had been tired and she wanted him to rest.

"Pretty little Mummy," he had called her, and he had been very much in love with her.

He could remember how, when he was very tiny, she would always undress him and put him to bed herself. And then she would listen whilst he had faltered his prayers, prompting him with a word here and there when some part of the prayer escaped him. Then, when he was safely tucked away in bed, she would stand at the window looking out, from behind the lace curtain, into the garden, and he would feel happy and safe, knowing that she would not move away until he was asleep.

She had spent hours showing him picture-books. All pictures had fascinated him. When he was very young a book could not interest him unless there were copious illustrations.

Sometimes his mother would hold a pencil in his tiny fingers, and together they would trace the lines of some illustration in one of his baby-books. And when it was finished he would clap his small hands in an ecstasy of glee, and then hold up the tracing with a comic little expression, of achievement and wait for her to say, "That's wonderful, Geoffrey. You're getting to be quite an artist."

Dear, sweet, pretty little Mummy. She had been so young to die, and for a while he had wanted to die just to be with her again.

Life had seemed very empty without her, and there had been no regrets when he had been packed off to preparatory school. The big Bayswater house had been very gloomy when she was no longer there, and sometimes at night, when sleep would not come to him, he would forget for a moment and glance quickly at the window to see if she was there. . . . Then he would feel very lonely and small and unhappy, and when at last sleep came to ease his tormented little mind, his pillow would be damp with the tears that had trickled down from under his closed eyelids.

His father had been kind, but he had not had much time to spare for his son. Always there had been some new business enterprise that needed his attention; some urgent undertaking to assist him in making the money that he spent so lavishly and carelessly.

Mr. Manners had been a man who savoured life to the full; he had craved enjoyment and he had been prepared to pay for it.

After the baby had arrived he had been disappointed in his wife. She had so obviously preferred being with her son and tending his wants, to dining and wining at the gay restaurants or visiting the theatres that were the very breath of life to Mr. Manners.

It was disappointing, because he could not enjoy himself when he was alone or when he was with a member of his own sex. He needed the company and admiration of a woman before he could expand and attain the full measure of his generous, overwhelming personality.

So that after his wife had died, Mr. Manners had been very quiet and reserved for a discreet interval, and had then discovered for himself some new feminine diversions. He had not married again. He was not deterred from taking this step by any sense of loyalty to the memory of his wife, but he cherished his freedom, and revelled in each new conquest.

They were no hole-and-corner affairs that he indulged in. He displayed his lady-friends in a proud and open manner. He brought them to his house, introduced them to his friends, and even introduced them to his son.

They were usually very kind to Geoffrey, saying that he was "a sweet little boy," and that " he wanted a mother's care and love," but Mr. Manners would only smile indulgently and did not bring a new Mrs Manners to the Bayswater home.

Before he went away to school, and afterwards when he was at home during vacations, Geoffrey came to look upon these comings and goings of his father's lady-friends as a part of the daily round.

Since the day his mother had died, his father had always insisted that he was old enough to do grown-up things; most evenings they would dine alone together, and that was the only time during the day that they saw each other. But sometimes, when one of his father's friends came to dinner, he would sit at the large dining-table, longing to be allowed to go to bed, and yet striving all the time to look wide-awake and interested. He would listen to the boom of his father's great voice, and smile at his witticisms, only vaguely understanding them. And he would compare the arch-glances of his father's current conquest with the arch-glances of her predecessor.

The dinner would drag on, and sometimes they would say things that he did not understand, and his father would turn to his companion and say, "The boy's old enough to understand these things now."

Then, after dinner, they would go into another room where there was a big grand-piano, and sometimes the ladies would play or sing, and he would sit on a chair and look at the clock and wonder if he closed his eyes just for a moment whether they would notice At last his father would say that it was time for him to go to bed, and he would thankfully say his "good-nights" and hurry to his own room. He would hasten to undress and get into bed, and then his eyes would turn to the curtained window that looked down into the garden and he would imagine that his mother was there as she had always been...

He would say his prayers, as he had so often repeated them after her, and at the end he would say, "God bless Daddy, and God bless Mummy," and then he would add a little prayer of his own that he had said since his mother had died, ".... and keep her safe until I come."

When he was older he left his preparatory school and went to the old-fashioned public school in the south of England that his father had attended before him.

He resented the dragooning of his schooldays; the insistence they displayed in forcing his attention upon dead-languages, abstruse mathematical calculations. He longed for some subject with living, human interest to which he could devote his energies. He was bored by study.

It was during his holidays that he had accompanied his father to the theatre and then to supper at the Savoy. Always, there had been one of those strange beautiful women. Admiring his father; being kind to him. But by then he had ceased to wonder, he had only that sense of feeling awkward, the sudden access of boredom.

Then there had been nearly three years at Oxford — be had been happy there. He had flourished in the easy companionship, the generous opportunity for sporting activities, but he had been bored by study, as he had been bored at school.

He came down from Oxford in his third year. His father died suddenly and when the estate was settled there was very little for Geoffrey. There had been nothing parsimonious about his father; he had had extravagant tastes and hobbies. . .

Mr. Manners had died happy in the thought that he had given his son every opportunity. It was not his fault if his son had wasted his time at Oxford and had nothing more to show than a reputation for being the best "scrum-half" for years, a more than useful fast bowler, and a useful "doubles" player at tennis.

Geoffrey missed his father, but there had been no time for regrets. Life had become a serious thing — he had his living to earn.

So in this effort to earn a living he had drifted into advertising, as most people engaged in advertising have drifted into it.

As Geoffrey had not been trained for anything, and had always had some vague idea that when the time came he would go into his father's business, for a while he was at a loss to know where to turn for a job. And then, as at school, the only thing that had really interested him had been a sketch-book and a pencil, he garnered the fruits of his spasmodic learning by applying for, and getting, a job in the art studio of an advertising agency. He took the job with a smile on his lips and a sense of complete unconcern in his mind. He would not have cared if the job had been with an engineer making technical drawings of machinery, or with a publisher producing coloured illustrations for children's books. He dribbled on for quite a while, until suddenly, he became interested; he craved knowledge of the subject, as a man craves knowledge of his lover —of the past, the present, the future. He worked hard to learn, and discovered how little, compared with many of this world's undertakings, there was to learn.

But his knowledge grew. He learned of the chicanery, the bluff, the graft, the impressive but false façade that had been built up by the Goliaths around him. He cast away his pencil and brushes and "went in for Advertising." His jobs were many, and varied; he danced light-heartedly over the pitfalls that encompass the downfall of so many, until, many, carefree years after he had first been paid to put a pencil to paper, his feet found firm ground. Or rather they found the soft, luxurious carpet which decorated the office of the Advertising Manager of the British Dominions Manufacturing Corporation. "A coming young man," the Board of Directors had agreed when they appointed him; much, it must be confessed, to Geoffrey's surprise.

So here he was at thirty, tall, wide-shouldered; still playing most games competently, but now excelling at none; occupying a fairly responsible position and finding himself comfortably situated.

He had inherited his father's black waving hair, and clean strong features; from his mother he had his blue eyes, white teeth and a smile that said "Hallo" in the cheeriest possible way.

He was popular with men, and as a general rule he preferred their company. It was not that he disliked women, but often with women, especially those he had just met, there was a feeling of shyness, of embarrassment. It was not noticeable to others, but he would be aware of it, and it would make him uncomfortable.

His clothes were expensive, well-cut, and fitted him to perfection. He was very attractive, with his broad shoulders and slim hips; his dark hair that caught and reflected the light; his blue eyes that were usually smiling, but looked as if they could grow hard and cold with anger, or perhaps hot and vibrant with passion.

He was slow in making advances to women, and yet, at first sight, one imagined that he would be so different. Taking them confidently, casually ... It could be very puzzling to women — this lack of initiative where their sex was concerned. Often they would decide that he needed encouragement, and then there would be the meaning smile, or glance, or gesture. . . .

And from these smiles, and glances, and gestures, would spring his embarrassment, his discomfiture.

Women could be so quietly insistent on physical things — suggesting, wondering. . .

There were many women he had met who had attracted him very much. He was attractive enough to have been emotionally involved on more than one occasion. But they had been no more than little bright flickers of flame where there were possibilities of such a white burning heat ...

He had preferred his relationships to be on a friendly basis — it was awful how quickly women could become possessive — but there had been times when friendship had wandered hand-in-hand with passion.

Nevertheless, there had been nothing that he had even tried to magnify into a semblance of real love.

He was wondering a little about this as he finished his second Martini and glanced at his watch. He was surprised to find that he had been sitting at the bar for more than twenty minutes. He drew his slim gold case from his pocket and selected another cigarette. He flicked his lighter into flame, and for a moment he held the cigarette case in his hand, regarding it. It was a beautiful case — a present from Sir Highley Nitely. A gift from Sir Highley Nitely of Nitely Advertising Ltd., to Geoffrey Manners, Advertising Manager of the British Dominions Manufacturing Corporation. Sir Highley Nitely had handled the advertising of the British Dominions Corporation for many years, but never, until Geoffrey's advent as Advertising Manager, had the relationship between the two organisation's been so smooth and untroubled, or the advertising so consistently successful.

Sir Highley had been grateful, and the gift was an expression of his gratitude. It was a gift typical of Sir Highley, tasteful, expensive and sophisticated. The engine-turning of the case was of a most unusual design; most things that emanated from Sir Highley were unusual. Why, thought Geoffrey, even his name was unusual; Sir Highley liked it that way. The Highley had been his mother's family name, and he had been christened William Highley Nitely. So, at first, it had been just W.H. Nitely, and then later W. Highley Nitely, and now Sir Highley Nitely — the William lost far in the limbo of the forgotten past.

It was as Sir Highley's guest that Geoffrey was here tonight. In a few moments he must make his way, to one of the many luxurious private rooms adjoining the main restaurant; rooms whose names featured romantically the art of William Schwenck Gilbert and Arthur Seymour Sullivan, and whose very decoration thrilled in you some half-remembered fragment of Princess Ida or the Sorcerer. Rooms in which "big-business" so often held the floor; where deals in thousands, in hundreds of thousands were haggled and bargained.

Tonight, Sir Highley the uncrowned king of British publicity, Sir Highley the exhibitionist, the opportunist without equal, would put over another advertising deal. Sir Highley with his charm, his blandishment, his shocking sexy frankness, would cajole, and bluster, and talk, and talk his way into another enormous advertising contract with its 10 per cent remuneration for Sir Highley.

Ten per cent. It was the very heart throb of the advertising business — its strength and its weakness. Its strength because it created wealthy men like Sir Highley who could carry the name of advertising into the counsels and heart of industry and commerce; and its weakness because it exposed advertising to the racketeering curse of split-commissions and unwise spending.

2

Sir Highley Nitely waited, his expression a mixture of jovial bonhomie and suppressed indignation. His face, however, as he came forward to meet Geoffrey, beamed with its usual expansiveness, and it was with a wealth of good-will that he grasped the younger man's hand and said, "How are you, my boy?" Then like a shining summer sun disappearing behind a sudden scudding cloud, his face and mood changed, his indignation bubbled, he threw harsh staccato sentences at Geoffrey.

"Just had a message. They're not coming. Darn cheek! Who the hell do they think they are, anyway? I'm as big a man in my line as they are in theirs — aren't I?" This last almost appealingly, as if he wanted Geoffrey to bolster up his own undoubted importance.

Geoffrey murmured, "Of course you are, but they probably had some very good reason. . . ."

" Good reason," cut in Sir Highley, "fellow 'phoned, and burbled some inane balderdash about getting to a shooting party tomorrow or something — I've a mind to tell them to take their blasted contract and — Well, anyway, there's still plenty of time, have to fix up another meeting. Sorry you've had a journey for nothing, my boy, but you can help me a lot to convince these fellows; if you tell them what I have done for British Dominions, and just pile it on a bit, you know, why, they'll be tumbling over themselves. . . . So don't let me down when I do run 'em to earth, will you?"

Geoffrey watched Sir Highley with amusement — the mention of the contract had returned him almost immediately to his usual amiable self, and he could almost hear him thinking, "After all, I'm too big a man to be upset by a thing like this, ignore it Highley — they don't appreciate you yet — but once you've got the contract—"

He turned his winning smile on Geoffrey, "Care to stay and have dinner with me, my boy?"

Geoffrey considered. Dinner with Sir Highley. Dinner with this shortish, inclined to be fleshy, excitable, enthusiastic, energetic personality. As slickly turned-out- as one of his own advertisements; his well-cut suit; his immaculate linen ;his pearl stick pin in a silken tie; his fine head with its carefully tended silver-grey hair; his seeming-air of "All things are mine; ask and ye shall be given."

And having considered and the answer, being "No," he said, "Well, it's awfully kind of you, sir — but, if you really don't mind – "

" I quite understand," Sir Highley's glance was almost sly, "surprise her, eh? Don't forget, if you get stuck in town — too late to get back or anything — there's always my flat. Seldom use it now — very discreet." And chuckling, he shook Geoffrey's hand, murmured something about ringing next week to fix a luncheon date, and bustled through the door leaving Geoffrey in the deserted room, feeling for all the world as if he were the disappointed host, and Sir Highley the departing guest.

3

Geoffrey sauntered into the corridor, drawing a cigarette from his case, and whilst he fumbled for his lighter, paused to gaze at some tiny figures from "The Mikado" that postured prettily in their glass case set in the wall.

He wondered what to do. Sir Highley had been wrong. He did not feel in the least inclined to surprise any of his several female acquaintances.

Then, standing there wondering what his plans for the evening should be, he heard, coming from a door along the corridor, the hum and murmur of animated, crowded conversation; the chink of glasses; sporadic bursts of high-pitched laughter.

A sudden inexcusable curiosity to ascertain the source of all this gaiety consumed him. He walked slowly up the corridor and found that the door was partly open. He tried to peep round it, but someone apparently was executing the same manoeuvre from inside. He found himself staring into a pair of large grey-blue eyes; hurriedly he withdrew. The owner of the grey-blue eyes followed him into the corridor, making way as if to allow him to enter.

Geoffrey stood uncomfortably silent.

"Aren't you going in?" said a low voice with a soft attractive American accent.

"Er . . . No, not exactly," stammered Geoffrey, "you see I . . . well, as a matter of fact, 'I was just being inquisitive."

"But you should go in," said the soft, attractive voice, "they're really having lots of fun — lots of drink, anyway — one of America's brightest stars having a cocktail party, reception for the press you know."

"Film star?" enquired Geoffrey, rather foolishly.

"Oh, of course!" replied the owner of the grey-blue eyes, "only a film-star would rate a party like this, these days even an opera singer has to be a film-star as well, to get the gentlemen of the press and the sob-sisters together this way. But Miss Lesley Travis isn't an opera singer, just a film actress. This is her party. Why not go in? Wouldn't you like to meet her?"

"No, really," said Geoffrey quickly," I don't usually make a habit of gate-crashing parties, it's just that — well, I was at a loose end and wondered what was going on, that's all. I was just trying to look round the door when you. er. . . . By the way, were you trying to slip away when I...?"

"Yes. I was," she interrupted him very demurely. And after a pause, during which she subjected him to an apparently favourable scrutiny, she continued, "I'm at a loose end too."

And then she began to talk animatedly, rapidly, "You see I don't know London, or in fact England, at all. I only arrived here to-day on my way home after my first holiday for years" Then absently and with a sigh, Southern Italy" Then brightly again, "Just one night in London, Southampton to-morrow, and then home to the good old United States. But I would so love to have lots and lots of fun to-night, to laugh and dance and be happy and forget everything except that I'm young and that work won't start again until tomorrow"

Geoffrey regarded this fascinating, excited creature with bewilderment and pleasure. Her enthusiasm was infectious, he felt that this evening would be something very much out of the ordinary. "Would you consider me unforgivably presumptuous if I asked if you would allow me to show you a little bit of London? I can promise you dancing, I think you'll have fun, and maybe you'll laugh and be happy ...."

She flickered a quick smile in his direction, "I should consider you unforgivable if you did not ask me," she said.

For a few moments he surveyed her loveliness and she laughed up at him. Then he seized her by the arm and swung her down the corridor, "Let's go, he said.

....

Once more in the car Geoffrey regarded his companion. "I suppose as this is your first visit to London it's no good asking, 'Where to?' — however, you choose," and proceeded to recite the names of half-a-dozen of London's gayest and most exclusive haunts.

The tiny perfumed figure beside him snuggled herself into the high collar of her fur wrap, "Oh! no, none of those – what I want to do is to go to the little tiny places. I want to get away — right away — from bowing head-waiters, pile carpets, and central heating. Take me somewhere where they haven't even heard of caviar and the waiters don't flip the wine list at you with a Nothing-less-than-champagne' look in their eye.

"Right" said Geoffrey, "Soho, here we come."

4

To dine at The Golden Pheasant is always a pleasurable experience; to dine there as the guest of one who is a friend of the proprietor, Monsieur Dairieux, can be an occasion.

Monsieur Darrieux greeted Geoffrey with one of his best smiles and a characteristic jerky little bow. His "Goo' Devning Meester Manners," and his somewhat theatrical gesture as he indicated a table, was a sign to the hovering waiters that here was a special customer who must at any cost have special attention, and that every dish before being served, must first receive the personal approval of Monsieur Darrieux.

It is indeed somewhat strange that The Golden Pheasant is so little known. It is true, of course, that Monsieur Darrieux prefers to cater for the few; but it is true also that he supplies only the most excellent food and wine at the most moderate prices, and accordingly among the comparative few that represent his clientele are many who can afford more but are well aware that they cannot fare better.

You must realise when at The Golden Pheasant, that the enjoyment of good food and good wine should be the sole reason for your being there at all. It is useless to hope for a band, and unnecessary to fear that one must suffer sudden black-outs whilst a cabaret does its best to distract your attention from indifferent victuals.

Those who dine away from home because of the opportunities afforded to gaze upon the famous or to shudder at the notorious;

would find but little to satisfy them at The Golden Pheasant, for here the tables are set between high backed seats, each forming an alcove at once discreet and cosy. Each table accommodates four; more often shelters two.

Geoffrey thanked Monsieur Darrieux for the table he had indicated, and into this comfortable retreat he shepherded his companion; across the softly lighted table he surveyed her with unconcealed admiration and pleasure.

In the car she had adjusted a small veil so that, much to Geoffrey's annoyance, it partly concealed the upper part of her face, but now with a quick movement of her hand she swept it upwards, and laughingly returned his admiring gaze.

Beneath a gossamery fragment of a hat, her hair billowed out in a fair cluster, falling long on to her shoulders; a small oval face; white teeth strong and well matched; a nose straight and delicately formed; and those large grey-blue eyes. Without a doubt her eyes were enchanting, captivating; unusually large, they seemed to hold a world of changing expressions, a host of haunting experiences too wide and too extensive for eyes so young. A face, animated, mobile and dramatic.

"Well?" said a soft and enquiring voice.

"Fascinating," replied Geoffrey, and in response to her gesture of disbelief, he protested, "Really, I do mean it."

"Why! thank you, kind sir — I think you do. Don't you think that we should introduce ourselves? After all, such charming compliments from a stranger. . ."

"Geoffrey Manners, at your service," he said, endeavouring with some difficulty to make a mock bow across the table, "and M'amselle?"

A waiter, hurrying forward in response to an impatient gesture from Monsieur Darrieux, interrupted them before she had time to reply.

"Will you order for me — Geoffrey," and when she spoke his name he was unaccountably thrilled ; he suddenly became aware how happy he felt at having this lovely creature so near to him, and for a moment he was filled with the strangest tremor.

Geoffrey ordered carefully.

"That sounds lovely," she said as the waiter withdrew, "I think that French is such an exciting language for food – even though I can't understand half of it."

He found her delightful. "Tell me about you, your name, what you do. Everything about you – your lifetime in a nutshell as it were."

She regarded him with friendly amusement; he had suddenly become a very earnest young man and somehow it appealed to her. "But surely, that's asking rather a lot, isn't it? Is there a woman who could compress her life story into a nutshell? And surely there must be lots and lots of things so much more interesting to talk about than just me!"

But Geoffrey was adamant, and when he tried he could be most attractively persuasive, and he tried his hardest now. So in the end she capitulated, and though perhaps there was a ghost of amusement in the smile she gave him, her voice was sincere enough as she said, "Well, I suppose I must begin, as all good fairy stories do, with 'Once upon a time.' Well then, once upon a time a little girl named Phyllis Peters was born in a small town in America. I won't trouble to describe it, because it was just like a hundred other small towns in America. Quiet, happy, self-centred maybe, and no doubt, to a stranger, sleepy. But it was a pleasant enough place to grow up in, and in due course Phyllis was old enough to go, with lots of other little girls, to the local high school. Then, in due course, with lots of other girls, now not quite so little, she left school and went out into the big world to earn her own living. Well, that little girl was me, and for a short time I pounded a typewriter without interest but with reasonable success. My mother, dear soul, had died whilst I was still at school, and Daddy had struggled along on his own to bring me up, but he had never been strong and after mother died he seemed to get much worse, and when at last I finally persuaded him to see a doctor, it was very serious indeed. It was his lungs, and only chance was to get away from the dry and dusty little town, where we lived for so long, to a place where there would be sunshine and air that came from the sea. The people that Daddy worked for were awfully good, as soon as they heard about it they arranged for his transfer to one of their branch offices in Los Angeles. If it hadn't been for Daddy's illness, I should have been the happiest person alive, to me Los Angeles meant Hollywood, and Hollywood is a fairy place to lots of American girls, and I was no exception.

"But in the end California and Los Angeles didn't seem to be much different from my own home town. I still pounded my typewriter; still spent too much of my time in a dismal office when I would have much preferred be out enjoying life. Then...." she hesitated a little"...there was the greatest tragedy of my life — Daddy died. Quite without warning, and just when he seemed to be getting much stronger, I was heartbroken, and, truth to tell a little terrified. I still felt something of a stranger in Los Angeles and the thought of living there alone frightened me. It seemed as if there was to be no limit to my misfortunes, for hardly had I recovered from the shock of Daddy's death, than I lost my job! The following weeks were the unhappiest of my life; alone in a strange place, and without a job, I felt that the fates themselves were against me. Of course, I know now that I must have exaggerated my plight, because Daddy had not left me entirely unprovided for, and there was no possibility of my being in urgent need. But I have never forgotten those days, and even now, if ever I become depressed or dissatisfied I think back to them, and tell myself how lucky I am to-day."

She looked up from the table, on which she had been tracing little wavy lines with her finger nail; her expression was half whimsical, half enquiring, "But I must be boring you – though you insisted, you know ..."

Geoffrey had given her his undivided attention, "Please go on," he pleaded now, "it makes me feel, just a little, as if I had known you for a long time, and that we're not really strangers any more."

"Well there isn't really much more to tell. I had registered with an employment agency, and one day they telephoned to say that there was a vacancy for a stenographer at the Inter-Continental Film Studio in Hollywood. I applied for the job and got it. That was the beginning of everything for me.   I ...Well I got the job of personal secretary to Lesley Travis, the film actress. It's the job I have now and I'm really ever so happy, and I think that I have nearly everything I want."

"You are a lucky girl, then." said Geoffrey.

"Yes, I know I am .... except that sometimes .... well, sometimes I get so tired of films, films and films. I seem to get so terribly tired and sort of – old..."

"Old!" laughed Geoffrey, "you old! Why, don't be crazy ..."

"No, don't laugh at me," she said, "I'm happy now, and when I'm happy I look young and I feel young, but when I'm tired, and sometimes I do get so very, very tired, I have that awful feeling of growing old – of being old."

Geoffrey laid his hand lightly upon the slim fingers, that had now ceased their restless tracing on the tablecloth, and gave them a slight but friendly pressure.

"There's an easy solution to that, you know," and in response to her look of enquiry, "we shall just have to continue keeping you happy that's all."

She gave him a warm smile, and he held her hand for a few moments longer. They chatted away oblivious of everything but themselves. She told him how disappointed she was that she could spend only one brief day in England, but Lesley Travis, after her first holiday for years had to get back to Hollywood where they were waiting to start her new picture.

Phyllis was enthusiastic about Italy. Spring came so early in Southern Italy. It had been wonderful! There had been warm sun on the Riviera; the cathedral in Milan; Venice with its canals and gondolas and palaces; they had motored to Rome and Florence through olive groves and the fragrance of sun on vineyards; and there had been Naples and the Bay . . . oh, yes, it had been wonderful. But at times all that beauty had been marred, when one saw the dragooning of the Italian people; the arms outstretched in interminable salutes; little boys drilling with miniature rifles; pictures of Mussolini plastered everywhere. ...

For England, on such a brief acquaintance, she had mixed feelings. Her train to London had passed through country pretty enough, and to her mind toy-like with its tiny fields and hedges and trees, and such a cared-for and protected appearance; but in London itself, running from the suburbs to the terminus, the drabness and desultory poverty of so many of the tall, gaunt houses backing on to the railway had appalled her. She wasn't going to be unfair to England, she said, she knew that every large city had its squalor and poverty, but, like so many Americans, she had thought of England as a sort of reflection of England's history; of kings and castles; thatched cottages and colourful countryfolk; Windsor Castle and the Tower of London; Westminster Abbey and Hampton Court; history and tradition. Were they really there? she asked him, just as they had been for oh, so many, many years. She loved old things, old furniture, old buildings, she confessed. She told him, after a great deal of encouragement, of her own secret ambition. She told him that one day she wanted a cottage in England of her very, very own. A cottage with a thatched roof, oak beams, an inglenook, a solid oak door, and oh ! everything that really old cottages did have. A cottage of her own so that one day, perhaps, when there was less work and more leisure, she could, for a month or so each year, make it, and England, her home. A place to which she could escape, to rest and be alone; to see England in the spring. She told him all that her dream-cottage meant to her, and asked him whether he thought it was a crazy ambition.

Geoffrey thought that it was rather an ambitious ambition for a private secretary, even a personal secretary to a film star, but he recalled dreams and ambitions of his own which had been quite as aspiring as a dream-cottage in a foreign land, and in the sweet content of her closeness and listening to the soft music of her voice, he was only aware that he was glad that someday, somehow, she wanted to come again to England, and that if and when she did he might be with her again. But he realised that he had no desire to wait years and years until he could see her again; not all the years and years that must pass before she could earn a possible retirement; he wanted her now, whilst she was young and vivacious and lovely. So he started to plead with her not to go; to stay in England just a little longer. Somehow he felt that she was meant to play a very much more important part in his life than could be represented by just this one evening together.

But to all his pleadings she would give only a kindly refusal. It was quite impossible, she said.

"But why?" asked Geoffrey unreasonably. "Couldn't you get a holiday or something and stay over for just a little while?"

Phyllis smiled and shook her head. "I'm afraid you don't know Miss Travis very well."

"I don't know anything about her," he replied, and then in a bantering sort of way said, "but if she is going to take you away so soon I don't think I'd like her very much at all – a regular slavedriver I'll bet!"

A shadow of annoyance momentarily clouded the pretty face. "But you must know something about her – *who* she is."

"No," replied Geoffrey, "until to-night I'd never even heard of her."

"You've never heard of Lesley Travis? Why, she's famous – it was her party I was at to-night." The annoyance was plain now. "You must have heard of her – only a little while ago she was described as quite the most promising of all Hollywood's younger actresses."

Geoffrey looked with surprise at the resentful loveliness which faced him across the table, he sighed, thinking how beautiful it made her look, and that probably it would be the first and last time that he would ever see her looking like that.

"Don't mind me," he said. "I'm really most frightfully ignorant about the most important things – come along, let's talk about you. You are real and lovely, not some exotic, temperamental Hollywood doll! Don't be annoyed – after all there's only to-night, don't let us spoil it."

"No, it's silly of me to be angry." she said, smiling again, "only Lesley is rather sweet, and when you've lived, talked and almost breathed films for as long as I have, well, you sort of measure everything's importance by the same standard. Let's forget all about Lesley Travis for to-night – Phyllis Peters is out for fun!"

....

And fun they had. Always, looking back upon that evening, was, for both of them, a somewhat hazy recollection of a rushing laughing kaleidoscopic pattern. Of night clubs with crowds swaying and jostling on dance floors which seemed no larger than pocket handkerchiefs; of clinking glasses which seemed to echo and re-echo into a babel of tiny bells; of men acting like girls, and girls looking like men; of a thousand conversations of which they were a part and yet had no part; of wine that bubbled and sparkled like their own heady intoxication of life and living. But always, through the phantasmic changing memory of that night, the recollection of their happiness was crystal clear. Happiness in each other; the exciting closeness as they danced; they revelled in their discovery of each other.

5

Relentlessly, it seemed to Geoffrey, the morning of another day intruded on their delight, the long fingers of the clock cast shadows on their gaiety. Soon she must go. He hated the inevitableness and finality of the forthcoming parting. He had an almost irresistible desire to plead again with her to stay. She was such marvellous fun. But, of course, it was quite impossible. You could not go around asking people to upset all their arrangements to suit you, just because you had had more fun with them than you had had with any one before in your whole life. People had to be in love with each other before they asked, or did, things like that, and he felt a little better when he had given himself a most emphatic assurance that he was not in love with Phyllis, however lovely and delightful she might be. It was, he thought, a typical and tantalising stroke of fate that things had turned out this way, but nothing that he could do would alter them, and so the sooner she was safely back at her hotel, and he bracketed her away as a very delightful memory, the sooner he would regain his peace of mind.

But it wasn't quite as easy as that. First of all he could not, however hard he tried, imagine her going out of his life altogether, and secondly, and most important, Phyllis had no desire to go home.

When he suggested that it was perhaps time for him to see here to her hotel, she was clinging to his arm, and she pleaded so charmingly for just a little longer – to see just one more place, that Geoffrey found himself protesting, with a vehemence that surprised him, that the last thing he wanted to do was to let her go – now, or ever.

6

The Bag o' Gold Club opened at midnight and closed with a service – a breakfast service, which was very convenient for its many patrons who decided that going to bed was a waste of time, anyway, or alternatively, who had no time to spare for bed.

A badly hung, artistically crude representation of a bag of gold swung fitfully over the door which Geoffrey pushed open to admit Phyllis. They found themselves in a tiny, black draped hall, in the roof of which glowed a dim and totally inadequate electric bulb. From behind the hanging black draperies emerged a negro, very battered as to face, but very correct as to dress in his black tie and dinner jacket. As he moved forward it seemed to Geoffrey that the whites of the negro's eyes and his white collar and shirt front had jumped out of the surrounding blackness and hovered before him like a disembodied spirit.

In response to a guttural enquiry Geoffrey explained that he was not a member of the Club but that a very good friend had given him an introduction.

His friend's name? Mr Michael O'Hara. "Oh, the fighting Irishman - why, certainly, sir - this way. Ten shillings each — if you would like to sign the book, sir?"

And, drawing aside the black hangings, the negro led them into a narrow passage which was in turn hung with the funereal draperies.

A mighty tome, very dog's-eared and of doubtful cleanliness was indicated to Geoffrey by the negro, who, having watched him enter his own name and a fictitious name for his companion, accepted the proffered note, and handed them into the charge of a second coloured man who had appeared like a wraith from the surrounding gloom. Without a word he led them down the narrow passage, which ended in a flight of narrow stairs. On the stairs they paused involuntarily, bewildered at the curious sight spread before them.

A vast room, of irregular shape, comprising what had once been a series of cellars, lay under a pall of tobacco smoke so dense that in the farthest corners of the room people moved as in a fog. Around every wall, and covering the whole floor space, including a small but highly polished dance floor, people sat at little tables, talking, laughing, drinking and some even snoring. White and coloured guests appeared to be about equal. But there was no segregation into colour groups; white men seemed to favour coloured women ; the white women had coloured escorts. Geoffrey hesitated — pulling lightly upon Phyllis's arm as if to withdraw. She glanced at him, her eyes excited, and drew him on, down into the smoke and clamour of conversation. Their negro guide shepherded them to a table on the far side of the room, beckoned a waiter to them and withdrew. The waiter made no enquiry as to their requirements but, setting a bottle of whisky and a bottle of brandy upon the table, which was already furnished with a syphon and glasses, moved dismally away and was swallowed up in the smoke and packed humanity. Hardly had they time to glance around them at the bacchanalian revelry on every side, wondering at the blatant love-making that proceeded at almost every table, than the lights were dimmed, the band ensconced in a far corner, screeched a discord, spotlights played upon a doorway, and into the crowded room danced the cabaret.

The floor upon which they should have performed being now clustered with tables, they danced with difficulty between and around them, stooping to caress first one guest and then another. dancing lightly away from hands which reached out hungrily to grasp them. Six young negresses, each naked except for a gilt fig-leaf, postured and capered, their movements rhythmic but exotic, enticing and yet repulsive. Geoffrey was disconcerted to find himself embarrassed — he glanced somewhat apprehensively at his companion. But if Phyllis was embarrassed she gave but little sign of it.

When the lights had been lowered she had taken off her hat, with its tantalising little veil which made it so difficult to see her face clearly, and was now gazing bright-eyed, her lips slightly parted, at the animated scene before her. For several minutes she sat watching as if she were fascinated, and then, somehow, she seemed to sense that Geoffrey's gaze was upon her; she turned to him, and taking his hand whispered, "It's wonderful and horrible all mixed up — they're suggesting indescribable things in the strangest, loveliest way — I wouldn't have missed this for anything. I've so often heard about places like this, but this is the first time I've ever been to one." And then, noticing Geoffrey's look of concern, she hastened on, "Don't look so worried Geoffrey, it is a little — er — unusual, but everything is so different, so primeval, it makes me feel as if I'm peeping into a different world — please don't be upset."

Geoffrey smiled at her earnestness. "Me, upset? You should be the one to be upset — with me for bringing you here. I really didn't know the place at all; I should have guessed, I suppose, when Mike warned me that there are some pretty nasty lads here at times — a-word- and-a-blow type — the word's usually a swear word though and the blow comes first. Mike said not start anything, because too many of these tough gents here have an itch for jumping in to finish things. But seriously, darling, I don't like your being here, and when this display of ebony pulchritude is -over you're going home, even if I have to carry you out."

And, as if in answer to his suggestion, the lights flashed on, the dancers high-kicked their way into the oblivion of the doorway, a burst of applause swept round the room dying rapidly away as the clapping hands returned to their glasses and love-making.

One there was however, who left his glass untouched before him, who gazed at Phyllis with lustful and somewhat unbelieving eyes. His very stare was an insult in itself, thought Geoffrey as he surveyed the low-browed powerful stranger. His elbows rested on the table, his massive shoulders hunched, large hands supported his chin, as he leered at Phyllis.

She became aware of his scrutiny and hurriedly put on her hat and drew the little veil over the upper part of her face. As she did so the bulky figure pushed back his chair and reeled towards her .

"Drunk," thought Geoffrey, and a little impish voice seemed to echo in his ear "Don't start anything—" The man, gigantic he seemed to Geoffrey when he reached the table, swayed gently as he stooped towards Phyllis, "Well, well," he said, "fancy meeting you. You're prettier than your pictures. How about a lil' kiss, eh?" His face moved closer to Phyllis, his hand reached out to grasp her shoulder. She sat white and still, obviously frightened at the sudden assault. As the man's head stooped low over the table Geoffrey deliberately broke a bottle of whisky over his skull.

The noise of the breaking glass and of the man's body as it hit the floor was followed by an uncanny silence.

"Criminal waste of good whisky," said Geoffrey, as he assisted Phyllis to step over the massive, but now recumbent body.

With a feeling as if his stomach had temporarily vacated its usual position, Geoffrey escorted Phyllis across the crowded floor. Nobody moved.

The immaculate negro showed them to the door.

"The whisky will be two pounds." he said.

7

Geoffrey was unusually silent during the short drive to Phyllis's hotel. He stopped the car near the embankment entrance, and she let him take, and hold, her small hands. He said, "I'm so sorry that had to happen. Did you know him?"

In the half light her beauty and nearness was enthralling. Her voice was very kind and sympathetic as she spoke, "No, Geoffrey. I've never seen him before – let's forget that part; we have so many happy things to remember about to-night." Her lips were very close as she spoke. Then his arms were about her, his mouth upon hers. He was acutely conscious of the warm, softly rounded body as he pressed her to him. For a long moment their lips clung together. It seemed to Geoffrey that the world stood still. The darkness and stillness that surrounded them magnified their consciousness of each other. Very gradually they drew apart. Geoffrey looked down on that lovely face, no longer smiling but infinitely tender. He spoke slowly, "Our first kiss – and it says 'Good-bye'"

"Yes Geoffrey – 'Good-bye' – but let us stay here just a little longer – I don't want this lovely night to end." She snuggled down against his shoulder; the perfume of her hair was all about him. He held her close and they sat silent together. Until at last the first lights of the dawn streaked the sky beyond the river; and London's buildings silhouetted against the early light.

Softly Phyllis moved away from him. Almost before he was aware of her intention she had kissed him lightly, jumped from the car, and with a flurry of the revolving doors she was gone.

CHAPTER 2

In the days that followed, Geoffrey was strangely restless. His old amusements and recreations seemed dull and uninteresting. Nothing was changed and yet everything had an air of inconstancy. He was glad he had sent the flowers to Phyllis at the boat – somehow it seemed to make their parting less definite – and yet he had a heavy, despondent feeling that he would never see her again. He realised how little he had known about her during the short time they had spent together; he had not even an address to which he could write. Not, he assured himself, that he really wanted the address .... The incident was closed. A charming interlude with a lovely companion. There had been others – they had been soon forgotten.

He did not realise then, just how much he missed her; how great the longing for her would become. He was only then aware of the strange emptiness and lacklustreness of things – without really knowing why.

And so he spent long hours alone; sitting before the fire at his flat, or walking the brightly illuminated streets, lost in the surging crowds. Alone, yet glad of his aloneness, to let his mind range free to try to find himself again, and to rid himself of the gnawing, aching emptiness.

And then one evening, among all the glittering, shining lights, a name unblinking and staring, stopped him; jarred something within him. "Lesley Travis." For a moment he could not remember. "Lesley Travis?" he said to himself. And then, "Why, yes, Phyllis worked for Lesley Travis!" His curiosity grew as his heart bounded.

He surveyed the cinema on which the name was blazoned in electric lights. The "blurbs" screeched at him, "Lesley Travis in her greatest role." "Lesley Travis in 'Path to Glory.'" He entered the luxurious and heavily carpeted foyer. It might have been the entrance to a millionaire's residence; so cunningly contrived; cunningly conceived. For such a small sum one could become a part of all this. Little wonder that millions every week lost their everyday cares and worries in the make-believe world of the films. Luxury and romance. The ambition of youth; the lodestar of half the women of the world.

Somewhat gropingly he found a seat in the half-darkness. His entrance had been well timed. A tiny fantastic creature cartooned its way across the gaily coloured screen, aided and abetted in incredible adventures by companions no less fantastic than himself. The living coloured phantasy ran all too quickly to its close; the hero triumphant – evil despondent in defeat.

The screen flashed in a momentary whiteness; darkened again to display a certificate proclaiming that the British Board of Film Censors had passed a film entitled "Path to Glory" for exhibition to Adult Audiences. Its purpose served the certificate was withdrawn, whilst in the background an orchestra, of Hollywood-alone-knew how many pieces, played with gradually increasing strength. To this dramatic introduction there flashed on the screen the shattering information that "Inter-Continental Productions" presented Lesley Travis in "Path to Glory" with Anthony Anthony. And then, some together, some singly: a cast of players, the producer, the director, the novelist (from whose original story someone imagined the film had been made), the writers of the screen-play, extra dialogue by, gowns by, the sound director, the assistant sound director, montage effects by – and many more. Credit where credit is due – even at the risk of boredom. Such a store to set by a little credit title.

The film really started. Not too well, thought Geoffrey. Anthony Anthony was inclined to gabble his lines, and he had quite a lot to say in the early moments of the film.

And then Lesley Travis. Geoffrey went rigid, his hands involuntarily seized the arms of his seat, he felt as if he had been plunged suddenly into cold water. Lesley Travis was Phyllis Peters. Or rather, Phyllis Peters was Lesley Travis. He gazed spellbound at the screen. He thrilled again at the sight of her image. Question after question trampled and thundered through his brain. "Why had she not told him?" "Why the deception?" "Why? Why? Why?" And then suddenly it seemed not to matter; watching her seemed almost like being with her again. Half-remembered little gestures which he had tried so hard to recapture, but which had always evaded him, were there again in reality. The way she inhaled deeply, and then took the cigarette from her lips with a wide sweeping arc of the hand, brought a flood of memories. He watched entranced. She was magnificent.

Later he learned that it was a performance which set the seal of stardom upon her short but promising career.

As a darling of Society faced with a tremendous problem she soared to a mighty climax. From gaiety to deepest sorrow, her portrayal of living emotions was superb. Geoffrey was astounded that the unassuming, seemingly unsophisticated Phyllis Peters could be so competent, nay brilliant, an actress. He was suddenly proud of their brief friendship. Watching her on the screen he knew the reason for his restlessness during all these past week. He was in love! In love with Phyllis Peters. Hopelessly in love with Lesley Travis, film star!

2

As he walked slowly from the cinema he thought, "Now I can write to her - ask her why she didn't tell me." But even as the thought came to him he knew that it was impossible. To have his letter opened and read by some mechanical secretary who would class it as another of the hysterical outpourings of some heartsick "fan." To have his letter acknowledged with the laconic statement that if he would send a small part of a dollar Miss Travis would be pleased to send him her autographed picture. No, that would be unbearable.

And it was more than probable that it would happen, he thought, as he recalled the case of his friend, an actor of no small repute who had created a character on the London stage. When, subsequently, the play had been made into a Hollywood film, his friend had written a letter of congratulation to the actor who had played his original part, and had received just such a reply!

He felt that Phyllis - Lesley-would not want him to write. That was why she had kept the truth from him - why she had left him so suddenly. An evening's amusement perhaps, but not a tiresome intrusion upon her life. "Well," he thought, "perhaps it is best that way."

But he felt better now that he knew the reason for his loneliness; the disquietude of his mind, his restlessness.

It was like finding one's feet upon an old and well known pathway, after having stumbled for too long over rough and unknown ground. Even though you knew that the path could never lead you to your heart's desire, it was good to have the feeling of knowing oneself and of going forward again.

On his way home he bought an evening paper. In his flat before the fire he idly scanned the pages. The one devoted to London's entertainments held his attention. Quite a large space advertised Lesley Travis in "Path to Glory." But what a poor and uninspiring advertisement it was - what a puny tribute to a magnificent performance, to a magnificent film. He surveyed the advertisements for other films. It was a class of publicity which had been outside his sphere, but he was struck by the mediocrity of them all, the obvious lack of imagination, their sameness. Always he returned to Lesley Travis ; he felt indignant that so little was told when there was so much to tell. The advertisement should at least have captured a little of the spirit of the film's achievement, of Lesley's performance. He realised from the code number that it was an advertisement from Sir Highley Nitely's organisation - he remembered that Sir Highley was the agent for the gigantic chain of theatres of which the cinema he had visited was one.

He had an appointment with Sir Highley for the following day, and would at least have the satisfaction of telling him what a rotten job of work his organisation had done in advertising this film. With this thought in his mind he went to bed. Sleep did not come at once, although his mind was more restful than it had been for many days. Lesley Travis filled his thoughts and he was glad. She had never seemed so near, now that she was far away and quite beyond his attainment. It was a poignant sweetness. He would never have believed that he could have been so happy in so hopeless a love; he was wondering about this when he fell asleep.

3

The following morning was bright and crisp. It suited Geoffrey's mood admirably. He had the strangest, happiest feeling, as a man might have who had achieved a long-sought ambition, and meant to spend the rest of his time enjoying his success. He could not understand the feeling at all. From all that he had heard an unrequited or hopeless love should make one despairing, dull and morose. Instead he had a zest for work, for life. Besides he had something to tell Sir Highley.

It was later that day that Sir Highley received him in the mahogany panelled, heavily carpeted, luxuriously furnished room which he belittled by calling his office. Sir Highley was seated in his magnificent and sumptuously padded swivel-chair, behind his broad and highly polished mahogany desk. He was toying idly with a heavy brass letter opener. His desk was gloriously innocent of papers. A blotting-pad with gold corners; a gold cigarette box; an automatic table-lighter; a fountain pen holder with two pens in swivel sockets; a siphon of soda in a silver stand with a cut-glass tumbler standing stiffly to attention at the side, completed the furnishings of the desk. And, of course, it was a very large desk, and all of its highly polished surface was winking at the electric light, which hung above, as if it were saying, " Other desks may be made to work on - but not me! Oh! No!" And it still went on winking, even when Sir Highley pushed the gold cigarette box towards Geoffrey and told him to help himself. And then the cigarette box started winking at the light, and all the other glittering things on the desk joined in, and Geoffrey felt that he only had to listen to Sir Highley talking, anyway, so that it really didn't matter, and he could relax and look round the room, and wait for Sir Highley's pretty secretary to bring them in some tea. And he realised that this was the way he always felt in Sir Highley's room. It was a nice way for Sir Highley to have his visitors feel if he was going to talk business to them, and Geoffrey wondered if other people felt the same way he did, and if it was the room that did it. So he looked round the room, but beyond the heavy curtains at the windows, and a very elaborate table by the far wall upon which a tall vase held a great sheaf of white lilies, that sent a heady fragrance round the room, there was nothing. Geoffrey decided that it must be the combination of Sir Highley and the room; they suited each other so very, very well. Sir Highley sitting behind his desk, reminded Geoffrey of a fairy at the top of a Christmas-tree, or .of one of those little figures you see right on the top-tier of a wedding-cake.

    " Don't you think so ? " interjected Sir Highley, right into the middle of Geoffrey's day-dreaming, and Geoffrey realised that he had not the faintest idea what Sir Highley was talking about, and that was awfully rude, so he started to listen to what he said. Anyway, Sir Highley never started off on the business you came to see him about. He always aired a grievance or two, or flaunted a triumph, or gave you his opinion about something or other, and if he could scramble all the things you really had to talk about into the last minute or two - well, you did not really trouble quite as much as you might have done, and there wasn't much time to argue, and so Sir Highley usually got his own way. And this time it was another grievance. Apparently some Company or the other were changing their Advertising Agents and Sir Highley had been invited to put in his ideas. Well, up to there, it had been quite all right, because only one other firm had been asked to submit their ideas, and as Sir Highley said, "We had them absolutely licked to a frazzle on ideas, my boy, absolutely licked. But I lost the account on the dirtiest, crookedest deal you ever heard of. Yes, the advertising manager of this concern was pretty dissatisfied - only getting seven-fifty a year and you know what they spend on advertising, and his firm didn't want to pay him any more, so my honest competitors pointed out to his Directors that whilst, of course, they couldn't pass back any of the commission they would get for placing their business, if they got the account they would need a new man to give them the right angle on things, and this firm's advertising manager was the very man for the job, and they would pay him a thousand a year and let him stay on with his firm and carry on just as if nothing had happened. The firm would save seven-fifty a year, so that they should be happy, the manager would get his thousand, so that he would be happy, and my 'friends' would be happy to get the account, so that everyone would be happy."

"And," cut in Geoffrey, "so as not to spoil this universal happiness and good-fellowship they gave them the account."

Sir Highley's indignation bubbled. "Yes! Just shows what you're up against in this business. Why, if the fellow had only told me I'd have given him twelve-fifty like a shot! "

This somewhat unexpected climax left Geoffrey rather limp. He thought he would try and steer Sir Highley round to the matters which he had come to discuss, but at that moment tea appeared under the direction of Sir Highley's secretary. Sir Highley rose to assist. "Just put the tray on the desk my dear, we'll manage the rest," and he gave her an affectionate little pat and watched her with interested eyes until the door closed behind her. "Jolly neat and clean-looking those white collar and cuffs aren't they?" And then, falling seemingly into retrospective mood, he mumbled, almost to himself, "It's what attracted me to my third wife - always looked , neat and clean in white cuffs and collar .... " Then pulling himself up, he motioned towards the tea and cried "Help yourself, old man. My! it must be getting late, let's see, what did we have to do? " And so, without delay, and all in the space of time that it took Geoffrey to dispose of one cup of tea, they settled numerous matters outstanding between the British Dominions Corporation and Sir Highley's Agency. The speed with which they disposed of them would have astounded (and possibly worried) Geoffrey's directors; in fact, he was a little surprised himself.

And then as he rose to go he remembered the advertisement for "Path to Glory." Taking the paper from his pocket he laid it on the desk in front of Sir Highley. He pointed to it, "You're responsible for that, aren't you?"

"Yes," replied Sir Highley wonderingly.

"Well, I saw the film last night. It's good, jolly good - and dam' well acted, especially Lesley Travis, and you, or your people, advertise it like that, I think it's an absolute disgrace, that's all!"

Sir Highley appeared somewhat puzzled, "After all, I don't see why you should worry yourself, it's not a bit in your line really, and . . ."

Geoffrey wished he could tell him what he really felt.

Why, the thing was a blasted insult to Lesley, but he could not very well blurt out, "I'm in love with Lesley Travis and you're not doing her justice." So instead he said, "It's just that the whole thing is so incompetent, why, it doesn't tell you anything at all about the film - the real film I mean. Look here, I'll show you ... have you got a piece of paper anywhere?"

Sir Highley produced a large drawing-block from a drawer in his desk. Geoffrey drew it towards him and roughed out an advertisement.

All his desire to give expression in some way to what he felt for Lesley, to that wonderful acting of hers, surged within him. His many years of drafting advertisements stood him now in good stead. His pencil flashed and turned across the paper. He captured something of the spirit of the film; something of the character that Lesley had created. Of course it was rough, but there was no denying its intrinsic merit. As an advertisement for a film it was startlingly different from any other advertisement that Sir Highley had ever seen.

"There," said Geoffrey, slipping his pencil into his pocket and pushing the drawing-block towards Sir Highley, "that's some idea of what I mean ... can you understand?"

Sir Highley seized the pad eagerly, studying it in silence, rubbing his chin with the first finger of his left hand, whilst he held the pad in his right. His finger made rasping noise on his face as he rubbed against the grain of his beard.

"This is good, my boy - very good," he said at last. Do you mind if I keep it?"

"Of course not," Geoffrey replied, and feeling somewhat self-conscious about his recent outburst, followed up with, "I'll confirm those points we discussed by letter," shook Sir Highley's outstretched hand and made for the door.

Sir Highley continued to gaze at the lay-out.

4

That evening, for the first time in his life, Geoffrey knowingly paid to see a film twice.

He thrilled again at Lesley's every appearance on the screen. He watched hungrily for every gesture; listened intently to every intonation of her voice. More than ever he knew that he loved her; loved her to the exclusion of every other woman. A hopeless love, and she would never know, but he welcomed it; held it fast, and imprisoned it deep within him.

But, walking home, he saw fit to chide himself – it suited his mood. He told himself what a fool he was. Like a schoolboy joining the ranks of juvenile minds that have a "crush" on a beautiful shadow on the screen and sigh soulfully over pictures of their favourites in magazines produced by people who know their follies; who wrote letters which were seldom, if ever, read; who endangered their favourites' very lives and limbs whenever they were bold enough to come among them.

Especially foolish in his case. To have known Lesley in the flesh and to have emerged from the encounter with his heart untroubled, and then to fall in love with her screen shadow! It was foolish almost to the point of insanity. In his present mood he refused to acknowledge what he now knew to be true - that he had loved Lesley since the moment that he had first looked into her grey-blue eyes.

5

It was just a week to the day, after his meeting with Sir Highley, that Geoffrey sat in his office gazing somewhat unseeingly at a list of runners in the two-thirty race. He found it difficult to concentrate upon the horses, because at the same time he was trying to make up his mind whether to lunch at Simpsons, or to go to the club, have a snack, and play off the third round of the snooker handicap. He had almost decided in favour of the incomparable roast mutton which could be obtained only at Simpsons, when his mind wandered back to the two-thirty race. He sat there wondering whether to put a couple of pounds on "Blonde Lady" (because the paper-boy had said that it couldn't lose) but at the same time realising that the real trouble with the horses he backed was that they just couldn't seem to win. He was just thinking that, if it could be arranged, he could make quite a nice income from owners of racehorses by getting them to pay him not to back their horses as an insurance against certain failure, when the 'phone bell rang, and after confirming to three separate female enquirers that, "Yes, this is Mr. Manners," Sir Highley's voice boomed out asking him how he was, and what he was doing for lunch, all in one sentence. About ten seconds later Sir Highley, still booming, finished the conversation with, "Right! Savoy Grill, one-fifteen," and Geoffrey had a luncheon appointment. He thought rather wistfully of the roast mutton and the red-currant jelly, and of the snooker handicap, but decided that, as Sir Highley would be paying for lunch, he would put the two pounds on "Blonde Lady" after all.

6

A wise man of Geoffrey's acquaintance had once remarked, that if he was unfortunate enough to find himself without a job, he would beg, borrow or steal enough money to lunch with some frequency at the Savoy Grill, listen to the conversation around him, and from the resultant information would make a good living. Whether as a result of blackmail or of turning to advantage overheard business secrets he had never made quite clear, but, thought Geoffrey, as he glanced around him, there was probably a living in it whichever way you went to work.

Sir Highley, true to form, had not even touched upon his real reason for wanting to see him. At the moment he was occupied in airing another grievance. "Trying to pinch my account, that's what they were doing. Blasted American Agency feeding up my clients with a lot of 'bally-hoo' talk about market research. Market research - bah! Lot of underpaid little men knocking on doors and asking if you use tooth-paste or powder, and if so, why? Rubbish! I told 'em so too! I said, 'Gentlemen, I won't spend a lot of your money trying to find out whether your product is popular in Manchester and lousy in Leeds; whether spinsters like it and bachelors loathe it; I'll spend your money selling *more* of it! That's what you want, isn't it? What do you care who uses it, as long as they use enough of it, and go on using it?' I'd got 'em there, my boy. That's what they wanted all right, finished up with a vote of confidence in me .... That's what you want in this business ... confidence. Tell 'em you know and they don't. They can't disprove it anyway.

"Now for some coffee and a brandy," said Sir Highley, changing the subject. When it was on the table in front of them and cigars were lighted, he went on to talk about the advertisement that Geoffrey had drafted for Lesley's film. It was, he assured Geoffrey once again, "Very, very good." Something new in a field which had for years been hackneyed and uninteresting. It was so good that he had shown it to Mr. Levi Shamberger, the Chairman of the United British Colossal Cinema Circuit, and Mr. Shamberger thought it was good. In fact, Mr. Shamberger thought it was so good that he wanted to see some more like it; more along the same lines for other films that would soon be showing in the circuit. That was where Geoffrey could help, if he would. Nobody in Sir Highley's organisation could quite capture the spirit of the thing, and reproduce the freshness of this new idea, as Geoffrey had done. Would he do some more for other films? If he could, and would, nobody could quite tell where it might lead, but in any case, just to oblige Sir Highley ... ?

Geoffrey had not the faintest idea whether he could do a similar sort of thing for other films. It had been because of Lesley that the other one had been done, and without her as a sort of inspiration - well, he wasn't at all sure. He could not give that reason to Sir Highley, however, and it would seem a little ungrateful to refuse without some good reason, for after all he was a charming old boy, and so Geoffrey said that he would try.

7

So Geoffrey saw a lot of films and created advertisements for them. When, after his interview with Sir Highley, he went to his first trade-showing, he imagined that he was going to feel just like a film-critic, and wondered what to look out for. Actually, it didn't turn out a bit like that. He just sat there, as he had always done in the past when he had visited a cinema, and enjoyed the film if it appealed to him, and felt somewhat bored it if didn't. Then afterwards, if it was a film that he had liked, he remembered the part that he had liked most of all, and if it was a film that he thought rather boring, he remembered the part that had bored him least of all, and these parts formed the foundations of the advertisements that he put down on paper. But it was the novelty of their presentation that made them so good, for good they were. Geoffrey was rather amazed at his own facility for the work. But if Geoffrey was amazed, Sir Highley was delighted. When, some weeks later, he examined the results, he became almost affectionate; he bubbled with enthusiasm. With his arm around Geoffrey's shoulders he almost hugged him. Geoffrey found it all rather embarrassing. He was too well acquainted with Sir Highley's sudden enthusiasms to pay much heed to his muttered, "I can keep their account for ever with stuff like this, they're bound to spend more, much more!"

And so it came as something of a shock when Sir Highley asked him if he would go with him to meet the Board of Directors of the United British Colossal Cinema Circuit, under the

Chairmanship of that figure well known in the entertainment world, Mr. Levi Shamberger.

8

The boardroom of the United British Cinema Circuit in their building (known as Colossal House) in Wardour Street, was, in Geoffrey's opinion, and, in fact, in the opinion of all who were privileged to enter, stupendous. It was quite obviously the very grandfather of all boardrooms; nothing more luxurious, or more the essence of a boardroom, had ever been created by any set-designer for any moving picture. Almost involuntarily you glanced hastily around for a sight of the cameras and arc-lights and listened for someone to shout "Turn 'em over .... "

The magnificence of the setting in no way overshadowed the magnificence of Sir Highley's entry. He swept in like a headmistress entering an infants' classroom. He gazed at the assembled Board of Directors. They were his valued and respected clients, but - was he not Sir Highley ?

He greeted Mr. Shamberger with an air of respectful equality. He introduced Geoffrey. He accepted, with a gracious acknowledgment, the chair indicated to him by Mr. Shamberger. Geoffrey occupied the chair which was indicated to him, though he did not quite see the point of making so elaborate a recognition of a common courtesy. Sir Highley produced his case and lit a very fat and expensive cigarette. They awaited Mr. Shamberger's pleasure.

Mr. Levi Shamberger was a massive gentleman. Something over six feet in height and well built, he betrayed his Hebraic ancestry only by his nose, which, though cast in a somewhat gentler mould, retained, nevertheless, an undeniable likeness to the beak of a bird of prey. His small eyes, close set, darted sudden and suspicious glances around the room. He looked like a man who was forever on his guard. He was unaccountably restless. He slithered about in his chair, resting first upon one arm and then upon the other.

Mr. Shamberger's restlessness and meticulous attention to detail, had gained for him the chairmanship of one of the largest cinema combines in Great Britain.

Hailing from Yorkshire he had founded in the London suburbs a small chain of cinemas, which by reason of their luxury and the liberality of the entertainment provided, had been immediately and equally successful. In those early days Mr. Shamberger had driven daily, in his high-powered car, to every one of his cinemas to carry out a regular inspection. Every member of his staff had been engaged personally by Mr. Shamberger. His usherettes had been a by-word. When a new usherette was needed Mr. Shamberger lined up the applicants and requested them to display their legs; not just to the knees, but all of their legs, every inch of them. Those who refused were no use to Mr. Shamberger, and from the remainder, the owner of the prettiest face and the shapeliest legs emerged in due course as a Shamberger usherette; a thing of beauty and a joy for many. A creature to be yearned for; a creature to thrill you (should you be a male) as she accepted your ticket and guided you to a seat. Only Mr. Shamberger had any true conception of the number of misunderstood husbands and misguided bachelors who visited his cinemas to gaze upon the loveliness he provided, and who later hoped to do something more than just gaze.

It was, after all, a detail, but Mr. Shamberger had known the value of detail then, and he knew it now. That was why his advertising received his personal attention and the attention of his board.

Having lunged violently in his chair two or three times, and having apparently decided upon the impossibility of getting really comfortable, Mr. Shamberger addressed the meeting in a voice which bore unmistakable testimony to the county of his birth.

"Well, gentlemen, the next item on the agenda is the question of our advertising appropriation for the next three months. That's why Sir Highley's here," indicating Sir Highley with a nod of his head. "He's got some new stuff to show us this time. I've had a look at some of it already, and I don't mind telling you that I think it's good. This young man here," indicating Geoffrey with a further nod of the head, "Mr. Manners, he's responsible for it and I asked Sir Highley to bring him along. Got the stuff with you, Sir Highley ? "

Thus abruptly addressed, Sir Highley drew, from a magnificent blue binder which he had placed upon the table before him, the result of Geoffrey's work during the past few weeks. In silence he handed them to Mr. Shamberger. In silence Mr. Shamberger passed them one by one to his colleagues. They also subjected them to silent scrutiny. Geoffrey began to feel somewhat uncomfortable. Whilst he wasn't terribly concerned with what they thought of his efforts, this total lack of comment was becoming embarrassing.

The specimen advertisements completed their journey from hand to hand round the table and returned to the chairman. Everybody waited for him to break the silence. Mr. Shamberger wriggled in his chair, darted a vicious glance round the room, which encompassed the whole gathering, and said, "Well, what do you think of them?"

Geoffrey was both gratified and amazed at the unanimous chorus of approval which burst from the assembled Board of Directors. Sir Highley expanded with pleasure, it was obvious that he regarded it as a personal triumph and achievement.

Mr. Shamberger handed the lay-outs back to Sir Highley. "Best thing you've done for us, Sir Highley. I don't mind saying now that it's lucky for you that you brought those along with you to-day. As a matter of fact we haven't been too well satisfied with the stuff you have been doing for us lately, and we have considered making a change - only considered it mind - but . . well, anyway, this new idea alters all that. If you can go on turning out stuff like this for us you need not worry about keeping our account, and, if that young man there had as much to do with it as I think he did, you'd better fix things so that he can go on doing it, because if you don't, I'd probably have an offer of my own that might interest him."

Geoffrey decided that it was quite an interesting meeting after all.

Sir Highley, who had had a very considerable interest in the meeting right from the start, boomed in his best platform manner,

"It's certainly encouraging to hear you say that, Mr. Shamberger. It's very difficult stuff, you know, this film advertising, hard to find a new angle, but we've got it here all right .... Now, about the appropriation for the next three months, Mr. Shamberger ... ? "

"Same as usual," interposed Mr. Shamberger, "but if this new scheme does what I think it's going to do, perhaps we'll be able to find something more a little later on. Well, unless there is anything else, Sir Highley .... "

This polite but obvious dismissal passed airily over Sir Highley's head, he plunged immediately into a welter of statistics of the number of free columns of press matter he had obtained on behalf of the United British Colossal Cinemas; of editorial mentions; of photos; of this and that; in fact, a quick-fire barrage of 'what-I've-done-for-you,' all of which was designed to, and in fact did, impress at least one member of the board sufficiently for him to remark, upon Sir Highley taking his leave, "A live wire that fellow - he's the man for us."

After the somewhat elaborate ceremonial of leave-taking, Geoffrey and Sir Highley, after falling precipitately down through the centre of the building in an electric lift which started and stopped with disconcerting suddenness, made their way to Sir Highley's luxurious, if somewhat ostentatious, car and relaxed in the soft upholstery.

Sir Highley sighed contentedly, but Geoffrey had a thousand questions to ask. Sir Highley swept them aside. "My boy, from now on you work for me. You're the only one to do this particular job in the way that it's got to be done. Don't bother about your firm, I'll arrange things with them, old Potter (the chairman of that so casually considered undertaking) is a jolly good friend mine, I'll fix it. You're a lucky man, more money and working for me, why, there are men who'd give their arm for the chance .... "

"Oh, it's not as easy as all that." Geoffrey countered. "There's all sorts of things to be considered, my present job, the future - I can't just jump into this without any consideration at all."

And so they argued on, as the car nosed its way from Wardour Street through London's traffic.

CHAPTER 3

1

SIR HIGHLEY provided Geoffrey with a magnificent office; an exquisite secretary. His financial appreciation of Geoffrey's efforts was more than generous. Geoffrey accepted the change with equanimity. He had ceased to be surprised at anything which happened in this near-crazy world of advertising. He scarcely troubled to wonder where this new step would lead him. Had he done so, it is doubtful if, even in his wildest imaginings, he would have supposed that he had taken the first step to Hollywood and Lesley Travis.

2

When the first of Geoffrey's advertisements appeared in print it stood out from the other mundane announcements like a blonde in a line-up of Harlem chorus girls.

Of course, his style was copied; but not equalled. In its own way his work was as unique, in its vigour and novelty of presentation, as a painting from the brush of a master. Once he had seen a film he had an uncanny facility for capturing and reproducing its strongest appeal.

His work was noticed. The appreciation of the Cinema Group grew; and so did Sir Highley's; and, of course, Geoffrey had no complaints.

But however much Sir Highley might value an account, and however remunerative that account might be, he was far too clever a man to give Geoffrey his office, his secretary, and his salary, for just drafting advertisements for one account.

Geoffrey soon found that he was handling a great deal of work which arose from many of Sir Highley's other accounts, and so well did he handle it that before long he found himself one of the most valued executives in Sir Highley's organisation. It was no surprise to Sir Highley to find himself with a new and valued assistant. He had had a pretty shrewd idea of Geoffrey's capabilities when he had first appointed him, and although the firm of Nitely Advertising Ltd., was a strictly personal business, insofar that Sir Highley liked, if possible, to deal directly with all his clients, there were many occasions when he had found himself wishing that he could be in two places at the same time if he was to retain what he described as the " personal touch in business."

But in Geoffrey he found a very able and personable lieutenant. One who knew Sir Highley's ways and who had had more than a glimpse of what he really thought, and of what went on behind the sonorous, prodigious exterior into which he had moulded his outward appearance, manner and voice. Geoffrey found a real affection for him; he worked hard and enthusiastically in his interests, and although at times he was pulled up short by some of the "ethics" of his mentor's profession, his loyalty to Sir Highley was pre-eminent. And Sir Highley, in his bluff and yet charming way, returned Geoffrey's affection. Sometimes he would watch him striding through the office, and notice the typists' heads turn to follow the passage of his handsome lieutenant; and whilst his eyes held much of envy, they were friendly eyes, holding something perhaps of a father's pride something of regret for his own youth now behind him and for the possibilities of youth which now escaped him

So with his added responsibilities, Geoffrey found great deal of pleasure and enjoyment in his work for Nitely Advertising Ltd.

Sir Highley, whilst bitterly refuting any suggestion which implied a superiority of American advertising methods, nevertheless confessed to a great liking for American office organisation. And as Sir Highley had a great liking, and weakness, for pretty and attractive females, his offices were conducted upon the America principle, and a high proportion of his staff were curvesome and comely representatives of the fairer sex.

Sir Highley was, at all times, a doughty exponent of "the place of women in business." It was a subject which, on many occasions figured as the main plank of his public utterances. Privately he was equally enthusiastic, but on the private occasions his mind was inclined to wander from business.

Apart from Sir Highley, Geoffrey found that there were only four people who really counted in Nitely Advertising Ltd.

Pre-eminent among these four was Miss Lovejoy, the general manager. Miss Lovejoy, whose duties we multifarious - ranging from office-mother to whip-cracker-was a round chubby virgin of some forty summers, who maintained under the most trying conditions an equable and unruffled countenance. Miss Lovejoy could not, even in her younger days, have risen to the standard of attractiveness that Sir Highley normally demanded in the women who surrounded him; but, against this, she could set an efficiency and a clear-thinking business mind that steered the Nitely offices through the constantly recurring periods of trouble and turmoil which beset them. Trouble and turmoil were as naturally present in the Nitely offices as noise in an underground railway or peace and quietness in a deserted church.

If Sir Highley was the mainspring of Nitely's, then Miss Lovejoy was the governor - controlling, guiding, regulating.

Second only to Miss Lovejoy was Miss "Laddie" Arthur, the production manager. In private life Miss "Laddie " Arthur was Mrs. Oswald Whistler, the wife of Mr. Oswald Whistler, the notorious and brilliant poet, who periodically emerged from self-sought obscurity with a new and scintillating offering, or a shocking and scandalous escapade.

Mr. Whistler had occasioned the raising of more than one eyebrow when, upon the occasion of the presentation to the world of his much-commented upon "Remunerated Lover," he announced that in order to get to the heart of things he had slept for the space of thirty days and nights with a Parisian prostitute, who, it transpired had had a "heart of gold."

But Miss Arthur remained fond of her eccentric husband despite his foibles, and as the financial return of his chosen labour was spasmodic, and occasionally non-existent, she had also to support him.

"Laddie" as she was invariably called by Sir Highley, was a beautiful woman; she had caused Sir Highley many moments of despondency, but she had also given him many moments of exhilaration. Miss Arthur was smoothly and handsomely dark; graceful and statuesque. She had a flair for transmuting Sir Highley's evanescent ideas into tangible selling advertising. The combination of her beauty, and her ability to convince Sir Highley of his own brilliance, proved quite irresistible to her employer.

There was occasionally some slight friction between the Misses Lovejoy and Arthur, but this was of a very minor nature compared with the other grinding discords with which the office abounded.

Then thirdly, mincing daintily behind Miss Lovejoy and Miss Arthur, came Mr. Errol Thackeray. Sir Highley sometimes described Mr. Thackeray as his statistician, sometimes as his "visualiser" - whatever that might mean. It would, perhaps, have been more accurate if Sir Highley had described Mr. Thackeray as a seer.

Mr. Thackeray would disappear with the most abstruse technical problems; the most complicated mathematical calculations, and in due course would emerge with a brilliant monograph, or a statistical and mathematical masterpiece, either of which could be only remotely understood by anyone other than Mr. Thackeray himself. But Sir Highley would triumphantly flaunt the result of Mr. Thackeray's labours in the startled faces of his clients, and by his insistence upon the infallibility of Mr. Thackeray's dogmatic conclusions, or of his overwhelming calculations, would frequently gain new business, expand an existing account, or bolster-up a languishing connection.

In person Mr. Thackeray was very tall, neat and dapper. He had very highly-polished finger nails, long curling eye-lashes, thinly pencilled eyebrows and his walk was faintly reminiscent of a lady in a tight skirt hurrying to catch a bus.

Sir Highley, who found Mr. Thackeray's general appearance and mannerisms unbearable, was, nevertheless, captivated by the unending flow of pseudo-scientific and mathematical mumbo-jumbo that emanated from his exquisite being.

Mr. Thackeray had a wonderful superiority-complex and as, in addition, he was in the way of being something of a snob, he regarded Geoffrey as a rather low species of commercial intruder and scarcely deigned to acknowledge or accept him. But as Geoffrey could muster only a very minor enthusiasm for Mr. Thackeray, or for his eloquent dissertations and breath-taking conclusions, and as he was always vaguely troubled by the indefinable hint of the erotic in his dapper colleague, he experienced only a fleeting concern at Mr. Thackeray's coldness.

Last, and most emphatically least, of the Nitely quartet, was Mr. Harry Wimper, chief artist and head of the Nitely studios. Mr. Wimper was brilliant. His brilliance was recognised but unrewarded, and it was entirely his own fault. Mr. Wimper was a little man with a peaky face, pale-blue eyes and thin fair hair that drooped listlessly over his broad forehead. In his queer high-pitched voice he frequently proclaimed that, "these days one was lucky to have a regular job," and seemed to exhibit an expression of permanent surprise that Sir Highley should consider him worth the ten pounds that he paid him every week.

Actually, to Sir Highley, Mr. Wimper was worth every penny of five times ten pounds a week, but he was more than content with the salary he received, and in controlling Sir Highley's large and industrious art department he realised a long hidden craving for power and authority which was as a balm to his sorely troubled mind. For Mr. Wimper had a very large, formidable and overpowering wife.

These four then, were the most prominent of Geoffrey's colleagues. With Sir Highley they controlled the activities of the hundred odd other souls that together made up the staff of Nitely Advertising Ltd.

In the beginning Geoffrey found life at Nitely's a rather rushing, breathless experience. Everything was executed at the double. All day there would be a constant coming and going of Nitely messengers with letters, blocks, messages or proofs, each bearing upon the wrapper the flamboyant Nitely label, and returning with more blocks, messages and corrected proofs. Artists would be called upon, at a moment's notice, to produce inspired masterpieces which coincided with Sir Highley's ideas of dignified art work! The media department would be given a few hours to evolve a campaign in the press giving a national coverage (with particular regard to the agricultural areas) and Sir Highley, sitting ponderous and very business-like behind his great desk, would shout after the breathless and panting "space-buyer" who was hurrying away to carry out this latest rush order, "And you might give an exact estimate of the cost, y'know, with all the discounts and everything." And as this last request would bring a pair of startled eyes flashing in his direction, Sir Highley would deliver his coup-de-grace by saying, "Don't forget, I must have it by four o'clock, you know!"

In all this feverish, troubled maelstrom of activity Miss Lovejoy was as a rock of sanity. Day after day there would be new love-affairs, quarrels and jealousies. Miss Lovejoy would be called upon to intervene in all of them. Her round chubby figure would trundle rapidly from room to room, from department to department, criticising, encouraging, adjudicating.

Everybody loved Miss Lovejoy and in return Miss Lovejoy loved everybody.

Dark-haired, beautiful Miss Arthur was in a different category. Most of the male staff loved Miss Arthur but in return she did nothing about it - well, scarcely anything, because, after all, Sir Highley was hardly a member of the staff.

But, in spite of all the constant rushing and bustling, the Nitely offices housed a very efficient organisation, and Geoffrey found that, with the exception of Mr. Thackeray, the staff were a very pleasant and happy crowd to work with.

Sir Highley went to great lengths to foster the team-spirit. "Nothing like it for efficiency !" he would proclaim, and in an effort to further the spirit, encouraged the universal use of Christian names among his staff.

Sir Highley made a great point of being a leader in this friendly fashion and would stride through the office saying, "Good morning, George ! Good morning, Ivy! Good morning, Dick! That's a pretty dress, Myrtle," and the only unfortunate result of his insistence upon the universal use of Christian names was his own habit of confusing, in the case of the junior and less prominent members of his staff, Tom with Dick, and Dick with Harry. It was a little embarrassing at first to walk with Sir Highley through the offices and studios, and to hear him greet Tom with a boisterous "Good morning, Harry !'' and then five minutes later to return, and stand behind Tom called Harry, and to hear Sir Highley say, "That's a nice piece of work - keep it up and we'll soon make something of you, Dick, my boy!"

But whilst, at all times, the team spirit and love-thy-neighbour spirit was encouraged, and was regarded as the key-stone of the organisation, nothing in the whole year could compare with Sir Highley's master-piece - the dinner and dance that he provided annually for the members of his staff.

There was no doubt that these annual affairs were very well done. Sir Highley was generous and Miss Lovejoy was a most capable organiser. Miss Lovejoy would make all the arrangements for a superb dinner, an excellent dance floor and a first-class band, and Sir Highley would lean back and rejoice in the credit, and the gratitude of his "one big happy family."

The annual fiesta was looming large on the horizon shortly after Geoffrey went to Nitely's. Miss Lovejoy was constantly bombarded with questions as to "Where is it going to be held ?" "Whose band are we having this year?" "Who are you getting for the cabaret ?" But to every eager questioner Miss Lovejoy would return an enigmatic smile and a tantalising "Wait and See."

Nitely's staff dance was always a well-attended function. Quite apart from its popularity with the majority of the staff, attendance was almost a point of honour and duty.

On the day before the dance, Geoffrey was in Sir Highley's room discussing some problems in connection with one of the new accounts, when the great man, who obviously had something on his mind, turned to him and said, "Are you taking anyone to the dance to-morrow?"

"No," replied Geoffrey, and then as an explanation, added, " you see, you have so many attractive girls here that I'm rather looking forward to a good time."

Sir Highley nodded absent-mindedly. "Quite. Quite," he said.

Then he looked up and continued, "Would you mind taking 'Laddie' - you know, Miss Arthur. I'm in a bit of a hole really. You see I'd sort of given her to understand that I'd be taking her along, but now my wife's decided that she ought to be there, and it's going to rather difficult for me if. . . . "

Geoffrey interposed. "Well, if you like I'll ask her if she will come with me, but she may not care to, you know."

Sir Highley beamed. "Oh, that'll be quite all right he said." I've told 'Laddie ' how things are, but I can't bear to think of her having to go alone." He sighed heavily. "A woman like that shouldn't have to go anywhere alone."

Then, with the thought that another difficulty had been successfully surmounted, he brightened considerably and said to Geoffrey, "Why don't you run along and ask her now ?"

Miss Arthur was busily engaged upon redrafting some advertisements for a face powder that was apparently of a texture so fine that it could be compared very favourably with the powder on a butterfly's wings, and she glanced up with a look of enquiry when Geoffrey came in.

"Can you spare a few minutes?" he asked.

"Easily," said Miss Arthur, and took a cigarette from the case Geoffrey offered to her.

"About the dance to-morrow .... " he began.

"Yes, I'd love to come with you," said Miss Arthur, and inhaled cigarette smoke with every evidence of satisfaction. There was a look of shadowed amusement in her eyes as she regarded him.

"Thanks a lot," he said, "I'm afraid that I must have been rather obvious."

"Not at all. It was rather rude of me really. But I know Sir Highley so very well, and I guessed that he would put you up to something like this."

She smiled at him and he quite understood the way Sir Highley must feel.

"One has all sorts of odd duties, working for a man like Sir Highley, don't you find?"

Geoffrey smiled in return. "And some very pleasant ones," he said.

She looked at him with a new display of interest. "I think we may enjoy ourselves."

"I know that I shall," said Geoffrey."

"I may be a rotten dancer," she said.

He looked at her figure as she came round from behind her desk. "I don't think so," he said.

She walked with him to the door. "What time shall I call for you?" he asked.

"Well, we mustn't be late. Would seven o'clock be too early?"

Geoffrey said that seven o'clock would suit him very well. "Oh, by the way, what is the address ?" he added.

"No 44, Eglington Gardens, Kensington," said ' Laddie." "I'll be waiting for you."

3

No. 44, Eglington Gardens, was a large, old-fashioned mansion that had been converted into a number of modern service flats.

Geoffrey surveyed a line of bells each of which had a neat printed card below it. He found one bearing the inscription, "Mr. and Mrs. Oswald Whistler," and rang the bell. In a few moments "Laddie" was at the door, looking very lovely in a black velvet evening gown, which was revealing in its simplicity.

"Do come in and meet my husband," she said, and Geoffrey felt rather guilty about the orchids, reposing in their little cellophane box, that he had brought for her.

But Miss Arthur was delighted with the orchids. She took them from the box and held them against the front of her gown.

"It's very sweet of you to bring them," she said, and looked dangerously attractive.

They made their way upstairs, and into a small comfortably furnished flat.

In the far corner of the room Mr. Oswald Whistler was seated at a piano, but when they came in he leapt up, dashed towards them, shook Geoffrey's hand in a somewhat feverish and jerky manner, said, "A thousand welcomes. It is delightful to know you," and dashed back to his piano.

Mr. Whistler was of medium build, with rather sharp bird-like features, and a mane of iron-grey hair which persisted in falling over his eyes. The general effect, however, apart from the hair, was not unpleasing. Looking at him, Geoffrey thought that it would not be difficult to like him. But Mr. Whistler, having done his duty, appeared to have forgotten their existence. He was deeply engrossed in his piano. For a few moments he would sit very still and then suddenly he would leap into activity and pound violently upon the piano, discord and harmony alternating with amazing frequency. As suddenly as he had attacked the instrument he would stop, and seizing a pencil would write urgently and rapidly upon a scrap of paper which he rested upon the top of the piano.

His wife regarded him with a look blending affection and amusement, and turning to Geoffrey said, "He's forgotten all about us - he's working on another of his masterpieces - the music is for inspiration! Come along, we'll get along now."

At the door they paused and "Laddie" called out, "Good-bye, dear, we're going now."

Mr. Whistler paused before making a further violent attack upon the keyboard, and glanced up. "Have a good time," he said, "I hope that it is a good play!"

"Laddie" glanced at Geoffrey with a quick smile and spread her hands in a gesture of despair. "And to think I spent thirty minutes this evening explaining to him why Sir Highley gives an annual dinner and dance for his staff."

At the Splendide Sir Highley and Lady Nitely received their guests. Sir Highley beamed with an air of bountiful provider, whilst Lady Nitely looked a little bored, a trifle supercilious, and very benevolent. Lady Nitely had for too long, and much too recently, been accustomed to meeting upon equal terms the class represented by Sir Highley's more junior employees, to allow her, upon an occasion such as this, to return once more to their level. Before her marriage Lady Nitely had been Miss Winifred Worplesden, a manicurist in the Oxford Street firm of hairdressers and beauty specialists that Sir Highley favoured with his custom. Even now, Sir Highley invariably addressed her as "Winnie" - a habit that she found especially irritating and, in fact, considered exceedingly undignified. But to Sir Highley, Miss Worplesden had been Winnie long before she had been Lady Nitely; his fondest memories were of Winnie, and so Winnie she was likely to remain. As a manicurist Winifred had been in receipt of a more than moderate income. An income which was sufficient to allow her to clothe her undoubtedly attractive person in smart clothes of the latest fashion. Her income had been higher than that of her fellow-workers, and she had once been known to confess (but not to Sir Highley) that the income of manicurist was very largely dependent upon a carefully applied psychology. When questioned further she had explained that a black dress, relieved here and there with a touch of white, was the regulation wear in her place of employment. There were, however, no regulations as to style, and Miss Worplesden had worn her skirts short - tantalisingly short, and low-cut necks - tantalisingly low. As she stooped demurely over the masculine hands that were placed eagerly into her care, even the most astute student of psychology would have hesitated before believing that Miss Worplesden had been heard to proclaim, "The lower the neck, the higher the tip!"

In the end she had, with very great success, graduated from Oxford Street to Sir Highley's Mayfair flat. She had not been one whit disturbed by the knowledge that before her there had been three previous Lady Nitelys, two of whom were still living; or that she occasionally encountered them enjoying themselves on their part of the Nitely income; or that one of them had, in the past, been the object of her own ministrations designed to enhance her acknowledged beauty.

And so, on this evening when she could enjoy her triumph, she stood with Sir Highley, her air of condescension graduated to a degree. She greeted Miss Arthur in a manner which reminded Geoffrey of a tiger putting on its very best manners in polite society, and his own reception he could liken only to that of a young and untried courtier (who yet showed possibilities of amatory dalliance) being presented for the first time at the court of Tudor Queen Elizabeth.

The dinner that followed was excellent. Sir Highley made a speech congratulating the staff upon their work during the past year; congratulating himself upon having such a staff; and congratulating the staff upon having Sir Highley. He prefaced his remarks by a crisp statement of his intention to say only a few words, as he knew that everybody was anxious to get on with the dancing, but in fact, he spoke for forty minutes. Considering that it was Sir Highley, this was not at all bad, and satisfaction was apparent on every face as they made their way to the ballroom.

Sir Highley led off the dancing with Lady Nitely and gradually, as shyness and trepidation were overcome, the floor filled. Geoffrey and Miss Arthur watched these initial efforts with considerable interest. Sir Highley slipped round the floor with a smooth, though mechanical ease, acquired late in life from a painstaking professional instructor; Mr. Wimper paraded miserably with his overpowering wife, walking backwards in long straight lines round the outside of the floor and turning abruptly at every comer; Miss Lovejoy trundled contentedly in the arms of a tall junior member of the staff who she was trying hard to make feel at home, but who was, at the moment, conspicuous only for his very red face and awkward feet. The younger members of the staff alone seemed to be thoroughly enjoying themselves, having swung into the execution of complicated Palais-de-danse steps - a standard admittedly far above that of the shuffling and hesitant performances of many of their more established colleagues.

When Geoffrey swung Miss Arthur on to the floor for their first dance, he was conscious of an uncontrollable thrill as he clasped her warm, perfumed body. It was the first time, since his meeting with Lesley, that he had held a woman in his arms. With the soft rhythmic melody of the band, the smooth delightful ease with which his partner followed his every step, and her exciting beauty, his mind was full of bitter-sweet memories of the night he had held Lesley in his arms and had danced with her. Dance followed dance, and together they swept effortlessly round the floor. He was happier than he had been for a long time. There was something strangely sensual and voluptuous in these facile movements that they made so perfectly together. It left his mind free to wander and imagine that it was Lesley in his arms. He had no idea of what thoughts, if any, filled his partner's mind; she was relaxed and compliant in his arms. Between dances they chatted idly together, and if, as the evening drew on, he was aware that as they danced her body pressed closer to him, he gave no sign of it, and they still spoke only of casual things.

Towards the end there was a Scottish Reel, in deference to the wishes of Mr. Thackeray. Mr. Thackeray's Scottish ancestry in combination with alcohol and music called out the wildest in him, and always it culminated in his desire to demonstrate his proficiency in this Scottish dance. There were but few performers and Mr. Thackeray led the way. Around the floor the others gathered to watch, their faces expressing amusement, boredom, impatience or admiration. Faster and faster went the music and faster and faster went the dancers. Fastest of them all went Mr. Thackeray. The dance approached its climax; Mr. Thackeray was whirling round at terrific speed until, tragically for Mr. Thackeray, his feet slid forward and described a curving arc in the air; his back hit the dance-floor with a resounding thud, driving from his exhausted lungs what little air remained. There was a deep silence in the room. At last, from the depths of the serried watchers came an unknown youthful voice; a voice whose owner had perhaps suffered at the hands of the superior Mr. Thackeray. A very distinct, "Now let us see you plot a graph of that!" echoed hollowly across the floor.

In the end everyone voted that the whole evening had been an unqualified success.

5

Geoffrey braked the car to a halt outside No. 44, Eglington Gardens. Miss Arthur, who had been very silent during the drive home said, "I must thank you for an unexpectedly lovely and enjoyable evening."

Geoffrey said, "Thanks to you, Laddie; every moment has been most delightful."

He drew his cigarette case from his pocket. "A last cigarette before you go?" he asked.

She thanked him and took a cigarette, waiting for a few moments until the lighter on the dash glowed a bright red. She inhaled deeply on her cigarette and then said suddenly, looking straight ahead of her, "You rather despise me - for Sir Highley and everything, don't you?"

Geoffrey was jolted out of the easy friendly association that they had known all the evening. "Why! Good heavens, no! Of course not. I hadn't even thought of it, and if I had I most certainly should not have felt ... well, the way you suggest."

In the half-light, thrown by a street lamp a little way up the road, she tried hard to see his face whilst he was speaking.

"Honestly?" she said.

"Honestly."

She laughed. He was not sure if it was a note of bitterness or of amusement in her laugh.

"Why should you think a thing like that?" he asked.

"Oh, you've been so charming and yet so - so stand-offish. Almost as if you wanted to like me and there was a barrier between us. I'm afraid that I'm a rather strange person; unmoral, I think would be the correct term to apply to anyone who lives as I do - with an almost complete disregard for the ordinary conventions –

but I suppose that the first term that would occur to most people would be immoral. But I'm not really, you know. It has been a strange life for me with Oswald. He's fond of me in an odd, preoccupied, complaisant way, and I - I've never really got over the mad headstrong infatuation I had for him years ago. I don't mean that I'm still infatuated, or anything like that, but it left something behind - love, I suppose, although if it is, it is a detached, impersonal sort of love; something like being fond of a brother or a sister - affection without being in the least bit physical.

She threw her cigarette out of the window, and for a few moments watched it glowing on the pavement.

"Of course, Oswald does the most outrageous things, and I do things that I suppose I should be ashamed of - but I'm not. It seems to me to be just some small consolation, in this queer life of mine, to be able to love, and to be loved, without feeling that I'm cheating or hurting anybody.

"At first, when I found out about Oswald, I was almost crazy with jealousy, and so hurt that I felt sick. But he went on doing those things, and gradually, I came to realise that the things he did, didn't mean anything to him; that he was just going through life experiencing everything as it came along, hoping that among those experiences he would find something that he would consider worthy of setting down on paper. Then I realised that he didn't care about me - about what I did I mean. I won't say that I rushed out and flung myself at the head of the first attractive man I met, but when, some time later, somebody did come along, well, there was just nothing to stop me. That's why, to-night, I was half hoping that you would want to make love to me, and why, if you had tried, I should not have stopped you. Now do you despise me? "

She saw him shake his head. "No," he said, "a short time ago I should probably have fallen head over heels in love with you, and then I should have regarded your lack of convention as the happiest thing in the world, but now, well, now .... "

"Now there is somebody else?"

"Yes, in a way."

"What do you mean - 'in a way'?"

"Oh, she is in America, and for all I know I may never see her again."

"You love her?"

"Yes."

"And she loves you?"

"No, she couldn't - you see she's miles above me, quite unattainable."

"That wouldn't stop her loving you - didn't you ever ask her?"

"No."

"Couldn't you tell? But, no, of course you couldn't. Oh, I don't mean to be rude. I've met men like you before. The only way you would know if a woman was in love with you would be if she came right up and told you so. Isn't it? You just can't believe that anyone can be in love with you, can you?"

She ·twisted round and drew her legs up under her, so that she was sitting facing him.

"Listen. I know women and to a lesser degree I know men. You don't need me to tell you that women are queer creatures, but there are some men, one happens along every so often, that have a strange indefinable attraction for almost all women. Some women, when they see a man that attracts them and it is a man they want, will go straight in and try to get him without caring what other people think, but there are others who resent the attraction and fight against it, why I don't know, but there it is, and sometimes it will make them quite cool and aloof, rude almost, to the poor unsuspecting man who is so unwittingly the cause of all the trouble."

Geoffrey smiled, and she seemed in the darkness to sense his smile, because almost at once she continued: "Oh! I'm not trying to say that you have some fatal and irresistible attraction - but there is something about you that makes women want you - especially if they get to thinking about you and what it might mean if you were not really as casual and disinterested as you appear to be."

"But I'm not casual," he said.

"No, but you appear to be. Oh, I suppose I shouldn't be talking to you like this, but somehow I just had to tell you that you don't need to be so humble about any woman - not even this one in America, that you mention almost with bated breath. I'd say that it was an even chance that she thinks just as much of you, as you do of her."

"If I told you the whole story I don't think that you would say that."

"Well, we'll see," she said, and then switching on the dash light, cried, "Heavens, look at the time! I must get in now, if I'm to be fit for anything to-morrow."

As she was putting the key in the lock he put his hands on her shoulders and said, "I've been very happy tonight, my dear, perhaps you would come out with me again sometime?"

She slipped round so that she stood facing him.

"Any time," she said.

He waited until the door had closed behind her, and as he walked back to the car he felt strangely elated.

CHAPTER 4

1

As a normal and healthy young man, comfortably situated, Geoffrey enjoyed life. His sporting and social activities continued and developed. His love for the far-away Lesley cast no shadow on his life, but always he was aware of it. Of course, it did alter things considerably. Whilst he did not avoid the company of attractive women, he avoided complications which led inevitably to kisses - or more. Amorous interludes had lost their thrill; every woman he met he compared quite brutally with Lesley, and always there was something about Lesley ....

At this stage, the only woman whose company he really enjoyed and who was prepared to accept him without questioning his lack of initiative, or resenting his apparent indifference to the more obvious feminine attractions, was "Laddie" Arthur. Many were the pleasant and delightful evenings that they spent together, and she provided him with the light and gay companionship that he needed. She knew that he was grateful and tried hard to amuse and entertain him. His gallant and courteous behaviour towards her was sufficient reward; restoring her self-respect and making her happy in a rather strange, almost exalted, sort of way.

But, apart from his friendship with "Laddie," he discovered that he enjoyed the opportunity of being alone. Many week-ends he would spend touring alone in his car . Travelling fast or slow to suit his mood, the exhaust note bubbling behind him, he could relax and live again those short moments with Lesley. His mind would wander into fantasy, with Lesley as the central figure.

He was especially happy spending the evenings at the small inns he found on the way; drinking ale with the "locals" and playing darts. Life then was very simple and enjoyable.

But although he enjoyed these solitary excursions he was far from being a dreamer. He found a new interest and an outlet for his energies in flying. He joined a flying-club and pegged away practising during every hour that he could spare.

He practised incessantly, with all the enthusiasm that he could bring to bear when he was vitally interested in anything. There was no boredom, not even in the constant repetition of the routine manoeuvres which were necessary for him to acquire proficiency. But he wanted more than proficiency, he wanted perfection; but, as in flying perfection was unattainable, he tried for something as near to perfection as was within the limit of his capabilities.

There were hours that he spent in taking off, circling the field, landing (often, in the beginning, with a disappointing bump) taking off again, and repeating the whole process. There were magic hours when the ground slipped away below him, the "stick" between his knees, the roar of the engine in his ears, the scream of the wind in the struts. Flying came naturally to him. Right away he found himself banking into simple turns and automatically keeping the nose of the plane fixed steadily on the line of the horizon.

Then there was the great day when he had been for a short trip round the flying-field and landed, and his instructor jumped down and said, "Right, Mr. Manners, take her away!"

For a moment he had wanted to lean over the side and shout, "Don't be so damned silly - I'm not ready yet!" But before he had really had time to think about it he was in the air, and then the only thing he had time to think about, was how he was going to land the plane, and to keep on reassuring himself that he had done it dozens of times before and each time quite successfully, but failing completely to find any consolation or hope in his own reassurance. Then after a spin round, when the plane had seemed much faster and more willing, lighter and more tractable, with only his own weight to carry, he had come in and had made a perfect three-point landing.

After that there had been no more fears. His energies had been devoted to learning all that he could about flying; to gaining an even greater proficiency.

He found that he was too restricted in relying upon the club planes for his continued practice and enjoyment, but he did not feel justified in shouldering the expense of a plane of his own. So in the end, with two other convivial companions, he became the part-owner of a not-quite-new "Moth."

Sometimes two of them would fly together, but Geoffrey liked best to take the plane up alone, when he could practise more complicated manoeuvres - like figure eights and taking the plane in and out of tail-spins.

Soaring alone in the plane with nothing but the clear blue sky above him and the earth pin-pointed to tiny lilliputian dimensions far below, he found more thrills than ever before in his life. He became a very good pilot; he could more than hold his own with most of the week-end flyers he encountered.

But that was before knowing how to fly really meant so much. Before hordes of planes with their ugly crosses and obscene crooked swastikas cast a shadow over Europe. Before those "week-end" flyers were called upon to play their part in tearing and slashing the much vaunted "Luftwaffe" from out of Britain's sky.

2

Whilst flying had tended to reduce the number of Geoffrey's week-end excursions in his car, the coincidence of a well-earned long week-end and a spell of especially fine weather tempted him to pack a bag and set out quietly on one of his carefree exploratory journeys. The warm sun as it beat down upon him as he drove along, set him longing for the sea, and that night he found a small and comfortable inn on one of the less frequented parts of the Suffolk coast.

The following morning, fortified with a gargantuan breakfast of home-cured ham and farmhouse eggs, topped off with crisp toast and marmalade, he ventured forth to wander where fancy might list to take him. Idly he sauntered along the cliff-top, pausing occasionally to pluck a stem of grass, which he would bite on for a while with every evidence of satisfaction; or to seize a stone and endeavour to cast it, over the deserted beach below, into the sea beyond. He had just watched one such stone disappear into the sea with a satisfying "plop," when he rounded a bend in the cliff and saw a cottage.

He knew somehow that it was Lesley's dream-cottage. He could see at once that it was genuinely old and, although his knowledge of architecture was limited, that there were many features characteristic of the Tudor period. The cottage nestled in a green hollow protected by a natural buttress of the cliffs. The sunlight glinted on the leaded windows; the flowers in the little garden, danced in the breeze. In Geoffrey's fanciful imaginings it seemed to wear the air of a disappointed host. As if it had got itself all ready to make someone really happy and comfortable, and then, after all, that someone had not materialised. Of course, it was really because there were no curtains at the windows, no sign of life about the place, and the little garden had an uncared-for, unkempt look.

A board, planted somewhat insecurely in the garden, announced that Messrs. Twitt & Willow, House Agents and Auctioneers, of Beccles, were prepared to enter into negotiations for the sale of the property, and that their offices were open for business between the hours of 9 a.m. and 6 p.m. from Monday to Friday, and from 9 a.m. to 1 p.m. on Saturdays.

Geoffrey pushed open the little gate and surveyed the cottage. He was more convinced than ever that it was Lesley's dream-cottage suddenly and wonderfully brought to life. He peered through the windows, and though his vision was of necessity restricted, the inside seemed to fulfil in full measure the promise conveyed by the delightful exterior. Just at that moment he wanted, more than anything else, to explore the inside of the cottage. He even contemplated returning to the inn and driving to Beccles with a view to hunting out Mr. Twitt or Mr. Willow (if those two worthy gentlemen did, in fact, exist) and obtaining possession of the key. He made a round of the cottage peering through every window. He wondered if it would be much of a crime to break one of the small panes of glass in one of the leaded windows, and gain an entrance that way. He completed his circuit of the cottage and found himself once more opposite the weathered oak door; there was an old-fashioned latch. He lifted it .... the door was open.

The inside was everything that he had imagined it would be. He stood before the inglenook fireplace and imagined a blustery wind outside with rain beating on the leaded panes, and a blazing fire and a comfortable chair inside. In his imagination he furnished the cottage with all the things that Lesley would like best. It was an idea that captivated; a new interest beckoned. Could he buy the cottage and· make it his secret hideaway? Translate Lesley's dream into his own secret world? And then perhaps someday .... ?

3

Messrs. Twitt & Willow proved most helpful. When, at nine o'clock on the following Monday morning, Geoffrey presented himself at their offices, neither Mr. Twitt nor Mr. Willow had arrived. A young gentleman, of some fifteen or sixteen summers, was the sole occupant of the office when Geoffrey pushed open the glass door. He was a somewhat remarkable youth, if only for his luxuriant and amazing growth of hair. Strawlike in colour and fibrelike in texture, it grew straight up from his head as if he had just experienced a frightful shock, or as if some strong electric current was holding it in its strange position. Geoffrey found himself wondering if the owner of the hair ever wore a hat, and if so, whether the hat rested on the hair, or whether the hair submitted to the indignity of its crowning, and bent itself unwillingly to its master's whim.

A mildly uttered "Yes, sir?" reminded Geoffrey that it was rude to stare, and rather reluctantly withdrawing his gaze from the strange tonsorial adornment, he enquired for Mr. Twitt or Mr. Willow.

"Mr. Twitt will be here in five minutes Mr. Willow will be here in ten minutes; if you want to pay rent I can take it; if you want to see about a house you'll have to wait for Mr. Twitt or Mr. Willow. Take a seat, if you please," said the youth almost without a pause for breath.

The hair and the eloquence were too much for Geoffrey, he sat down in the chair indicated.

The owner of the hair promptly forgot all about him, and returned with no little display of interest to the study of the strip-cartoons in the pages of a popular daily newspaper. Geoffrey lit a cigarette and glanced around; the notices of auctions and sales by private treaty he found far from inspiring. He wondered if Mr. Twitt would beat Mr. Willow in the morning "office-stakes" as so confidently forecast by his shock-haired informant, and at precisely five minutes past nine Mr. Twitt arrived. He greeted Geoffrey as if he were a long-lost friend, and ushered him into a small but comfortable inner office. Hanging his bowler hat and neatly rolled umbrella on a peg behind his desk, he turned with a brisk, "What can I do for you, sir?"

Whilst he explained about the cottage, Geoffrey regarded Mr. Twitt. He saw a middle-aged, well-built individual with a well-cultivated moustache brushed straight out and bristling, sometimes referred to as a "Guardee"; a sportive, brilliant club or old-school tie; hair a little thin on top, and a kindly and interested expression. During his explanation Mr. Twitt once or twice cut in with understanding remarks in a rather heavy cultivated voice, and occasionally, for no obvious reason, guffawed heartily. The guffaws caused Geoffrey some little concern, and he began to wonder if he was thinking of buying the local "haunted house."

On further acquaintance with Mr. Twitt, however, he discovered that the guffaws were, like Mr. Twitt's moustache and his tie, just part of his make-up of a jovial good-fellow; one of the best.

Geoffrey concluded his explanation about his interest in the cottage on the cliffs . . . "the one near Saltern village," he terminated.

Mr. Twitt was enthusiastic. "Ah! You've an eye for the real thing, sir," he said, "a piece of property as genuine as any ever handled by the firm of Twitt and Willow."

Between occasional guffaws he continued to enthuse. Mr. Willow, a small bearded gentleman, who had since arrived, and had evinced considerable interest in the proceedings, enthused also. They conducted a duet of praise.

"Quiet and secluded," said Mr. Twitt.

"Perhaps a little off the beaten track," ventured Mr. Willow, "but, if you have a car, that's no handicap" (Geoffrey's car having been parked outside, and plain for Mr. Willow to see).

"Excellent state of repair," countered Mr. Twitt.

"Nice piece of ground - not too large, not too small," Mr. Willow subscribed.

But not even the combined sales-talk of Messrs. Twitt and Willow could dissuade Geoffrey from his purchase.

Once his intention was clear, Mr. Twitt and Mr. Willow were most helpful. In the shortest possible time Geoffrey was, to all intents and purposes, the virtual owner of "a unique, old-world seaside cottage," which, for some reason or other, had apparently never been properly christened, and for want of a better name had become known simply as "The Cottage."

4

Many were the week-ends and holidays that Geoffrey spent at his cottage; it became his hobby and his escape. He spent hours searching for the furniture he felt Lesley would have liked. He recalled every detail of everything she had told him about her dream-cottage. He laboured long to build reality from a dream. And when at last it was finished it was very lovely; and it was deep in his affections because of Lesley, and for itself.

And then he turned to the garden. He loved the long and quiet hours spent digging and planting. The sun beating down, warm and comforting; the smell of the newly turned earth; the sough and sigh of the sea behind him.

Thus it was one day, standing in the garden with the flowers he had tended all about him, in his own world which he had created out of his love for Lesley, he gazed beyond the cottage to the sea. The sun glinted on the water in a thousand places, like a host of silver seabirds darting and resting. On this so lovely day the sea was happy and friendly; in the sunlight and the breeze the water danced before his eyes. The dancing water. He found the words strangely appealing; they seemed to "belong"; to "belong" to Lesley's cottage. And so he decided that "The Cottage" should have a name - a real name - "The Dancing Water."

5

Geoffrey painted the sign himself; a hanging sign it was; to hang from the little tree; from the branch just above the gate, and when it was finished and in position he stood back to survey his handiwork. As he contemplated with a measure of satisfaction that there was no jarring-note; that the sign was in harmony with the atmosphere of the cottage, his contemplation was disturbed by a scuffling and puffing just behind him. Seeking the cause of this encroachment upon his solitude, he turned, and at the same moment, a diminutive but sturdy and chubby young gentleman grabbed at his trousers. A large golden retriever, tail a-wag, continued to nuzzle a questing nose into the young fugitive's shoulder blades, whereupon the object of his undoubted but unwelcome affection, turned a pair of supplicating blue eyes upwards to Geoffrey's face and at the same time held up his arms to be lifted into safety. Geoffrey stooped, and lifted him so that he sat in the crook of his right arm. "Well, young fella', what's troubling you, eh?"

The owner of the bright blue eyes, now seated comfortably out of range of the questing doggy-nose, replied, "Uh-uh-uh-gwog-gwog-grr!" Apparently considering that he had given a concise and lucid explanation of his presence, and of the recent difficulty from which he had been extricated, he began, from the more lofty elevation in which he now found himself, to evince a lively interest in his surroundings. Geoffrey looked along the sandy lane that led to Saltern village, but there was no sign of the owner, or owners, of his two visitors. There was nothing for it, thought Geoffrey, but to get his coat and carry his young charge back towards the village, and enquire at the cottages on the way if they had any interest in this small and highly attractive bundle of humanity. He was too small and somewhat uncertain on his legs to have come far on his own, so Geoffrey pushed open the gate, and carefully shutting the rather too boisterous retriever outside, where he promptly sat down and pushed his nose through the bars of the gate, set the young man down on his feet. The young man scuttled up the path to the cottage, dropped on all fours to negotiate the step, and disappeared through the doorway.

Geoffrey followed him inside, and found him with his eyes fixed on a jug of home-made lemonade which stood upon the table. When Geoffrey appeared, a tiny, podgy finger was pointed at the jug, and a voice demanded, "Dlink!" When the necessary glass was procured and the lemonade was being poured, the small person suddenly dropped on to his well-padded bottom and held out his two hands to receive the glass. His round and rosy face was displaying considerable satisfaction, when Geoffrey heard a voice calling, with a shade of alarm and anxiety, "Bobby! Bobby! Where are you?" Glancing down at his young charge, who continued his refreshment without interruption, Geoffrey went outside the cottage just in time to see a young, attractive woman, reach the gate and address the dog, who jumped up to meet her with a somewhat woebegone expression on his face.

"Prince! You naughty dog; where has Bobby gone?" said the young woman, this time with a note of relief in her voice.

"Good-afternoon," said Geoffrey, "he's inside - drinking lemonade. Won't you come in?"

She favoured him with a most attractive smile, and opening the gate passed through, carefully shutting the retriever outside, much to his ill-concealed disgust.

The young man called Bobby had just finished his lemonade as his mother came through the door, and discarding the glass held out his arms to her. "You naughty boy," she said, gathering him up into her arms with a flurry, "how could you frighten your Mummy so?" And she kissed him on his rosy cheek with so much obvious love, as to render quite useless the chiding tone in her voice.

"Thank you so much for looking after him," she said, turning to Geoffrey, "I have so much trouble trying to take care of both of them. They seem to encourage each other to be as naughty as possible, and how they both managed to get out of the garden to-day, I really don't know."

They lived in the cottage just around the bend in the road leading to the village, she told Geoffrey; and he told her that he only used his cottage at week-ends, and she said that she knew; and he showed her over it, and she fell in love with it almost at once, and in the end they all stayed to tea.

The following week-end Geoffrey went to tea at the little cottage just around the bend with Mrs. Knight (Elsa Knight she told him) and Bobby and Prince the retriever, and enjoyed himself immensely. He was surprised when he found how sparsely the cottage was furnished, and how frugally they lived; and that they lived alone.

After that, they met whenever Geoffrey was at the cottage, and Geoffrey fell in love with Bobby, and brought him toys and sweets from London, and Elsa fell in love with Geoffrey; but he never knew about that.

Their friendship came to mean a great deal to him; his visits were more frequent because of them; he found a thousand little ways to help.

Sometimes, when Bobby had gone to bed, they would have long conversations together. He discovered that her husband had been killed fighting with the International Brigade in Spain. She told him about her husband. He wasn't a "Red" she said, but he had been something of an idealist; he had believed that if the world would not do something to stop the horrors that were going on in Spain, then the world would itself suffer those same horrors, only magnified a thousand times. He hadn't wanted his baby to grow up in a world like that; to suffer the horrors that had been suffered by the babies of Madrid. And so he had gone. Gone to try, so he said, to help to cut out at its roots, the filthy cancer of fascism; he had died in trying, and a nation that just went on blindly practising "non-intervention," had scarcely noted or mourned his passing. He had been young when he died, and had left her very little on which to live, but somehow they managed; the three of them. There were no relations to whom she could turn, and as working meant leaving her baby, she would not do that, and so she managed on the little that they had, and had her baby with her, and was happy watching him grow into the sturdy little man that his Daddy would have loved had he known him.

One Saturday evening, after they had spent a long and happy day together, he told her about Lesley. She was the only one to whom he confided his secret. When he had finished telling her about their brief time together, and the cottage, and what it meant to him, he looked at her, wondering whether she would think him a fool, and aware, deep inside him, that if she did, it would spoil something between them that he valued very much. But she only smiled in her lovely, friendly way and said, "Poor old Geoff. You have got it rather badly. Haven't you?"

When he had filled his pipe, and it was burning well, he rose ready for the short walk back to his own cottage. He put his arm around her shoulders and gave her a friendly, grateful squeeze. She longed to turn in his arm and kiss him; to tell him to forget such fanciful yearnings; to tell him that here was someone real, and vital, and alive, within his grasp; someone who loved him more than he could ever know. But instead, she only said, "Good-night, my dear, don't forget to say 'goodbye' before you go to-morrow."

But later, when she was in bed, she fought hard to keep back the tears. She lay there with wide-open eyes, staring through the window into the darkness of the night, her hands pressing her breasts, as if they hurt her. And as she recalled all that he had said; remembered the soft light in his eyes when he spoke about Lesley, a deep sob shook her. The tears, so long held back, were no longer to be denied. They ran, unheeded, from her eyes; soaking into her pillow.

Elsa, for the second time, was saying good-bye to love.

CHAPTER 5

1

AND so life slipped smoothly by. Geoffrey's work was good, sometimes brilliant. His leisure restful and contented. For many months nothing came to disturb the even flowing tenor of his life.

Until one day he met Mr. Abraham B. Harlam, Jnr., European "Big Noise" of World Wide Pictures and Studios Inc., the centre of whose universe was, as may be guessed, Hollywood, California.

The meeting appeared casual enough to Geoffrey; it was far from casual to Mr. Harlam. Mr. Harlam didn't believe in casual meetings; casual meetings wasted time, and time was precious to Mr. Harlam, who had so many things to do. So if you met Mr. Harlam, and he stayed longer than to say, "How d'ye do?" and "Good-bye!" or one of their numerous American equivalents, you could be pretty sure that Mr. Harlam had taken some trouble to arrange the meeting long before. He said far more than, "How d'ye do?" and "Good-bye!" to Geoffrey; in fact, it took him the whole of a long and protracted luncheon to say what he had to say, and to ask the questions he had to ask.

Geoffrey was a little surprised, but not bewildered; nothing that happened now, he thought, could ever bewilder him again.

During the year he had worked for Sir Highley and had become more and more responsible for the handling of the United British Cinemas' account, he had, not unnaturally, made a number of friends connected with the film business. He had regarded it as in no way unusual for one of these friends to invite him to luncheon, and to find, upon his arrival at the rendezvous, that his friend was accompanied by a third party. But he had regarded it as somewhat unusual, when the usual introductions were over, for that third party to assume full responsibility, not only for the luncheon, but for things generally and to monopolise the conversation, and to ask questions of an undoubtedly personal nature.

Mr. Harlam appeared unusual; in fact, was unusual, because he dispensed with all the preliminary skirmishings when he conducted an interview; he came straight out with his statements and questions, as if he had only five minutes to spare before he had to rush and catch a train. But for all that, he had a way of avoiding any appearance of abruptness, and was very likeable.

He was a small man, with dark smooth hair, and dark brown eyes. He affected rimless glasses with many-sided lenses which are popular with many Americans of the quieter type. He had a soft, smooth and persuasive voice.

He said that he was aware that Geoffrey had been responsible for planning the United British campaign, and that he had produced the rather "different" announcements that were a feature of the campaign. Geoffrey probably knew that many of the films shown by United British, were produced by World Wide Pictures and Studios Inc.? He did? Good! World Wide had been favourably impressed; in fact, very favourably impressed, by Geoffrey's presentation of their productions. They had indeed come to the notice of Mr. Solomon Silverwin (Mr. Harlam hushed his voice here) who *was* World Wide. Mr. Silverwin thought they were the best he had seen. The best was none too good for Mr. Silverwin, and for World Wide. Whilst, as Mr. Harlam pointed out, exhibitors usually waited. with impatience for the products of World Wide Studios, World Wide did indulge in a certain amount of "selling" for their productions. He accepted, with becoming modesty, the view that he understood was held generally, that the pictures produced by World Wide were without doubt, colossal, dynamic, enchanting, and without equal in the world of films, yet nevertheless exhibitors had sometimes to be convinced that they should rent them, and the public in their turn convinced that they should see them.

Mr. Silverwin, that great man, held the opinion that to date, Geoffrey had discovered the best approach for bringing about at least one of these desired objectives; the second would seem to be a natural corollary. As Mr. Harlam had already stated, the best was none too good for Mr. Silverwin, and at the moment, in his own particular sphere, Geoffrey was the best. So would he go to Mr. Silverwin? To World Wide? To Hollywood? To a three-year contract? Would he?

It was not Mr. Harlam's fault that he failed to offer Geoffrey the greatest inducement of all. He might have said, "Would Geoffrey go to Hollywood? Hollywood, where Lesley lived, and worked and played?"

2

Mr. Harlam's offer presented Geoffrey with the most momentous decision of his career. Without the tremendous influence which Lesley Travis unknowingly exerted on his decision, there is but little doubt that he would, not perhaps without some regrets and some misgivings as to his wisdom, have rejected Mr. Harlam's offer. But the possibility of meeting Lesley again, and of renewing on perhaps some more permanent basis their brief but intimate friendship, would not allow him to dismiss the offer lightly, or in fact to reject it at all.

Viewed strictly from the material point of view, he knew that if he did accept he could anticipate but little monetary advantage. Not that the financial aspect of the three-year contract he had been offered was ungenerous, the dollars represented therein - converted into sterling - would, in fact, represent some slight increase on his present considerable remuneration. But he knew that his real interest, his real ability, was more than just this flair of his for film advertising. He had done too well on the executive side not to realise this. The never-failing enthusiasm which he had brought to bear in the solution of the problems of Sir Highley's clients; the new campaigns he had planned; the new products he had launched upon the troubled competitive waters of commerce; were all there as milestones on the road of his progress; milestones which, as he looked back, had something of the aspect of guide-posts, pointing the road he should follow, which they knew and he knew, was the right one for him to follow. But all these things, cast in the balance against Lesley; were as feathers without weight or substance. Secretly, he knew that his decision was already made. One thing only weighed in any measure against Hollywood; his loyalty - nay, he admitted - his affection, for Sir Highley. A Sir

Highley who had of late placed even more confidence in him; who had deputed more and more of the important undertakings to him. Geoffrey was fast becoming, after Sir Highley, the key-man of the Nitely organisation. No false modesty prevented him from recognising this, or from realising that it was so, because he had so successfully grasped the opportunities which had presented themselves. But he knew also that it was Sir Highley who had provided the opportunities and it was not in him to be ungrateful. And so he would not admit, even to himself, that the struggle was over and that Lesley had won. Instead he told himself that he would keep an open mind and take his problem, or at least a part of it, to Sir Highley.

And so that night, Sir Highley dined with his protégé, and Geoffrey told him about his American offer. He was convincing, without being maudlin, in his assurances of his gratitude for all that Sir Highley had done; he explained that he was not foolishly casting away the substance to grasp at a shadow; he analysed critically and dispassionately the possibilities of the alternatives before him, and left no doubt as to where he felt his real opportunities and fortunes lay. But whilst he made no effort to explain about Lesley (he had not mentioned her name to anyone but Elsa) he made it clear to Sir Highley that for strong personal reasons he was driven to accept.

Sir Highley was a sympathetic listener; his reaction to the whole suggestion was quite at variance with anything that Geoffrey had anticipated. He surprised Geoffrey when he told him that he had known about the offer for some days. He obviously enjoyed Geoffrey's astonishment, and his eyes held a friendly, humorous twinkle as he said, "I'm glad you didn't accept without telling me about it. You see, after all that you've told me, I know that you're going to accept, and frankly I think that you're making a mistake. But I can see that it's not just your own personal advancement that's driving you on. I can't imagine what mysterious private reasons you can have for wanting to go to Hollywood, unless," and here he chortled heartily, "you're aiming to become a film-star! But, anyway, Geoffrey, go ahead and accept. Opportunities always seem so much more desirable going, than coming, and if you let this one go, especially as you have such a weighty personal reason, you'll regret it, and then you'll be dissatisfied, and dissatisfied you won't be a damned bit of use to me, anyway! "

He paused for a few moments, and then continued in a warmer and more confidential manner, "But seriously, my boy, I've grown fond of you in my own peculiar sort of way, and apart from my business there's not much that I am genuinely fond of, and so you and my business sort of go together. You know I'm sixty, and although there's lots of life in the old dog yet, lots ... and there's more than one lady will vouch for that ... I know that it won't be long before I'll have to take things a bit easier. I want to take things easier, and when that time comes I'd sort of looked to you to take over a bit more. You know, you've really made yourself confoundedly useful about the place, and although I'm not going to say that Nitely Advertising Ltd., is going to stop like a rundown clock, or even slow-up when you go, things are going to take a bit of readjusting, and I'm not looking forward to it. I've already said that I think you're making a mistake, but, mark you, I'm not saying that the experience won't do you a whole heap of good. As a matter of fact, if this thing hadn't come along, I should have wanted you to go to America, anyway. I don't think the 'Yanks' have got any 'corner' in advertising - they haven't! If it comes to that I think there are a lot of things we can teach 'em quite a bit about, but they're more advertising-minded all of 'em, as a nation; they're slick and enthusiastic and they think big. You've got to live among them to appreciate it; I did, and it taught me a hell of a lot. So in advertising, almost more than anything else, I think a spell in the States is a jolly good thing. I go there every year, not only because I handle a certain number of American accounts - and it's always well to show your clients that you have a personal interest in them, apart from selling their stuff over here - but because I like the place and I've lots of friends there. Nobody can say that I've ever objected to combining business with pleasure - or vice versa - and that's what my American trips have always been - business and pleasure. . . . "

He let this last word linger on his tongue as if savouring a bouquet, and then as if it started a train of thought continued, "And their women are wonderful . . . wonderful.. . "

He sighed, and leaned back in retrospective mood, "But all women are wonderful, though some are more wonderful than others, and American women are so . ... Now, that little hat-check girl at the La Cigale ...." He ruminated with considerable satisfaction. "I must tell you about her sometime," he went on, "but it's you we're talking about now. Yes, you go to America - it'll do you good. Go and get your experience, and get this mysterious 'something' out of your system.

"But before you go, will you make a bargain with me? No, don't interrupt me," as Geoffrey made as if to reply, "listen to what I have to say first. You've been offered a three-year contract, right ? Well, it may go well and there may be another three years at the end of it, but, on the other hand, it may not. And if it's like a lot of other Hollywood contracts you may be 'out' in six months! I don't think you will - but you may. Well then, what I'm asking you to do is this, at the end of the three years, or before, for that matter, whether you're a great success or ... or otherwise, make a bargain to come back and work for me again. I don't think that I shall lose on the deal - the experience will do you good, and I shall have you back just about the time when I think I shall begin to need you most. Now what do you say?"

"Yes! By God, yes!" said Geoffrey. "You know, sir, excuse me saying it, but you really are a damned good sort."

Sir Highley only smiled.

3

When Mr. Silverwin wanted something, he wanted it right away, or if that could not be managed, with as little delay as possible, the very minimum of delay. And so Geoffrey found himself with very little time to spare before making his departure for the States.

Of all the things he had to leave behind him, his beloved cottage caused him the greatest concern. He was determined not to part with it, and yet he knew that the kindly old soul who had trundled twice weekly from Saltern to the cottage to keep it clean and neat, and who had "done-for" him on the occasions of his week-end excursions, would scarcely, in his prolonged absence, keep the place as he was determined that it should be kept.

And so it was, with uncertainty still in his mind and seemingly no solution to his difficulty, that he came again to the cottage for his farewell visit.

Then, that evening, with Bobby at his feet playing happily with his latest present, and with Elsa Knight watching him across the table, the solution of his difficulty was suddenly crystal-clear. "Elsa," he said," I want you and Bobby to come and live here whilst I'm away. You know that you love the place almost as much as I do, and it's so much more suited to your needs than that little place you have down the road. You'd be doing me a favour too; you know that I'd never let this place for any Tom, Dick or Harry to live in; in fact, I'd never let it at all, but if you would only come and live here, be a sort of resident housekeeper or guest or whatever you like to call it, everything would be just perfect. Besides, I'd know then that I won't lose touch with you, or with Bobby, and I feel that I have almost a proprietary interest in that young man, especially after the plans we have discussed for him and ... everything."

Geoffrey's announcement of his imminent departure, made earlier that evening, had shocked Elsa far more than she had thought possible. She had known that gradually she had looked forward more and more to his visits to the cottage and to the time they spent together, but only the sudden realisation that this was in all probability the last, that there would be no more, had shown her just how much he meant to her; how often he was present in her thoughts; how intimately he was woven into the rather lonely pattern of her life.

When he had told her about his Hollywood contract, he had made no mention of Lesley (they had not spoken of her after the confession that he had made on that evening that seemed so long ago) but woman-like she knew that it was the thought of Lesley, the hope of meeting her again, that was taking him away from her. For a little while she had experienced a sudden feeling of jealousy for the far-away Lesley. Until now, she had seemed unreal, a dream-person from the pages of some romantic novel, but now with Geoffrey going, she had somehow materialised as someone very real and very lovely; someone with whom it would be easy to be in love; someone of whom it would be easy to be jealous. But when the first sharp feeling of her disappointment had passed, and when she saw Geoffrey as he had always been, a kind and generous friend; playing with her son, or talking with his eager, boyish enthusiasm; she knew that she had no place for jealousy, only for love. The love which she had captured and imprisoned deep in her heart; a love which he had not glimpsed or even guessed at.

And so she agreed, and the sudden happy light in his eyes was her reward.

4

Sir Highley seldom missed an opportunity; and so, at almost their last conference before Geoffrey left for America, he had a minor favour to ask.

"I'm a bit worried about that tinned meat account of ours," he began, "you know, that 'Wham' stuff. In Chicago they don't seem to think that they're selling enough of it over here. It took me a long time to convince that bunch of hard-headed Americans, that a British agency was obviously the right choice to sell their stuff on the British market, and I don't want them to go slipping back and give the account to the offspring of one of their own agencies. It's not the money so much - although it's not to be sneezed at - but it's the prestige point of view. Can't have accounts leaving Nitely's and going to Taylor-Allgoods or Denham Lewis's; they've got quite enough pull on us already, grabbing off all the fattest accounts of the American firms. No! somehow we'll have to hang on to this one." He twisted one of his fat, expensive cigarettes in his fingers as if seeking inspiration. "Mind you, I don't think they'll ever sell a helluva lot of it over here. We don't take to canned meat. Canned fish or things like that, yes, but not canned meat. Must be a sort of 'hang-over' from the war - you know, too much 'bully-beef ' and that sort of thing - they've never forgotten it and fought shy of it ever since. I'll get Thomson to work on a new angle, he's pretty good with stuff like that ... must let 'em see we're trying anyhow."

"Now it occurred to me," continued Sir Highley, "that if, instead of going straight from New York to Hollywood, you could manage to stop off at Chicago, you could call on these 'bucks' and sort of jolly them along. You know, just tell them that we're working like blacks on the job, and we're not a bit satisfied with the progress it's making, but that I've got something really good coming along; something that will make the good old British public sit up and take notice and start buying 'Wham' like a lot of real live Americans. Of course, you'd better tell them that I've still got to put the finishing touches to it; it might take Thomson a few days to get his 'inspiration,' but that doesn't really matter; it's the personal touch that counts. They'll be tickled to death to think that I've sent somebody all the way there to see them, and I'll write a letter in advance, and lay it on a bit thick about having their account at heart, and that it's only by personal contact and discussion that the best results can be achieved, and so forth, and so forth .... "

And so it was that when Geoffrey left England bound for Hollywood, he knew that his rapid journey across America would, at least, be interrupted for a few hours in Chicago, and as it was his first visit to America, he look forward to it rather than otherwise.

CHAPTER 6

GEOFFREY sailed for America on the *Normandie*. Since Mr. Harlam's offer, things had rushed on at such a speed, there had been so much to do, that there had scarcely been time to pause and think. But now, as he stood watching the last faint haze of the coastline disappearing into the shadowy horizon, he had a sudden, sharp pang of homesickness; he began to wonder if this was not perhaps the craziest thing he had ever done; and he seemed to hear, above the noise of the sea, and of the *Normandie* as she cut through, the sea, the voice of Sir Highley, sonorous and wordly-wise saying, "Personally, I think you're making a mistake." And then Elsa's, so friendly and concerned, questioning, "But is it wise? When you have so much here .... " And even Bobby who had said, "Don't go away Uncle Geffwy! Don't go away .... " Oh, this business of going away and leaving things and people, it was the devil! If only he knew that he would see Lesley again. If only he knew that she would be glad to see him - or even remember him! But why should she? It was so long since they had spent that brief night together. Wasn't he reaching for the moon? Or rather, he thought, reaching for a 'star.' What a foolish, silly sort of thing to do! But it was a foolish, silly thing to fall in love with a film-star. But he had. And every surge and impulse of this giant liner was bringing him closer to her. What was it that Don Quixote had said about the mad ambition of a man in love? Well, after all, Don Quixote had no monopoly in tilting at windmills!

But in those early hours of the voyage there was no time to be long despondent. There was too much scurrying on every hand. Too much exploring and "finding out." There were so many, many people. The *Normandie* was so large. It was a bit depressing at first, that vastness. He thought "It would take me weeks to learn to find my way around this cavernous, floating palace, and there's only five days in which to find out all about it, and to enjoy myself at the same time." But it wasn't hard to find the way to the American-bar, and with a couple of brandies safely tucked away inside him everything seemed a great deal brighter.

It was odd how, occasionally, that sense of "vastness" would make him feel vaguely uncomfortable. He had first experienced it when he had seen the vast mountains of luggage waiting to be taken on board. It seemed impossible that people could want to take so much with them. He had quite a bit of luggage himself - mainly clothes - but compared with some of the collections, he might have been taking a week-end trip, or so it seemed. Nobody seemed to have gone quite so far as Eugene Pallete in the film "The Ghost Goes West," when he took along a complete dismantled Scottish castle, but there were many apparently who had made a bid to run him a fair second,

Geoffrey had been a little concerned when he had discovered just how many trunks would be needed to take with him the clothes he had acquired. He had thought it wise to take a fairly extensive wardrobe - he was not quite sure just how he would like American clothes; not even those "individually styled and tailored in the English fashion," by a "custom tailor" - whatever that might be.

It transpired, however, that vast as the *Normandie* was, he found that he had plenty of time during his crossing to discover many occupations in addition to looking round his floating home.

It was surprising in how short a time one became quite accustomed to the gargantuan ark, with its sumptuous and lavishly distributed fittings of mother-o' -pearl and onyx.

The swimming-pool, with its pale blue tiles, he found had quite an intimate air about it; but the main dining-room - that was too much! It was impossible to take it all in at one glance. There was just an impression of an enormous expanse of cast-glass panels, that just went on, and on, seemingly for ever; and in the centre of this crystal wilderness, dominating in solitary magnificence, the statue of a woman. To dine there, with the gigantic central statue watching him consume every mouthful, made a mockery of the meal; it seemed ridiculous for such small, insignificant creatures to be so fastidious about such a relatively unimportant matter as eating!

But, for all that, it was a very pleasant and comfortable crossing, and when at last he was on deck for his first sight of the world-famed New York skyline, he could not suppress a feeling of sorrow that he would soon be saying good-bye to this so lovely lady of the sea.

He had been prepared to be quite blasé about the celebrated skyline. So many films had featured it in all its magnificence; so many Americans had enthused about it; so many visitors to America had raved about it, that he felt that it was going to be like seeing an old friend. But in reality it was everything, and more, than they had said. It was in very truth a glimpse of a new world. New York is not America, but New York's skyline is the symbol of America.

It was a rather strange sensation, standing on the deck of the *Normandie*, watching that skyline. Everyone who has been to the movies has experienced it through the medium of the screen. Geoffrey had that rather peculiar sensation of having "done it all before." Strange, he thought, how many films indicated an Atlantic crossing in the same way. A quick shot of the liner scudding across the ocean; an equally rapid one of her docking; and then, perhaps, something a bit longer showing the passengers disembarking. But somehow they always seemed to muddle it up. The liner scudding across the ocean would perhaps be the *Rex*; the liner docking might be the *Bremen*, and more likely than not the passengers would disembark from the *Mauretania*. The film people seemed to think that the great, big goofy public didn't notice things like that, but many of them did, and it very often spoilt an otherwise excellent film. Why on earth, he thought, if they had to use this stock material, they couldn't choose material showing the same liner, was beyond comprehension.

They did it with railways too; especially in British pictures. They would give you a glimpse of a main line Pacific flyer breasting an incline, or roaring out of a tunnel, with prodigious exhaust and every indication of pent-up power and speed, and then, what purported to show the same train steaming majestically into the terminus after a non-stop journey, would prove to be a picture of some suburban "local" chugging into the station hauled by some weary old locomotive that probably first saw the light of day in about 1895.

They had at least stopped making the more obvious errors, like showing the hero getting into a taxi wearing a light suit and getting out of the same taxi at the end of his journey, wearing a dark one, but they still went on making silly mistakes, even in the most expensive pictures.

"I wonder," he thought," if when I get to Hollywood and offer them a bit of constructive criticism, they'll tell me why they do it, or whether they'll hand me the proverbial 'raspberry ' and tell me to mind my own b----- business?"

2

Geoffrey was met, on his arrival in New York, by a young man, wearing the most expansive and friendly grin and the most nondescript clothes, that he had ever seen in one combination.

The young man introduced himself as Jeff Middleton. Geoffrey gathered that he was something to do with the New York office of World Wide Pictures; something in the Publicity department, but just what position he occupied there he did not discover.

Mr. Middleton referred, at frequent intervals, to the "old man," a personage whom he apparently regarded with some considerable awe, and to whom Geoffrey discovered he was on his way to be introduced. The "old man" proved to be a Mr. Cooper, a benevolent, tiredlooking gentleman who welcomed Geoffrey with a lazy, " Mighty glad to have you with us," a friendly smile, and a cigar.

He told Geoffrey what the New York office did, and how it operated, in relation to the Hollywood "outfit," as he called it. The real centre of the film-industry was not Hollywood, but New York, he said. For this reason it was a pity that Geoffrey was not going to stay with them, but he would look forward to handling the stuff that Geoffrey was going to turn out for them, and he hoped that it would be as good as the stuff he had done on the "other side."

After a few more generalities and further assurances of welcome Mr. Cooper handed him back into the willing care of Mr. Middleton.

When Geoffrey told Mr. Middleton that he was not stopping in New York, but was leaving for Chicago the following morning, Mr. Middleton was despondent. Mr. Middleton had had pleasurable anticipations, so he said, of showing Geoffrey the town. With World Wide paying the expenses, and a real excuse to give his "trouble-and-strife" (that, he said in an aside, should make Geoffrey feel at home as it was Cockney slang for wife) he felt that he had been cheated out of a good time. But he soon cheered up again, and said that they would have to pack it all into one night. And they did.

Geoffrey saw more "Pent-house Clubs," "Rainbow Rooms," "Blue Rooms" and places to eat expensive food and to drink expensive liquor, than he would have expected to see if he had spent a month in New York. It was rather a pity really, that when, in the early hours, he arrived back at his "over-central-heated " hotel, the warm air, which felt damp like the air in a turkish-bath, should have made him feel so sick. It was rather a pity to lose so much expensive liquor in such a morbid and depressing manner; it was rather depressing to leave New York, after such a brief visit, with a "hang-over." And, as he climbed rather wearily into bed he shuddered as he contemplated the "hang-over" and, as it tran-spired, the shudder was justified. But he did catch his train for Chicago. Mr. Middleton stayed in bed.

When, after he reached Hollywood, Geoffrey received a letter from him it ran, ". . . it took my wife seven days to forgive me. During the whole time she hardly spoke a kind word to me, and didn't cook me a thing, so that they were mainly cold collations I had at home - she did at least give me plenty of 'cold-shoulder' and 'tongue'! But (and please don't think that I don't love my wife) it was worth it!"

In days to come quite a lot of people asked Geoffrey what he thought of New York. They were somewhat surprised when he said that he thought that the view from the 82nd, 92nd or 102nd (he wasn't quite sure which) floor of the Empire State Building was grand; that the rooms in the New York hotels were overheated; that he had a vague suspicion that the sale of wood-alcohol hadn't gone out with prohibition; and that one day he wanted to go to New York to see what it was really like. It was an unusual thing to say. But what else could he say?

<h1 style="text-align:center">3</h1>

The nine-hundred-odd miles that Geoffrey travelled from New York to Chicago gave him ample opportunity to recover. The luxurious travelling facilities of the Pennsylvania Railroad provided him with a new experience. When he arrived at Chicago he was his old self again; it was with a minimum of delay that he contacted Sir Highley's clients.   ·

In a taxi, on the way to his hotel, he observed with interest the gratuitous information addressed to the housewives of Chicago that, "With ' Wham' In The Can, You Have a Chef in the Kitchen." He decided that his best line to follow would be that advertising campaigns that sold "Wham" in the U.S.A. would not sell "Wham" in the United Kingdom.

In due course he enlarged upon this theme with considerable success. With his own charm, and several little tricks of salesmanship borrowed from Sir Highley, he had an exceedingly successful interview. The makers of "some of America's finest foodstuffs" sympathised with Sir Highley's problems; they deprecated the conservatism of an insular people. But even so, they insisted that there was no room for sentiment in business. What they wanted was results. "Give us ever-increasing sales," they exhorted, "and the sales-chart will be our charter of eternal friendship. But, "they repeated, "there's no room for sentiment in business. No room for sentiment. . . . "

That night Geoffrey dined with the president of the Corporation. After dinner, they tuned in the "Wham Hour" on the radio. In addition to "Wham" the announcer eulogised a food-product that was new to Geoffrey; one that had not yet been marketed in England.

"Why not try it over there?" he said.   ·

His host shook his head sadly. "Oh, no," he replied. "It wouldn't 'go.' It doesn't 'go' over here. It did once; my father built up the business on it. But the public taste changes, y'know. It's old-fashioned now - out of date. Doesn't really pay us to make it at all."

"Then why do you?" queried Geoffrey.

"First product, and all that, y'know. Sentimental reasons - purely sentimental!"

4

Even to a traveller in a strange and interesting land, it is difficult for a journey not to become boring when it is between two places so far removed as Chicago and Hollywood. Admittedly there is sleeping and eating, and stopping on the way, and comfort, and scenery changing and varied, but there are long weary miles of barren inhospitable sameness, when one longs for human companionship. And so Geoffrey welcomed a travelling companion; one who was going "all-the-way" with him. He met him in the observation car. He was a tall, "shouldery" man, about forty, with sandy-coloured hair, and friendly blue eyes. He wore a blue suit with a chalk-stripe, and brown shoes. The chalk stripes looked as if they might have been made with a piece of blackboard chalk, and as his ensemble was completed by a pink shirt and a many-coloured, jazz-design tie, the general effect was somewhat on the "loud" side.

He professed himself as interested to make the acquaintance of a Britisher; and as he represented a type that was new to Geoffrey they found a great deal to talk about.

He told Geoffrey that his name was Jack Donovan; Jack "Mouth" Donovan. "They calls me that because I shoots off me trap too much," he confided. During the long journey he lived up to his reputation. "There's a cop on this train," he said. "I can smell a bull a mile off - or anyone to do with 'em. I hates cops. It's because of them bastards that I'm leaving Chi. Not that they've got anything on me now, I'm clean. I've just finished a stretch in the can. The dirty swine goes and hangs a frame on me - picks me up and swears I'm carrying a rod. Yeah; ain't that sumpin'? Why, a guy can't just pay a friendly little visit to his old home town without getting picked up by those bastards. How d'yer ever know when you're in the clear, when they goes on pulling tricks like that? Still," he went on musingly, "Chi ain't what it was in the old days. No, sir. When they started crackin' down, me, I takes a powder - finishes up in Hollywood with the sweetest little racket you ever saw. Legal too. 'Course, one or two of our clients gets a little unreasonable at times. That's where I comes in - I reasons with 'em. I sort of points out to 'em that it ain't no good going and squealing their grief to the cops. That sort of thing ain't no good for a high-class established business."

He had quite a few more drinks before he confided to Geoffrey the details of the "high-class established business."

"We runs a school for aspirin' motion picture actors," he went on. " Correspondence or personal coachin'. You'd be surprised the way those suckers fall for it. 'Course we gives the outfit a grand build-up. Those what comes out for the 'personal' is guaranteed an introduction to a Studio and a film test. 'Course we got our own Studio - it's only a little two-by-four set-up - but it serves its purpose. We does turn out a short, or one of them int'rest things, now and again - just to show that everything's on the up and up - but if we used just one per cent of all the guys and dames what is interduced to us, we'd have to be as big as M.G.M. and United Artists all rolled into one! And do them suckers pay! Why, for a course by mail on motion-picture actin', and a guarantee that a picksher of their mug will be lodged with the castin' department of a studio they pays plenty. But the personal clients is the gravy. We got our own rooms where we boards 'em - they ain't cheap - we tells 'em nothin' ain't cheap in Hollywood; they pays us to have their pickshers took; they pays for the film-test; they pays for their lessons. Oh, it's a sweet little racket all right. 'Course, one or two gets a bit tough occasionally, but I soons straightens 'em out. 'What you got to beef about?' I says, 'you've had yuh lessons, ain't yuh? You've had yuh film-test? Yuh picksher's in the studio, ain't it? Now you go home and wait,' I says, 'you'll be hearin' soon - from us or from the studio.' Most of 'em goes sort of quiet like, and them that don't - well, I never did have much trouble handlin' suckers, anyway!

"What's your racket?" he asked Geoffrey. And when Geoffrey told him what it was that he was going to Hollywood to do, he leaned across and patted Geoffrey on the knee, " Well, ain't that sumpin' ," he said. "Ain't it surprisin' how some guys make their dough!"

Geoffrey was rather sorry when it was time to say good-bye. They would have to meet again soon, said "Mouth", Geoffrey would be tickled to death if he showed him the town. Geoffrey wasn't too sure - it seemed a bit too prophetic to him.

CHAPTER 7

1

"We're great on parties here," said Bill Grant to Geoffrey. "It's a pity that you're not a bit of a celebrity, or something like that, then we'd have thrown one for you. Still, you'll soon get settled down here, people are always coming and going and they make friends easy. You'll meet lots of folks at Lois Lamont's party - she's a grand woman - not much like the Lois Lamont of the films to be sure, I think she'd throw a fit if anyone ever pulled a gun in earnest, but she's tops. There'll be lots of celebrities there to-night, so if your fancy turns to seeing the film-famous in the flesh this'll be your chance."

Bill Grant was one of the junior executives of World Wide who had been deputed to show Geoffrey the way around. He was a very likeable and enthusiastic young man, and the weeks that Geoffrey had spent in Hollywood had not been wasted. World Wide Pictures and Studios Inc., was a bit overwhelming - even when taken in comparatively small and daily doses, but Bill Grant had proved an expert in pointing out the things that really mattered.

Strangely enough, the thing that had bored Geoffrey most of all, had been his first visit to watch a film actually in production. The miles of wires and cables that cluttered up the floor; the rushing and bustling about; the noise of banging and tapping and hammering, that was so strangely stilled when some stentorian voice yelled "Quiet," had all made him feel somehow as if he had wandered into Bedlam. He had been comfortable enough tucked away with Bill Grant at the side of the usual group of technical staff clustered round the camera, and he had liked it well enough when things went ahead without a hitch. But there were such long boring intervals when nothing interesting happened at all. The "dolly" would start tracking up from long-shot to close-up, and then it would require adjusting, and everything stopped while the job was done. Or they would be shooting a sequence on a polished floor, and, in between half-a-dozen rehearsals, somebody would jump out with a mop and start polishing away as if their very life depended upon it. Then there was a nail sticking out of some stairs that had been built on the set, and everybody started bawling for "Jim" to come and knock it in. Geoffrey did ask Bill why somebody didn't just get a hammer and knock it in without all the shouting, but Bill said something about "Jim" being a carpenter, and that knocking in nails was a carpenter's job, and about not upsetting the Union men, and seemed quite happy whilst they waited five minutes for "Jim" to get his hammer and knock the nail in.

Then they were shooting a scene where the hero was all upset, because his girl was out running-around with some other man, and he was being photographed sitting at a table lighting his first cigarette. Then they wanted to show him sitting at the same table with his tie askew, and his hair all mussed-up, smoking his twentieth cigarette, with a tray full of stubs at his elbow. But they hadn't got the ash-tray full of stubs. So everybody started smoking like mad and then stubbed out the cigarettes in the tray.

But when he had watched the same unimportant little scene rehearsed at least eighteen times, he hit a new low in depression. He began to long for the comparative sanity of even an advertising office. And, on one occasion, when he emerged gratefully into the open air, he confided to Bill Grant that he was glad his part of the job was concerned with the finished article and not in making films.

Bill Grant was a very good friend of Lois Lamont, the blonde wise-cracking star of so many "tough " films. Geoffrey had been dining with him when Lois had stopped at their table to invite Bill to her party. Lois was a revelation. Geoffrey thought that even though the camera could not lie, he certainly had the evidence of his own eyes that it could be guilty of the most flattering misrepresentation. Without intending to be rude, he had stared at Lois Lamont's face. On the screen Lois Lamont did not appear beautiful but she was undoubtedly good to look at. What trick of camera-magic was used to tone down those irregular features into the attractive face that the public were privileged to see upon the screen, was forever a mystery to Geoffrey. Her eyes were small, and her nose and mouth were large, but apart from the smallness of her eyes, individually, her features were good. The trouble was that they were so ill-matched as to make their assembly upon a single face one of the most obvious humorous mistakes of nature.

If Lois Lamont had not, as a result of her frequent appearances upon the screen, been so well known, a first sight of her face would have evoked in the beholder nothing more than an innate desire to laugh, which desire good-manners would have throttled at birth. But, expecting her to look just as she did on the screen, and being faced with the reality, was too much; it was a shock that left one speechless.

"Oh, don't mind my pan," Lois had said, interrupting his thoughts, and giving him a wide, friendly smile. "It's always a bit of a shock at first, but you'll soon get used to it - everyone does!"

Geoffrey had fidgeted with his napkin and wished that he could sit down. "No, really I - er--" he blushed.

"Now don't try and apologise," Lois had interposed, and turning to Bill Grant she had continued, "he's kinda cute – so good-looking and yet he still knows how to blush! Introduce me." She had decided to sit down, much to the relief of a waiter who had been hovering uncomfortably in the background nursing a chair, and she had stayed quite some time.

Then, before she had gone to join her friends, she had invited Geoffrey to her party and he had accepted with genuine pleasure.

"Well, I'll be seein' yuh!." she had said, reverting for a moment to the type she had made so famous on the screen, and had gone off to join her own party.

"She's a grand person, all right," said Geoffrey.

"I've an idea that she doesn't think you're too bad either," Bill had replied.

2

"Just slip into a tuxedo," said Bill, "and I'll be round and pick you up in about an hour."

Whilst he was shaving and dressing Geoffrey wondered about Lesley. During the weeks that he had been in Hollywood he had not had so much as a fleeting glimpse of her. His tentative enquiries about her had been quite unavailing, and he was beginning to wonder if, after all, he would ever meet her again.

Bill arrived right on time, and seated in his comfortable roadster driving into the hills, Geoffrey's thoughts once again turned to Lesley.

"Bill," he said, "I once met Lesley Travis in London - a long time ago. Does she get about much? I mean – I haven't seen her since I've been here and I wondered if you knew anything about her. I'd rather enjoy meeting her again - if she remembered me."

Bill screwed up his nose as if puzzling out the answer to an awkward question. "Well," he said, "she does and yet she doesn't - if you get what I mean. She's not a recluse or anything like that, but now I come to think about it, she doesn't get about a terrible lot, not to the usual functions anyway, and all that sort of thing. But I can remember running into her once or twice. I expect you'll meet up with her again sometime, if you're around long enough," and apparently considering it a matter of minor importance, he started to whistle softly to himself, and went on whistling until they pulled up in the drive of Lois' house.

Geoffrey and Bill were the first to arrive. They had come early at Lois' request, so that they could, as she said, ". . . have a few quiet, friendly little drinks before the 'wolves' arrived."

It was soon obvious to Geoffrey that Lois and Bill had a considerable affection for each other. When the guests began to arrive and the room to fill, Lois was busily engaged in the role of charming hostess, and Bill, quite naturally it seemed, was there helping her; doing all the little things that helped the party to run smoothly.

This left Geoffrey a little on his own, and whilst he had met a number of interesting people and had quite lost the feeling of being a stranger in a strange land, he was, for the moment, alone.

Snatches of animated conversation beat upon his ears like tiny waves tumbling rhythmically upon a seashore.

"... Worth two-thousand dollars of anybody's money - and told him that she'd found it .... "

". . . The sort of woman who thinks that wearing trousers makes her look effeminate!"

" I said, 'But darling, you can't be a virgin *and* wear a sable coat. . . . "

"Yeah. This guy Hitler'll stop lead, sure as grief .... "

". . . And everyone knows they gave her an 'Oscar' for *that* .... "

He had moved through this troubled sea of conversation and had collected a highball and was leaning with his back against the door that led on to the terrace, watching the new arrivals, when he saw Lesley.

She was just being greeted by Lois, and after they had exchanged a few smiling remarks, she moved slowly forward into the room, looking somewhat casually about her, as if undecided which group of her many friends to join.

She was breath-takingly lovely in a cool-looking gown of white organza, mistily printed with pink flowers and green leaves. The closely fitting bodice, which showed her figure to perfection, and the long full skirt made her appear to Geoffrey as if she were a Princess from some old-fashioned fairy-tale who had, for a short time, decided to join the mortals in their festivities.

He was seized with a most curious, breathless, empty feeling. This was the moment that he had waited for through all those long months, which had mounted to a year, and then almost to another, since he had last seen her.

Would it be best, he wondered, to go right up to her now and say, "Hello!" just as if it were only yesterday that they had met in London; or would it be best to wait until someone introduced them, and then to say to her, "I think we've met before - in London, wasn't it?"

"Hell," he thought, "I can't wait any longer. Whether she remembers me or not, I'm going to speak to her now."

Whilst these thoughts had been running through his mind, Lesley had continued to glance around the room, and, just as he reached his decision, she looked straight at him.

There was no doubt about whether she remembered him. There was an incredulous, happy look on her face, and he saw her lips move as she said his name softly, wonderingly. She came rapidly towards him holding out both hands in welcome. "Why, Geoffrey!" she said. " What are you doing here - in Hollywood?"

He seized her hands eagerly holding them tightly. For a moment he could not speak. He just stood there, holding her hands, and gazing down at her with a look of absolute adoration. She looked up at him, starry-eyed and happy, and he felt her hands trembling a little.

At last he said, "It's rather a long story really," and he thought how ridiculous it was that he should have so much difficulty in keeping his voice steady. He drew her arm through his, and continued, saying, "shall we go on to the terrace for a little while? It will be hard to tell you, with so much noise in here." She nodded her head in assent, and as he opened the door she disengaged her arm, moved ahead of him and waited, looking down into the gardens. He closed the door, and came up behind her, but she did not look round. He fumbled with his case and lit a cigarette.

"Cigarette?" he enquired. She shook her head. He drew deeply on his cigarette and said, "It's difficult to know just where to begin really, I ... "

She turned then and looked at him. Her eyes were suspiciously bright, and she was biting on her lower lip to try to conceal that it was trembling. He went on rather hurriedly, "I'm working over here now with ... " He paused again, and suddenly she was in his arms, and he was crushing her to him.

"Darling, darling," he whispered. It hurt a little, the way he held her, but she did not mind. It gave her a warm and happy feeling to sense his longing for her. Her head fell back a little. Her grey-blue eyes were even more lovely, with unshed, happy tears; through her parted lips he felt her breath, warm and sweet, beating upon his face. Her eyes closed, and her lashes were dark and curling against her fair skin. When he kissed her, it was as if a white searing flame was all about them; passionately she clung to him, within the shelter of his arms she looked frail and almost childlike. But she returned his kisses ardently, urgently. Their desire mounted to the stars.

When at last he released her, he thought that she would fall, and putting his arms about her, he led her to a low cushioned seat at the end of the terrace.

They sat there, with his arm still around her, while the tempest that had shaken them was gradually stilled. There was no need for words. The sudden blinding realisation of the depth of their love, the passion that had shaken them, were still too close and near to need the confirmation of inadequate words.

It was Lois who broke the silence, coming through the door with Bill. "What in the world are you two doing mooning out here?" she enquired.

They sprang to their feet feeling rather self-conscious. It was Lesley, happy and smiling, who said gaily, "Oh, we're old friends - and very good friends." And she looked up at Geoffrey with a tantalising smile, and slipped her hand into his.

"Well, I'm not going to be neglected at my own party," said Lois, and laughingly swept them back into the room.

It must have been a very good party - all Lois' parties were. But Geoffrey remembered very little about it. Outwardly, he was his usual charming self, mixing with the other guests, laughing at their jokes, taking his share in the conversation. But, all the time, he was aware only of Lesley, and whenever their eyes met he felt as if his heart had missed a beat, and she would wrinkle up her nose in the funny little way she had, and smile at him.

Lesley was radiant. People kept saying, "You look more lovely than ever to-night" or, "Why, Lesley! What have you been doing to yourself? You seem to get younger and prettier all the time!" And she would laugh and say, "Oh, I expect it's because I feel so happy to-night," and perhaps glance quickly towards Geoffrey.

Then, when it was time to go, Bill said that he was going to stay behind and talk to Lois for a while. "Why don't you take my car, and run Lesley home?" he said. "It's a wonderful night, and Lesley's house is right by the sea. The air will do you both good after being in this smoky room."

As the roadster rolled down the drive, they waved to Lois and Bill. "Don't forget, and start driving on the left!" Bill called out.

Lesley's house overlooked the sea. She led him inside and into the big lounge with its deep comfortable arm-chairs, and the big windows that looked out across the water.

"This is an occasion," she cried. "An occasion that calls for champagne. Now don't run away, and I'll be back in a moment." But before she could go he caught her to him, and for a moment she lay passive in his arms whilst he kissed her. Then very gently, she pushed him away. "No! No!" she said. "You'll have me all helpless again, if you do that, and I simply must have that champagne to celebrate – us!" And she broke away from him, and was through the door almost before he knew that she was gone.

As he took a cigarette from the box on the table, he heard her high-heels tap, tapping, away into the house, and then a door banged and everything was quiet.

It seemed an eternity before she was back again, bearing a bottle of champagne, wrapped in a napkin, and two glasses, which she carried with the stems between the slim fingers of her left hand.

She set the bottle and the glasses down on a low table, and flung her chinchilla wrap carelessly on to one of the big armchairs. One of the shoulder straps of the lovely cool-looking gown she was wearing had slipped a little, and after she had set it back in place, and swept aside a wayward lock of fair hair that had fallen in front of her eyes, she started to strip the gold-foil from the cork.

Geoffrey came and stood behind her and kissed her just below her left ear.

The cork left the bottle with a hollow, explosive sound; the champagne bubbled golden into the glasses. "This is lovely," she said.

Geoffrey gave a mock sigh. "Just a film-star at heart," he said. "Can't bear to be away from champagne for more than five minutes at a time." She wrinkled her nose at him.

She handed him one of the glasses and said, "What shall we drink to?"

"I shall drink to you," he replied. "To the loveliest and most adorable lady in the whole world."

She said. "I think I shall drink to love. To all the people in all the world who are really and truly in love."

"Then you drink to me," he said meaningly. "And to myself," she replied softly.

Geoffrey lifted his glass. "To you, Lesley."

"To love," said Lesley, and then added, "and to you, darling."

She sat down on the soft cushions of the deep settee, and motioned him to sit beside her.

"Now tell me, darling," she said, "what wonderful, delightful chance has brought you here to me?"

"Very well," he answered. "But before I do, I want you to tell me one thing. Why did you tell me that your name was Phyllis Peters? Why did you tell me that fairy-story about your life and ... everything?"

"So you haven't forgiven me for that?" she asked, shaking her head.

"Of course I have," he said, "if there was ever anything to forgive. But so often I have wondered why?"

"Well, it wasn't all untrue really. I *have* got a secretary named Phyllis Peters, and when I met you, and I realised that you hadn't the faintest idea who I really was, I thought that perhaps she wouldn't mind my borrowing her name for just a little while. You see, you seemed to like me such a lot, and ... " She broke off for a moment. "Oh, Geoffrey, it's so difficult this business of being a film actress. I am always finding myself wondering whether people really like me, just for myself, or whether it is because of all the glamour that they will insist on giving people who are in films. So that when I met you, and you did funny things to my inside - and to my heart - every time you smiled at me, I wanted to be ... oh, just anybody. But the story that I told you, except for the name, and that bit at the end about being a secretary, that was all true. I did get a job with "InterContinental" as a stenographer, but one day I was taking some letters for Chris Noble - the director - when he said casually that he thought I would photograph well. He arranged for me to have a test, and then they took away my typewriter and made me work much harder, learning to walk, and talk; and wear clothes and dozens of things like that. I just did everything they told me to do, and sometimes when I look around me and see all this, and sometimes when I see my name in lights outside a cinema, or see my picture in the magazines, I just can't believe it's really true. Any more than I can believe that it is really and truly you, sitting here beside me.

"And then, when you sent those flowers to the boat, addressed to Phyllis Peters, and I sat on my bed and looked at them and thought that I was going away from you, probably for ever, then I knew that I loved you. But it all seemed so crazy. I really didn't know a thing about you - what you did, your address, whether you were married - or anything."

Suddenly she sat bolt upright and looked at him, "You're not married, are you?" she said, with something vaguely like panic in her voice.

Geoffrey smiled, and shook his head. "Well . . . not yet!" he said slowly.

Lesley sank back into the cushions again. "I told myself that I would soon forget you. Or that you would write, perhaps to Phyllis Peters, or if you found out about me, to me. Why *didn't* you write, Geoffrey? Why, in heaven's name, if you felt the way about me," she paused and looked at him, "the way you seem to feel now, why didn't you write?"

"Oh, I wanted to," he said. "God, how I wanted to. But - with all those 'fan' letters you must get - would you have received it?"

"Oh, you sweet idiot," she said, and the soft warmth of her voice took away any trace of harshness from the word. "Of course I would. I told Phyllis Peters about you. I told her to look out for any letter that came from England, whether it was addressed to her or to me, and if it was signed 'Geoffrey,' to bring it to me right away. But nothing ever came, and I thought you had forgotten me. But I couldn't forget you. Oh, I've been so lonely sometimes sitting here in this very room thinking about you, and wondering what you were doing. Sometimes I've hated you. The way the memory of you would come stalking into this room, and smile at me and say, "Shall we dance?" or "You're adorable!" just like you did on that night so long ago. And then you would laugh at me, and go away, and leave me feeling lonely and tired. And then I would go to bed and determine to forget you. And for a while I would, until you would come marching into my dressing-room or my bedroom, without any regard for my privacy, and kiss me like you did that night in the car. Oh, Geoffrey," she said, "sometimes you've been perfectly horrible to me."

"Then I'll never be horrible again," he said, and holding her tiny hands, as if they were something fragile and very precious, he kissed the soft palms.

"Oh, you're incorrigible," she said. "Here you are, supposedly to tell me what you have been doing, and how you come to be in Hollywood, and right away you have me telling you all about myself, just like you did the first time we met, so that I still don't know anything about you. Anything that is, except that you're sweet, and that I love you very much."

He could not resist kissing her for that, and then glancing at the clock, he said, "It's getting very late, or rather, early, you know."

"Oh, bother the time," she said, "you're not leaving here until you dispose of all this mystery, and as for it being late, well, I'm a working girl myself, and if you do fall asleep to-morrow it will serve you right for staying away so long, and having so much to tell me."

"If you have no objection," he said, "I'll never leave you again, and to-morrow if I do anything except dream about you and how wonderful you are, and wonder why you should ever fall in love with me, I'll know that I'm really crazy, and that to-night didn't really happen after all."

He put his arm around her and drew her close to him. She rested her head on his shoulder, and he kissed the top of her golden hair. He thought how nice it was, that faint perfume of Schiaparelli, and then he told her about all the things that had happened to bring him to Hollywood; how, ever since that night in London, he had locked the memory of her away in his heart, and had wanted her more than anything else in the world. And, whilst he told his story, she snuggled closer to him and drew her legs up under her, like a schoolgirl, and the famous Lesley Travis was far away, and resting in Geoffrey's arms was only someone very young, very beautiful, and very much in love.

He reminded her of her dream cottage and told her how he had made it all come true, and of how he had furnished it with all the things that he thought that she would like, and had named it "The Dancing Water." How he had hated, almost more than anything else, leaving the cottage, because of the shadow-Lesley that had always been there; tending the flowers in the garden, or perhaps, sitting opposite to him in the deep armchair near the old inglenook fireplace. Of his hopes, that one day, she would go with him to see it all in reality and in very truth make it all her own.

Lesley worried a little about the cottage. What would happen to it, she asked, whilst he was away? So he told her about Elsa Knight and Bobby, and how they were living there and taking care of it.

They moved over to the big windows and stood, he with his arm about her, looking out over the sea which was still and quiet, and showed only as a faint silver line - a reflection from the now pale and waning moon.

"How long will it be," she asked, "before you can take me to my cottage? Can you look from the windows and see the sea - as we can here? But, yes! Of course you can. That is why you named it "The Dancing Water," isn't it? It's a pretty name. When you told me, it reminded me of an old fairy-story that my mother used to read to me when I was very tiny. It was a strange but lovely story full of fabulous creatures, wicked queens, and a beautiful Princess and her gallant Prince. I remember how pretty I thought their names - Princess Fairstar and Prince Chery."

She looked up at him for a moment. "But perhaps you know the story?"

He shook his head, "No, darling," he said, and then she looked back over the sea again and went on, "Well, before Chery could win Fairstar for his own there were many things that he had to obtain for her, and one of them was the Dancing Water. It was magic water hidden away deep in the heart of a Burning Forest, and Chery had many exciting adventures before he could bear the Dancing Water back to his Princess. But, at last, he brought it to her and wonderfully, it made her even more beautiful and kept her forever young.

"Oh, Geoffrey!" she cried, "you are indeed my very own Prince Chery, and have brought me the Dancing Water that will make me young again. Darling, with you, there will be no more of those horrible lonely nights. Lonely nights when I have felt so tired; a ghastly dragging tiredness that has left me feeling so worn-out - so old."

She laughed a little bitterly. "Old and worn-out, and I'm still only young! Yes, really very young," she said again, looking up at him. "But there have been five hard years of working, working, working to make the Lesley Travis of the screen; the only Lesley Travis that people seem to see, or want to see. Without caring about the real me. The real Lesley, darling, that you have found, and brought to life again. Yes, my dear, you are indeed the Prince Chery of my fairy-story."

"Then if I am," he said softly, "you are in very truth, the loveliest and most adorable Princess that ever was, since time began."

No measured time intruded on the night's loveliness as they stood together at the window. His arm was still about her; her hand pressing his close to the warmth and softness of her body beneath its flimsy covering. At last she detached herself from his encircling arm and moved quietly away. For a little longer Geoffrey gazed at the pale sequin-sky, the faintly silver-splashed sea, then he too turned away into the half-light of the room.

Lesley, lying deep in the soft cushions of the settee stared wide-eyed at the ceiling. As she heard him move, her eyes became alive again, all the sweetness and longing of her love were mirrored there; her lips were moist and a little parted. She did not speak but extended her hands towards him. Geoffrey took a sudden pace forward, seizing her hands and showering kisses upon them. · As his burning lips pressed hungrily into the tiny soft palms of her hands, her breathing became deeper, catching involuntarily as if she had been running. There was a beating in her temple and her breast that grew ever stronger; his breath was warm upon her hands as she drew him closer. Suddenly his arms went round her. Never had he felt so strong or she so weak. Her eyes closed. On her moist and parted lips came Geoffrey's, warm and vibrant; there was no time, no world, only their love. It surged about them like a rising, dancing tide; terrifyingly, exhaustingly. Slowly he released her. As she opened her eyes, they were moist, as her lips had been.

"Darling," he said, " I love you beyond hope, beyond understanding, if .... "

As she drew his lips down to hers again she was crying a little. The tide of their love swirled higher about them. He kissed her eyes, her cheek, her neck, moved lower to the soft rising curve of her breast. She drew her breath in tiny, tempestuous gusts, moving passionately, restlessly.

Geoffrey was beside her. They clung together, pressing closely; inseparable. His mind was lost in a wonderment born of his love for her and of her loveliness; if only he could pay some homage to her - to her love ...

The rising tide swept them on. They were lost to the world - their love was lost to the world for ever. The tide was full. The dancing water closed above them.

CHAPTER 8

1

THEY were married the following week-end. Very quietly. They went by plane to a little sleepy place, where a funny little old justice of the peace, who looked at them over the top of his glasses in a friendly sympathetic sort of way, made them man and wife.

At first Lesley had demurred at such a hurried wedding.

There was so much to plan, so much to do, so many things that would require attention, she said. But he had been peculiarly adamant. "I want to get married right away," he had said, and nothing that she could say would make him change.

"But, darling," she had remonstrated, "there's nothing in the world I want more than for us to get married. But why so soon?"

And at last he had whispered his reason to her.

She had laughed a little then. But it was a laugh that had a quality of tears about it. "Dearest, she said, "you really are most deliciously old-fashioned about some things! But," and she had held him very close, and she was not laughing any more, "I wanted it to happen. I wanted to *belong* to you."

But he had only held her in his arms and smiled, and kissed her lips, her eyes, her hair. And so she had agreed.

2

Lesley's marriage made good "copy." Even with the ever-darkening shadows that were falling across Europe, it was front-page news.

"Film Star Weds in Secret," said one report. "Lesley Travis Weds Scenario Writer - Romantic Culmination of Secret Love-affair," another announced.

"I rather object to that bit about the scenario-writer," said Geoffrey, when they were reading the newspapers at the breakfast-table. "Here I am on the front-page for the first, and probably the last, time in my life, and they describe me so that even my own friends won't recognise me!" They both laughed at that.

"You know," he continued, "this being married to a celebrity will take a little getting used to. Come to think of it, it's just as well that Lesley is your first name. Think what it would be like if it had been 'Pansy' or anything like that. I mean, if people do point to me when I'm with you, and say, 'My dear, that's Mister Lesley Travis,' perhaps they'll just raise their eyebrows and reply, 'Oh, really!' But if they nudged their friends and said, 'That's Mister "Pansy" Travis,' they might get entirely the wrong idea about me!"

Lesley wrinkled her nose at him. "Well, so far as I'm concerned they can use any names they like; outside the studio I am Mrs. Geoffrey Manners, and to me, darling, it is the nicest name in all the world.

"Not," she continued "that I intend to go on being Mrs. Geoffrey Manners if you are going to develop into the sort of husband who spends all breakfast time buried behind a newspaper." She laughed at him, and pushing back her chair, leaned over the table, and with a quick movement of her hand sent the newspaper flying.

There was a mischievous light dancing in her eyes as she stood watching him. He stooped and gathered up the paper, folded it carefully, and set it down upon the table. With equal care he folded his napkin and placed it upon the folded paper. "Young lady," he said at length, getting up from the table and moving round towards her, "I see that you will have to learn to have a proper respect for your husband."

Lesley moved round, keeping the table between them. Suddenly she darted away, but he had anticipated the move and caught her before she had gone more than a few paces. He swung her round into his arms and she stood there laughing up at him, with her fair hair all tumbled.

"Now," he said, "to find a punishment to fit the crime. I have heard that the back of a hairbrush - applied with discretion. . . . " He glanced around the room. "Ah, well, there's a very nice one in the bedroom," and he swung her up into his arms, and carried her towards the door.

He shut the bedroom door with a quick backward kick, carried her across the room, and very gently set her down upon the bed.

Her negligee was all disarranged, and she was so lovely lying there, that as he looked at her the merriment died from his eyes; he stooped his head and kissed her.

As his arms went round her she said, "Darling, you mustn't. Really you mustn't - after all we have only just finished breakfast, and . . . " He kissed her again.

Her voice was almost a whisper and her lips brushed his as she spoke: "You must not make love to me at this time of the day. You really must not make love to me so much. I should hate it if . . . " Once more his lips silenced her.

And at length, he said to her, "And what is it you would hate if . . . ?"

As her arms went round his neck she had just time to murmur, "I should hate it ... Oh, I should hate it if ever you should stop wanting to make love to me."

3

Sir Highley cabled his congratulations, and a letter followed close upon the cable. Sir Highley's letter expanded his congratulations in the most effusive terms; he referred to Geoffrey as a "sly-dog," and recorded, " ... No longer shall I speculate as to those mysterious 'personal reasons' which drew you so irresistibly to Hollywood."

On more general matters Sir Highley wrote: ". . . everything is going well at Nitely's. Of course, this tension in Europe between Germany and Czechoslovakia is getting worse, and to my way of thinking, is rapidly approaching a climax. 'Big Business' holds private meetings to decide what to do if war comes, and then proclaims loudly to the public that 'there will be no war!' Personally I incline to the view that their public utterances are correct - Britain is in no condition to go to war - there are people, who should know, who say that Germany's Air Force could blast Britain out of the sea!"

"So far as advertising is concerned, nearly everybody seems to think that, if there is a war, all publicity is going to take an immediate nose-dive into oblivion, and with the number of cancellation notices that even our own clients have got ready to shoot right in, if anything does break, I suppose the gloomy ones have an even chance of being right. But if the government are going to take the same short-sighted view, after all that happened in the last war, and everything that that little screaming Goebbels has shown us, I think that I shall begin to believe the worst .... "

But England and Europe were not alone in those summer days of 1938 in their horrible, down-dragging, sickening anticipation of war. The grisly fingers of a possible world-conflict spread their filthy touch as far as America. And whilst indeed, their touch upon the American people did not conjure up the awful possibilities that they did to the people of Europe, it did create something indefinable; disturbing and unsettling. Something of fear perhaps, possibly unrealised. But it was there, like a fear generated by a wild-animal call in a lonely place, or a sudden scream in the dark. A fear which manifested itself in urgent, strident calls for isolationism. Neutrality would be the new state to be admitted to the Union - inviolably and irretrievably.

They were days presenting to an Englishman in America something more than the usual difficulties.

"Why didn't England *do* something?" Geoffrey would be asked.

"Why didn't England bring Hitler up with a jolt?"

Useless to ask why it should necessarily be Britain's task? To ask if America would help?

The raised eyebrow; the quizzical glance, as if to discover in the individual the evidence of a decadent race; "But it's not America's business," was answer enough.

With the great Atlantic stretching its vast brooding miles between the old-world and the new, the sharp menace of a mighty fleet of bombers was blunted; lost its power of generating those sickening anticipations.

Lesley and Geoffrey had but little time for Hitler's rantings, but in the end it was Hitler, with his patience exhausted and dissipated in a flood of blood-curdling threats, who was responsible for their first quarrel.

4

All the sickening technique which had been employed so successfully in the case of Austria, was now paraded in an even more well-rehearsed version, to suit the peculiarities of Czechoslovakia. The fermentation of revolt within; the constant menacing, bloody threats from without. The hysterical screamings of the persecution of those of German blood. The demand that they should return to the Fatherland. "I demand only that territory which contains Germans - which is German," shrieked Hitler. "But what of our defence system?" asked the Czechs, and bravely stood firm. War was imminent. A horrible, murderous, cruel war, blasting women and little children in its blood-stained progress.

They sat together, Lesley and Geoffrey, whilst the radio, coldly and dispassionately it seemed, reviewed the latest news items of those memorable events in Europe.

"In Britain to-day," said the announcer, "trenches are being dug in the public parks. The green turf which has for so many years been carefully tended, is being ruthlessly tom up the distribution of gas-masks to the public continues . . . ."

Geoffrey rose and switched off the radio. He paced restlessly across the room, and paused, gazing unseeingly out of the window. Suddenly he flung round and said, "God, it can't happen - yet. They're not ready - they can't be ready. Not to meet those rotten, bullying swine on equal terms." He moved across to the radio and switched it on again. In the moment before it came to life he said, "I suppose they'll begin by bombing Prague - and perhaps Paris and London. By God, if they do .... "

The radio-voice interrupted him," .... It seems at this fatal eleventh hour that there is nothing, short of a miracle, that can prevent Europe from being once more plunged into war by the ambitions of a martial Germany."

Geoffrey reduced the volume of the radio-voice so that it was little more than a soft background of words.

"I can't bear to hear this reviewing of things as if they were happening on another planet," he said. "It's somehow like listening to Satan reporting all his earthly successes to a meeting of his Archangels. But it is loud enough like that to hear if there is any important newsflash."

He started to fill his pipe, jabbing the tobacco into the bowl with little jerky stabs of his first finger. He crammed the tobacco down too tightly. "Oh, hell!" he said in exasperation, when the match burnt out without the tobacco lighting properly, and he flung the pipe on to the table.

"Geoffrey-darling!" said Lesley, who had watched him with growing concern. "Don't be so irritable. I know how disturbed and anxious you must feel, but after all, this is all happening a long, long way away, and it can't really affect us so much."

"That's just it," he burst out. "It *is* so far away – I am so far away. I feel I should be there - in England, if this ghastly thing is going to happen."

She stared at him with wide, unbelieving eyes. "You? In England? Why should you be there? What could you do?"

"Oh, I don't know," he replied, "but I can pilot a plane pretty well. I should think that England is going to need all the flyers that she can lay her hands on!"

"Maybe," she said and there was a scathing note in her voice which was new to him, and unpleasant. "Maybe, but they'll need trained army-flyers and navy-flyers, not people like you who have trundled some slow old kite around during their week-ends."

"Oh, it's not quite like that," he replied. "Of course, I don't expect to jump straight into a 'fighter' and hare off like some modern flying Sir Galahad - but at least I should not be starting from scratch .... "

"I see no reason why you should start at all," she interrupted. "Your life is here now. Your work, your home, me - everything. I don't see why you should go and get yourself shot, or gassed, or blown to bits, just to save some Czechs or Slavs or somebody or other, that you hadn't even heard of until a little while ago."

"But that isn't the reason," he said with some heat. "It's Czechoslovakia to-day, but it will be Poland, or Denmark, or Holland to-morrow. Then it will be France's turn and England will be with her. We can't afford to wait until then. England has got a fight on her hands, and . . . and ... well, I feel I want to be there in it with her," he finished rather self-consciously.

"Oh, you're talking like the hero of some fourth-rate movie," she said, and flung out of the room.

In her bedroom she undressed slowly and climbed rather wearily into bed. But he did not come to her.

He refilled his pipe and sat listening to the radio. He waited, fearful and expectant, hearing a dozen times in his imagination an excited voice breaking into the programme, "It has just been reported that German aircraft have dropped bombs on . . . "

Lesley thought, "Oh, God. I never dreamed that I could be so miserable. This is worse than anything." Somewhere, deep inside her, she knew that if she tried, she could appreciate something of his point of view; that she could not doubt his love for her. But she would not try. She would not let herself think about it. "I won't lose him," she told herself again and again. "I won't let him go. I'll do anything. Anything .... "

She would not let herself cry, and when he did not come the bitterness of her unshed tears frightened her, so that for a moment she almost regretted her love for him.

In the morning she left for the studio without seeing him.

5

But if it was Germany's Führer that had set them apart, it was British Prime Minister Neville Chamberlain that brought them appeasement. An appeasement born of the greater appeasement he tendered to Hitler.

There could be no doubting the sincerity of the man who seemed too frail, too timid almost, to shoulder such mighty responsibilities; no shadow of doubt as to his overwhelming desire for peace. It brought something of cleanliness to a surrender which would otherwise have been sordid and degrading.

The world followed, with almost breathless interest, his flights to Germany; his conversations with Hitler at Berchtesgaden. There could be no mistaking the universal enthusiasm, the relief of millions of tensed nerves, as Chamberlain stepped from his plane when it landed near London, and waved above his head the pact that bore Hitler's signature.

And if, in far-off America, it was galling to an Englishman to witness a Prime Minister of England going cap-in-hand to a ranting and heartless dictator; if it was galling to listen to remarks about, "knots being tied in the Lion's tail"; Geoffrey would have been less than human not to have shared in the universal relief. To be thankful that he was no longer faced with a decision which might part him for ever from the one woman, the one woman in the world - the realisation was stark and almost brutal in its clarity - without whom he felt that it would not be even worth while for him to go on living.

6

On the day that the news came through, Lesley rushed home from the studio. Geoffrey was there waiting for her. As she flung open the door, she halted, and stood there looking at him for a moment. Then half-laughing, half-crying she ran into the haven of his arms. He held her very close, and she was only aware of the pounding of his heart, and of a flooding sensation of relief, which left her weak and trembling.

He lifted her in his arms and walking to one of the deep armchairs, sat down so that she was resting on his lap. For a long while they stayed like that and neither of them spoke.

At last he said: "Sweetheart. Let's be gay to-night. Let us be wildly and ecstatically happy. Let us go out and dance, and see bright-lights, and hear music, and celebrate. Let us celebrate all night, so that we can come back here and stand by the window, in time to see the dawn come up over the sea again."

"Yes!" she cried, jumping up. "Yes, and I'll wear my new gown - the white chiffon with the little knots of blue flowers - LaLaurie says that it's the most marvellous gown that he has created this season. You haven't seen me in it yet. Oh, I'll make myself beautiful for you!" And she was happy again, and young. And she seized his hand and started to pull him towards the door.

He stopped before they reached the door and held her slim shoulders. He looked deep into the soft grey-blue eyes. "Lesley," he said. "My very own Lesley. Never, never leave me again."

"Never, never, never," she cried, and flung her arms round his neck and drew his head down to her.

CHAPTER 9

HITLER bellowed forth at the Sportpalast in Berlin, "This is the last territorial claim which I have to make in Europe," and the world relapsed into something like its old easy-going ways. Perhaps a little more highly-strung, a little more on edge, but life could be pleasant once more without threats of immediate bloody upheavals.

It was easy, with Lesley, for life to be pleasant. Their work kept them apart quite a lot, but it made the time that they could spend together doubly sweet. Sometimes, when she had had a hard day at the studio or perhaps something had gone wrong, he would laugh away her irritation, or soothe her frayed nerves with all the love and tenderness he felt for her whenever he saw her looking so frail, and tired, and dispirited. And he would discover in her some new innocence of mind - some almost childish attitude to life - that had till then been hidden from him. And she would find in him some new sympathy, some new understanding, that bound her to him with even closer ties.

They were happy days that saw them to the end of the troubled year of 1938, and on into the early part of the new year. They worked hard but they played hard. There was a new joy in playing golf or tennis, in swimming or in dancing, now that they could do these things together.

And the facilities for enjoying oneself were legion. In this colony there was nothing too elaborate, too expensive to be achieved and enjoyed. One of the things that intrigued Geoffrey about many of the film-people that Lesley mixed with, was their complete control of money and of the things that money could buy.

Lesley earned as much in a month as he earned in a year, but they were sensible about it and they had no trouble about money matters. Geoffrey insisted on paying what he called the "household expenses," and whilst it made heavy inroads into his monthly cheque, it gave him a feeling of satisfaction, and Lesley could see that it pleased him and so raised no objections. Things like parties, and clothes, and her own car were, she said, things that she had to have to maintain her position, and that as she had to be somewhat extravagant in these things it was only right that she should pay for them out of her own money. Besides they were things that helped in her profession, and she just had to have something to put down as "expenses," otherwise it would all go in Income Tax, anyway.

This seemed a pretty reasonable argument to Geoffrey, and as some of the bills that appeared were quite beyond his capabilities, they soon fell into an arrangement that was equally acceptable to both of them, and made no demands upon their self-respect.

But there were many little things that he managed to buy for her, and the fact that she could, had she so desired, have bought them all for herself, did not seem to lessen the joy she displayed when he gave them to her.

One thing that he gave to her, she treasured far beyond its intrinsic value. It was a square-cut diamond ring. When he bought it, Geoffrey, at one stroke, reduced his bank balance by more than a quarter. But he was determined that this one gift at least, should not be overshadowed by the other lovely adornments that she had. It may have been a foolish extravagance but it pleased him, and Lesley loved him for it.

There was so much happiness for them together, that it seemed unnecessary for her to ask, as she did, whether he was quite happy in his new life, and if there was anything that he regretted leaving behind him in England. He had no regrets he said, but there were two things that he missed; the cottage, and the old, battered "Moth" in which he had had a third share.

That gave Lesley her idea. She had racked her brains to discover something that she could give him without running the risk of offending him.

One afternoon she was as excited as a schoolgirl going to her first "grown-up" dance. She hustled Geoffrey out into her car and refused to tell him where they were going.

When they arrived at the Aviation Country Club she insisted that they should go to the bar and have some champagne, and all the time she refused to divulge her secret, and laughingly refused to answer his enquiries as to "what all this was about." Then with her eyes sparkling she had led him out on to the field and had shown him the present she had bought for him.

It was a Beechcraft plane, and it looked worth every cent of the twenty thousand dollars she had paid for it. Geoffrey was breathless, and Lesley swept aside his half-hearted remonstrances at her extravagance.

It was a wonderful plane, as modern as the moment. With a 600-horse-power engine, and a retractable undercarriage, it had a top speed of more than 250 miles per hour; could climb to 30,000 feet, and was a joy to handle.

There were a few formalities before Geoffrey was recognised as a licensed pilot, but after that they enjoyed Lesley's extravagance to the full. It was play-time for both of them, but for Geoffrey, quite unknowingly, it was training for a hard and desperate venture still to come.

2

At his work, Geoffrey found himself established, and by no means unsuccessful. Even the reputed and much-boasted hustle of the average American office did not hold the terrors he had anticipated. He had been afraid that an interminable race with time; a constant snatching of seconds from the unrelenting progress of the day, would be something that he would find beyond his powers of resistance, something that would bring him down and brand him as a failure. But whilst the offices of World Wide hummed with activity, and whilst on the walls of the offices of the publicity department there were notices imploring one and all to "Do it Now," or enquiring, "Is It News About Us?" you did not require any greater resilience, any greater reserves of stamina or vitality, to work the "World Wide Way" than you did to work the "Nitely Way." And despite the stories, some true, some false; the publicity; the exploitations; the tie-ups with national advertisers; the ecstatic broadsides; the thousand and one promotion ideas for films, or the stars of films, that flowed from the offices in a never-ending stream, there was always time for a word or two with somebody on a subject outside the business of the moment, or to listen to a well-told yarn, or to try an experimental swing or two with the new mashie-niblick that somebody had just got from their "pro."

It was Douglas Martin, who of all the people in the World Wide offices had become Geoffrey's closest friend, whose duty it was to frown upon these "unworldwide-like" activities.

Douglas Martin was a sort of major-domo of the World Wide offices; a liaison between the many and varied departments; a man with a finger in almost everybody's pie. He was a small man, slim almost to the point of thinness. He was older than he looked, and his pale-blue eyes had seen, more than most, the vagaries of the ever-changing world of films. He would walk, with his slow and sedate step, from office to office, and his coming would be presaged by a rapid burst of noise from typewriters, or a sudden swirl of feverish activity. Sometimes, if his entrance was unannounced, he would stand quietly behind some misguided soul who, anticipating the joys of a coming vacation, would be engaged in the earnest study of a brochure of the attractions of some mountain or coastal resort; and there he would stay, with his eyebrows raised, and his bottom lip pushed out, until the delinquent became aware of his presence. When they did, and the brochure was hurriedly pushed away out of sight, he would continue to stand there for a few moments, nodding his head, something like an old mandarin doll, and then resume his dignified progress through the offices. Or sometimes he would wander out into the magnificent entrance hall, and stand, with his eyebrows raised and his bottom lip stuck out, surveying a cigar-butt which had been tossed by a careless hand and, missing the ash-tray, had rolled on the highly-polished floor. He would just stand there gazing at it, until some uniformed janitor would see him, and dash forward and remove the offending eyesore. Then he would move forward into the middle of the hall and survey "Greta," his most particular pride and joy. "Greta" was the name the staff had given to the huge gilded figure, something of a cross between a Winged Victory and one of Epstein's more advanced creations, which surveyed with a basilisk stare all those whose business or curiosity brought them to the offices which adjoined the World Wide studios.

The image of "Greta" appeared on the screen at the beginning and the end of every World Wide picture. Mr. Martin had made "Greta" his very own personal responsibility. Rumour had it that "Greta" had been carved from solid gold, and from the unremitting care which she received from Mr. Martin it might have been true. But it wasn't.

"Greta" was the central figure in a little pantomime that was played in the World Wide offices at the end of every working day. Regularly on the closing hour "Greta" would be covered with a snowy dust-sheet. A very junior member of the staff, who spent most of his day avoiding Mr. Martin, and when successful chewed incessantly upon a wad of gum and immersed himself in *True Detective Tales*, was entrusted with the job of robing "Greta" and making her comfortable for the night.

A minute or so before the hour, or perhaps a minute or two after, Mr. Martin would make his way slowly to the entrance hall. If he was a few moments early it was probable that "Greta" would be as yet unrobed, and in this event Mr. Martin would stand, in his characteristic attitude of suffering resignation, waiting for his minion to appear with the dust-cloth. On his arrival, Mr. Martin would raise his eyebrows and say, "Haven't I told you that this job has got to be done promptly every night? Why do I always have to hang about waiting for you? You're fired! Come and see me in my office to-morrow." Then he would wait to see that the job was properly done, and turn and make his dignified way back through the offices.

Sometimes, however, Mr. Martin would be a minute or so late in arriving to watch the evening ceremony. The dust-sheet would have hidden "Greta" from view, and only the tucking-in of a few straggling ends would remain to be done. In this event Mr. Martin would march forward with a stern expression on his face and say, "Haven't I told you never to put the dust-sheet on until I'm here? Why can't you do as you're told? You're fired! Come and see me in my office to-morrow." Mr. Martin was quite unable to appreciate that he was inconsistent. With an airy wave of his hand and a stern glance from his light-blue eye, he would effectively silence any remonstrations which referred to what he had said the night before, or the night before that. But as, in the morning, he had quite forgotten about firing anybody, no harm was done, and Mr. Martin frequently provided the staff with an amusing finale to an otherwise dull day.

It became a habit for Mr. Martin to spend at least one evening of every week with Lesley and Geoffrey. Sometimes, if Lesley was working late at the studio he and Geoffrey would dine alone together, and after dinner they would sit talking, whilst Mr. Martin consumed several very large whiskies, and wait for Lesley to join them. Or maybe, they would all manage to have dinner together and then go out somewhere. But Mr. Martin was at his best when, with a glass of whisky close to hand, he would reminisce about films, and people who had been, or were, in films.

Mr. Martin had been in the film business since the old Vitagraph and Biograph days, and he seemed at one time or another, to have done everything connected with films except appear in them. He would relate the most fantastic stories of those very early, crazy days in Hollywood, and his stories would be interlarded with references to Sweet or Swanson, Hart or Arbuckle, or to some other star of bygone days. Mr. Martin had been associated with Mr. Solomon Silverwin, the present head of World Wide, since his old nickelodeon days, but unlike Mr. Silverwin, he had grown tired of all the rushing and bustling, scrambling and fighting, and he looked on his job of running the offices for World Wide, as a sort of honourable semi-retirement.

Mr. Martin was inclined to be cynical about the film business. "No stability," he would say. "No stability. Take World Wide - one of the largest. What if it does value its assets at $100,000,000?

How are you ever going to realise them? No, the only real assets of a film company are the pictures it makes. The pictures it makes; the stars that appear in them; the guys that produce them; the technicians; the people that sell 'em and build up the stars. Of course, you can lump together their cameras; their studios; their sound-laboratories; their machine-shops, and all the miscellaneous bric-a-brac that they have collected, but of what value are they, unless they are producing films? And if the films they do produce are not winners - they're still worth nothing!"

Mr. Martin would pause and drain off a generous whisky. "You can put a million in the film business and make a million. But more often you can put a million in the film business and lose it! Film companies are like their stars; skating on the thin ice of bankruptcy to-day, coining dough to-morrow. Dames and dollars. The glamorous debenture. Make it in the east and spend it in the west!"

3

Hitler gave the world a renewed attack of jitters. In March he occupied Czechoslovakia. Geoffrey resigned himself to a coming war. He never mentioned the subject to Lesley, but he had long conversations with members of the English colony, and Douglas Martin, and Ronald Rawlings - his other particular friend.

Rawlings was a link with the old days in England; the days before Geoffrey had joined Sir Highley; the days when his chief concern was the advertising of the British Dominions Corporation and its numerous subsidiaries.

His first meeting with Ronald Rawlings in Hollywood had been in the studio restaurant. He had drifted in for a late lunch, and had seen Rawlings sitting alone at one of the small tables. He had sat down in one of the vacant chairs opposite to him and said, "Hallo! Remember me?" Rawlings had grinned in a puzzled sort of way. "I'm ... ." Geoffrey started, but Rawlings had said: "No. Don't tell me. I'll get it in a minute. I know who you are, of course. I saw your picture in the paper when you did that spot of lightning matrimony with Lesley Travis. I thought I knew you then, but I couldn't place you, and I thought that I must have seen you around here sometime. But I know you now, although I'm blessed if I can remember exactly where ....?"

"Remember 'Flans'?" asked Geoffrey. "The flannel trousers for every sporting, or informal occasion."; "God, yes," said Ronald Rawlings, "I've got it now, that day down at the photographic studio, when you got into everybody's hair, including mine, when you would have the photos taken your way, and not the way the photographer wanted them."

"Yes, that's right," Geoffrey confirmed, "but they did turn out rather well my way, didn't they?"

"I don't quite remember. But I do remember that you kept us so darned late that night, that I missed my dinner, and that after the most terrific row about something or the other you invited me out to supper as a sort of peace-offering. Quite a night that was, if I remember rightly. Let me see. The Cafe-de-Paris we went to, wasn't it?"

"Yes," replied Geoffrey," and you finished up with a very charming little red-head, remember? She said you were too good-looking for anything, and ought to be on the films. Quite prophetic in her way."

"Prophecy was by no means the greatest of her attractions. Blondes were your weakness then, I think. Anyway, you would insist that the girl with the long blonde hair, that sang with the band, had got 'something.' Had she? When you did manage to get her to the table, she consumed the best part of two bottles of champagne, and was calling you 'Geffwy, darling,' when you took her home!"

"Oh, those days are over now," said Geoffrey, "I'm a respectable married man, you know."

"And a very lucky one, married to a woman as lovely as Lesley Travis. But tell me. Hollywood is a long shot from London, what brought you here?"

And so Geoffrey had briefly recounted the events leading up to his arrival in the film-city.

"You remembered me all right then?" said Ronald. "Well, not exactly," replied Geoffrey, "I didn't really have to remember you. I've seen you in quite a few pictures since then. As a matter of fact, when you first started to hit the high-spots over here I scrapped one or two of those 'Flan' trouser 'ads' that I should have used again, because it seemed a bit like getting testimonial advertising without paying for it! By the way, how did you get started over here?"

"Oh, I was doing a bit in repertory in addition to the photographic work, and one of the World Wide scouts picked me out, and . . . well, here I am. Not a great deal of difference between your story and mine, really."

"Not really," said Geoffrey, "except that they don't pay *me* a thousand dollars a week." And they both laughed, and having finished lunch they went back to work.

After that they met quite a lot, and Lesley wanted to know when they had met before and what they had done in London; and she had laughed when they told her all about it. All, that is, except about the red-head and the blonde.

They went about a lot together, and Ronald usually brought along some charming companion to complete the foursome. He changed his companions with a frequency that was almost disconcerting. "If I'm seen three times in a row with the same girl-friend," he would complain, "the publicity department or the newspapers think they can scent a new romance. If I believe all that I've read in the papers, I've been engaged four times already!"

And so, with an undiminished exciting love for each other, and an ever-widening circle of friends, Lesley and Geoffrey paid little heed to the sullen, dark clouds of war, which were piling up and forming such a horrible monstrous pattern over central Europe.

CHAPTER 10

1

AFTER his boring experiences in the World Wide studios, Geoffrey had always resisted Lesley's invitations to visit her at the Inter-Continental studios and watch her at work. At last, however, he succumbed to her request, and it was arranged that he should call at the studios in the afternoon, watch Lesley at work on her new film, "Maestro of Manhattan," (subsequently retitled "Manhattan Symphony"), and afterwards that they would go out and dine and dance together.

He had duly followed Lesley's instructions, and had arrived outside the door of Stage 12, and was waiting for the red-lamp to dim and the warning-signal to stop its monotonous tick-tocking, when a most attractive voice behind him said, "Well, Mr. Manners! How are you?" He turned quickly, and almost collided with the girl who had come up right behind him.

Bumping into Mavis Lee could be an occasion fraught with distinct possibilities. To be brought, suddenly, into close contact with Mavis's slender yet curvesome figure; to look down into her brown eyes; to catch the faint fragrance from her jet-black hair; to see the white even teeth glistening from behind the red vivid slash of her mouth; could be a most disconcerting experience - at least to a member of the opposite sex.

"Why! Miss Lee," he said. "We haven't met since that little party at Lucey's."

"No," she said, and he wondered if, when she looked at men, there was always that warm, smouldering fire in her eyes. "We don't see much of you around here considering Lesley works here."

"I work as well," he reminded her.

"How's the grand build-up for World Wide going?" she asked.

But, before he could answer, the red warning-light went out, and the signal stopped wagging its admonishing finger.

"I'm going in to see Lesley," he said.

"Mind if I come? " she asked. He held the door open for her.

2

They were getting the camera ready for a big "pan" over the entire set, and Lesley's "stand-in" was taking the heat of the studio lights. Lesley saw them, and came straight over. "Hello, darling," she said, and glancing at Mavis, said, in a tone that was a little too casual to be friendly, "Hello, Mavis. Where did you spring from?" Then turning back to Geoffrey she continued, "I'm afraid I'm going to be late, dear. Everything seems to have gone hay-wire to-day. Still, everybody seems a bit fed up so they may decide to call it a day soon. Just wait around a bit, will you, darling?"

"Miss Travis," called a voice from the direction of the camera.

"Coming," she called out in reply, and giving Geoffrey a quick smile and wrinkling her nose at him, she left him standing there with Mavis Lee.

They found some chairs, and he could not help noticing the slim perfection of her legs as she sat down. "I guess she loves you an awful lot," she said. "I hope so," he said, without looking at her.

"I should think, maybe, you're kinda easy to love, at that," she said, and her voice was softer, more personal. He thought it best to ignore that remark.

Lesley was late. Very late. Everything seemed to go wrong. Lesley's co-star had achieved eminence in the film-world more because of the perfection of his profile, and the magnificence of his personal appearance, than for his acting ability.

The harassed director, having tried, at least a dozen times to get what he wanted, but each time without success, had carried out an almost grotesque pantomime of the scene he wanted played. Success still eluded him. He jumped up and walked in a wide sweep round the set. His circular perambulation brought him close to where Geoffrey and Mavis were sitting. As he went by, they overheard him muttering, ". . . why was he born so beautiful? Why was he born so dumb? That's it! Dumb. Dumb. Dumb .... "

And then, when at last they did get it right, the agitation of the constant rehearsals had produced a large number of wrinkles in the leading man's coat. He was playing the part of a very immaculate hero. "Look at that coat!" bawled the director. "It looks as if he'd been sleeping in it!" And there was a great scurrying, and tucking of cotton-wool inside the offending garment, until the wrinkles had been disposed of.

But nerves were getting a bit on edge, and tempers a little frayed, and Geoffrey thought, "No wonder she comes home feeling tired and irritable, with this sort of thing to put up with."

Mavis said that she must be going, and he rose to say good-bye. She held out her hand to him, and as he took it, she took a sudden step towards him, at the same time lifting his hand so that she stood very close to him, and the back of his hand was pressing against the rounded softness of her breast. She stood like that just long enough to say, "Don't forget me, will you?" and then swung away from him, pausing for a moment to wave her hand, before she finally disappeared from his view.

He was rather shocked when he sat down again to wait for Lesley, to find himself thinking of the way her heavy silk dress had swung from her hips as she walked away from him; and how much more attractive it looked when the dress could swing round such beautiful legs; and why beautiful legs always looked so much more wickedly beautiful when they were clad in such sheer gossamery silk; and when the seams were so beautifully straight down the back .... "

"That's all!" bawled a voice, and you could hear a sigh, like a man yawning and stretching in bed, run round the studio.

3

As he assisted Lesley into his car and then slid in beside her, he thought, "Breakers ahead, if I'm any judge of the way she's sticking out that pretty little chin." "It's too late to go out now," she said, "and I'm too tired. Let's go home."

"Suits me, darling," he replied, and set the car rolling. When the studio gates had closed behind them, he put his hand on her leg, and with his first finger traced little circles on her knee-cap. "Now don't sulk," he said. "When we get home I'll make two of the largest cocktails you have ever seen, then we'll raid the ice-box, and after that I'll tuck you up into bed nice and early so that you can get some rest, and get rid of those two tired little lines that will spoil that pretty forehead of yours." Then he took his hand from her knee and slipped it round her waist, and drew her near to him. He glanced quickly ahead, to see that the road was clear, and then lightly kissed the two petulant little lines she had drawn in her forehead.

Lesley made a half-hearted attempt to draw away from him. "Geoffrey," she said, in a tone she might have used in speaking to a refractory child, "how often must I tell you to keep your eyes on the road? Accidents can happen so easily!"

"Sorry," he said, "but I'm the one husband in the world that just can't resist kissing his wife in the car. If I get a ticket . . . well, it'll be worth it. Besides, I'll just take you along with me and say 'Look Judge, I hadn't seen my wife all day and I just had to kiss her. Look for yourself and see!' And then he would look at you, and probably sigh, and say, 'Case dismissed,' and take five minutes before he could get his mind back on to the next case."

Lesley thought. "I'm good and mad. I'm good and mad at things in general, and you in particular, you . . . . you . . . bluebeard! You, and that Mavis Lee flaunting her charms. Sitting there in the dark where I couldn't see you. No! I'm good and mad, and I'm not going to be jollied out of it by you, or by anything you can say!"

He was whistling softly to himself, and he had pulled her coat a little to one side, and through the thin silk of her dress she could feel his fingers beating a light tattoo upon her soft skin. Occasionally, at the end of a bar, he would give her a little intimate squeeze, and it would send a thrill running through her, as it always did when he touched her meaningly.

She thought, "I'll make him take his hand away." And then, "Well, perhaps not - it is rather nice. I'll just pretend that I haven't noticed."

Then she said, "What on earth were you doing sitting there mooning with that Mavis Lee?" "Mooning?" he said. "We weren't mooning - we were watching you!"

"Watching me!" she retorted. "It didn't look that way from where I was standing!"

"Darling," he said, "what nonsense you talk. Why, I've only seen the girl once before in my life - you were there when I met her."

"I don't see what difference that makes." She looked up at him. "After all, look what happened the second time that you met me!" "

"Oh, that was different ... that was .... Oh, I shan't even try to answer that. But Mavis Lee! Why, I couldn't even tell you what she looked like."

"That's a lie," he thought, "if I had to, I could describe her very well. Blast the woman. She was a disturbing influence. That was it. A disturbing influence. With her black hair and brown eyes, and that way she had of ... of ... oh, of being a woman. Queer, that one should feel so conscious all the time of everything ... of everything that ... er ... well, of everything that made her a woman."

He glanced at Lesley. She was looking straight ahead, but before he looked away again he caught just a glimpse of her little short upper-lip which was pushed forward rather petulantly. He loved that little short upper-lip of hers. Seen in profile, it made her seem so innocent-so young ....

"Dammit," he thought, "I should be downright ashamed of myself." And he was.

Lesley was saying to herself. "I won't be nice to him at all. I'm just going to teach him that he mustn't even *look* at another woman the way he looks at me! Especially a woman like Mavis Lee. It's all very well being feminine, but, after all, you could take that sort of thing too far! And Geoffrey, Geoffrey of all people standing there goggling at her as if she was brand-new; something just out of a cellophane package. Oh, he'd been perfectly beastly. I won't say a kind word to him for days, and days, and days." But she did.

When she had bathed, and put on something more comfortable, and when she heard the ice in the shaker making dull crunching noises, as Geoffrey jerked it to and fro, trying to keep time with the rhythm of a dance tune on the radio, and when he came behind her and kissed her below the ear, and gave her a cocktail, which he pronounced was a "Manner's Gloom-Raiser Special," and when he would insist on caressing her in his own intimate little way .... Intimate little caresses that sometimes made her heart start bumping away in the most disconcerting manner. She thought, "I'll just forgive him for to-night and then to-morrow I'll talk to him very seriously."

She closed her eyes. "Strange," she thought, "the way his hands are so soothing and yet exciting. Nice hands he had. Clean and strong and yet so gentle."

Geoffrey said, "You know, Lesley, the trouble with us is, that I haven't had you to myself enough. It's ages since we spent a whole day alone together. On Sunday we'll pack a picnic-basket, and take the car and go miles away from everyone."

Lesley murmured, "Yes, Geoffrey, that will be wonderful." She would have gone with him to the moon if he went on doing things like that to her.

4

It was a lonely, but idyllic spot that they found for their picnic. At one side, and just below them, the water gurgled incessantly as it tumbled and hurried between shining, black boulders. A green and weeping tree hung its branches, so that the farthest touched lightly upon the swift-flowing water, whilst others formed a shady canopy over a soft grassy slope that reached to the water's edge. The sunlight glinted on the water; a haze shimmered just above the earth, distorting everything into misty pictures composed of little wavy lines. Except for the water, which gurgled and splashed against the boulders, everything was silent in the afternoon heat.

Geoffrey lay on his back, a long stem of grass gripped between his teeth, his hands clasped behind his head, gazing unseeingly into the green leafy arch above him. Watching him was Lesley; her chin cupped in her hands, elbows resting on her knees.

It was Geoffrey who broke the silence. Unclasping his hands he rolled over on to his stomach, rested his weight on his elbows, gazed for a few moments into the grey-blue eyes which were fixed so lovingly upon him, said, "Darling," and rolled over on his back again.

"Darling ... what?" asked Lesley.

"Oh, nothing," he replied. "Just 'darling,' darling." "But," said Lesley, "you can't just say ' darling.' It's silly."

"Not at all," he countered, rolling over on his stomach again so that he could look up into her face. "You are a darling, so I called you darling. What's wrong with that?" "Well, nothing really, but it sounds sort of - incomplete like that. Just on its own."

"All right then," said Geoffrey. "Darling, you're adorable. Is that better?"

"Very much," she said, smiling happily.

"And you have adorable legs," he went on, tracing the soft line of her calf with the stem. of grass which he had taken from his mouth.

"Oh, you tell that to all the girls you make love to," she said, laughing at him.

"Adorable legs," he continued, as if she had not interrupted. "Such slim, dimpled, soft and adorable legs." Suddenly she was very conscious of the position in which she was sitting, and realised that lying as he was, he was not drawing upon his memory or imagination in describing her legs.

She felt the hot blood flooding to her cheeks, and thought, "Why on earth, after we have been married so long, should I always feel shy, when he talks like that? Is it the way he looks at me, or . . .?"

With the stem of grass he tickled the inside of her leg, where it showed white above her stocking.

"Geoffrey!" she protested, and there was a momentary tantalising glimpse of wispy chiffon as she moved her legs away. He looked deep into the lovely eyes above him.

Always when he looked at her, there was a slumbering, smouldering fire in his eyes. Now it kindled, and burst into a sudden dark flame. In a moment she was in his arms; she felt as if her strength - nay her very life - was draining away from her. She sensed the urgent, overwhelming passion that empowered him. Whilst there was still time, she protested,_"No, darling, no! Remember. . . ." But then his mouth was upon hers, silencing her protestations.

Suddenly she took fire from him. There was an aching, aching need to give - to give and to go on giving. To harbour and protect his love; to soften and assuage this burning, vital, tempestuous need of her.

A sudden breeze stirred the leafy bower that hid them. Unbidden tears forced themselves from beneath her eyelids. "Oh, God," she thought, "I never dreamed such happiness."

There was no yearning for anything beyond this.

....

As she cradled his head against her breast, she thought, "Was it thus his mother held him? Had any woman, even his mother, loved him as she did?" His eyes were closed now, but before they had closed, she had seen the peace in them; the flood of peace that she alone could bring, to extinguish for a while the smouldering fire, which, when it flamed, called her so urgently, helplessly, to him. She was lost in the wonderment of love.

There was only the noise of the water, and of the rustling of the leaves as a cool breeze fanned its way across the water. He stirred a little, and pressed his face more closely against her; through the thin silk of her blouse, she felt him kiss her. Then he was still again.

As she looked at him a wave of ineffable tenderness swept over her. A thousand thoughts fled pell-mell before the threat of the orderly marshalling of her mind. But first one, then another, were captured and held, and she surveyed them in a sort of dreaming wakefulness.

"Why? Oh, why should she love him so much? Why should this man, this man alone of all the men she had known, have the power to bind her to him with invisible chains that she could never break? What secret magnetism, what irresistible force drew her to him? What had happened in London, on that night so long ago? What secret hidden thing within them had merged so indivisibly? Why thereafter had his memory stayed with her so indelibly? As the memory of her had stayed with him. What was this something within her? For it was within; deep, inescapable. The very centre of her being. Nothing that life had held for her, or could hold, would ever approach this solitariness of desire; this all-embracing concern for another single living being. This interminable consciousness of him; - always there in her mind. Thinking, thinking, 'What is he doing now? What is he saying now?' That happy, happy, comforting thought that he loved her. The surge of her blood when he took her in his arms .... Oh, the incredible loveliness of loving, of being loved. Even when he took her so urgently, so passionately, there was something else. Something fine and clean. Like a clear white flame that would bum steadily - on into infinity. She was glad to belong to him; glad in his joy of her; glad that she was pretty, that he thought her beautiful. To see the adoration in his eyes. He had always thought her beautiful from the beginning. Would he have loved her if she had been different? Plain? Would that mysterious something have called them to each other despite everything ? Would she have loved him so much if his hair had not been so dark and waving? His eyes so blue? If he had not been so clean, so strong, so . . . so confident. Perhaps it was too late now for her ever to know that. But looks had mattered in the beginning. It was the way he looked that had first attracted her. It was later that other things had become more important. The things he said, his kindness and sympathy. He was so sure of himself, and yet, at times, somehow one sensed a shyness in him, a timidity almost. Especially when he was with women. Yes! That was it. That vague indefinable hint of shyness. It was his greatest charm. But was she right, after all, in trying to define it as shyness? Was it not rather that one sensed a doubt within him? A refusal to believe that people found him attractive? Oh, hell! Why not be truthful with herself? Not people - women. Yes, it was women who sensed that charm; who were intrigued that he could admire them, and yet be so hesitant in accepting or believing the messages of their eyes or of their lips. It was such a faint shadow, this inward doubt of his. A faint shadow, thrown by some intangible modesty, standing in the light of his own charm. Making you want to tell him . . . to make him believe. And all the time you felt that if he did believe you, that if he did understand that your eyes were not mocking him, that your lips were not laughing at him, then he would be quite imperious in his demands. As he was. But gentle and understanding. As he was. Oh, yes, she knew that other women had noticed him and wanted him. The too effusive acknowledgment of some small courtesy. The bold look or smile. The stolen glances. Thank God, he had eyes for no one but her. She had given him too much; put her heart, her very hopes for the future, so irretrievably in his keeping; had tangled her emotions so closely in the very fibre of his being, ever to contemplate losing him now. She would not lose him, she told herself fiercely. Not through circumstance or to another woman. She would not lose him. She would fight, and fight, until she dropped, but somehow she would hold him. At all costs she would hold on to this precious thing that had come into her life. Something that had made her young again; something that had made the skies more blue, the air more soft, the world more kind. Something that made her life worth while; gave it a purpose.

"And what of *his* love? Would that ever grow cold and unresponsive? Would the thrill in his eyes fade and grow dim? Would his joy that she belonged to him falter and grow less? Oh, no! No! Never that. She would not think of that. It was not fair. No word that he had spoken, no deed of his, made it fair for her to think such things. He loved her so much; was so proud of her. So proud of the success she had won. And he had never been jealous of the admiration, or of the many worldly possessions, that her success had brought her. Funny, at first, how that thought of jealousy had frightened her a little. It was so foolish of her to have been frightened. He was her most ardent admirer; her keenest critic; her greatest encouragement.

"He was successful too, she supposed. Not in this present job he was doing for World Wide. It was only the inflated values of Hollywood that made that at all worth while. It was not for *that* he had come, but always she would be grateful, grateful! He loved the work he had been doing in England. How enthusiastic he had been when he had told her; battling with his wits against the others;

looking ahead, always with the hope of catching a glimpse of the shadow of a coming opportunity; this appeal to the human emotions - everything that he understood so well. Yes, that was the work that he wanted to return to when he had finished at World Wide. She would not keep him from that. She could go with him, when the time came. Maybe she could work there. They were making good films in England now. Not just those 'quota quickies,' or programme fillers, but real films. Her own company were making films there. They had even flirted with the idea of sending her to star in one of their British productions. Oh, yes, they would manage all right. And Geoffrey liked America. He would be glad to come back. Somehow they would manage that too. And she would be able to help him so much. Business, especially his sort of business, was so personal. Was given or withheld by the few who were at the top. Social activities and contacts counted for so much. And people wanted to meet her .... Yes, she could help. Perhaps he would not welcome that. But, after all, she was his wife. She would, quite naturally, receive his friends, his business associates, in their home. Their home! Where would it be? Surrey, maybe. That was near London, wasn't it? Oh, she would make it beautiful for him. So beautiful that whenever he was away he would long to get back. When he was away. . . . Would she be lonely in England, if he was away, and she was not working? She did not want to be alone again. And yet there was no one in England. No one . . . yet. There might be by then. He wanted a son. She knew that. He had not spoken of it, but she knew. That little boy who was staying at their cottage - he loved him. She had seen that in his eyes when he had spoken of him. What love there would be in his eyes when he saw his own son; the son that she would give him. Even now? She wondered .... He had been so ardent - she loved him so. Even now his son ....?"

"Oh, Geoffrey, Geoffrey," she said softly, and kissed him. Her lips were warm. His eyes opened.

CHAPTER 11

1

LESLEY was away on location. Geoffrey sank his second cocktail. He looked disconsolately at the cherry, speared with a little pointed stick, resting abandoned at the bottom of the glass. "A modern heart," he thought, "pierced with a modern dart, aimed by a twentieth-century, chromium-plated Cupid." He looked up, and caught sight of his own reflection in the mirror opposite. "What tripe," he said, and scooping the cherry from the glass, took a pot-shot at his reflection in the mirror. The look of surprise which swept over his face, following this unprecedented action, confronted him somewhat mistily from behind the sticky splash on the mirror. "Now somebody will have something to say about that!" he thought, as he surveyed the damage he had wrought upon the once clean and shining surface of the glass. He wiped his sticky fingers upon his handkerchief, and swung away; taking a cigarette from a box upon the table. "Oh, hell, with Lesley away, this house is as dead as last week's sports results." Why the heck had he come home so early? "Oh, yes. Oh, yes," he said inwardly, "I didn't feel restless then, but I'm restless now. Confoundedly restless." He wanted Lesley - wanted her smile and the happiness she always brought him. It was deadly, that thought that she would not be there, smiling that warm, welcoming smile of hers, wrinkling her nose at him when he said something to tease her. Not to-night, or to-morrow night, or the night after that. Oh, when? When would she be back?

He glanced across at the radio, took a step forward, but halted and mashed out his cigarette. No, not that. He was not in the mood to listen to yet another review of one of Hitler's renewed wordy bludgeonings aimed at the heads of the stolid and long-suffering Poles.

The phone-bell whirred like a miniature fire-alarm in the loneliness of the room. He turned eagerly towards the instrument. It would be Lesley. It would be just like Lesley to call him when he was feeling low.

But it was not Lesley's voice that answered his eager "Hello?"

It was a girl's voice. Familiar, but somehow he could not just place it.

"Hello, Geoffrey?" enquired the voice. "Lonely with Lesley away? Guessed you would be. Listen, Bill and I are out on a party. Why don't you .... What's that? Who is it? Come now, don't tell me that you can't recognise the voice of your old friend Lois - Lois Lamont! Yes, I'm with Bill - we're just starting a party and thought that perhaps you would like to come along. Will you come? It's going to be a swell party."

Geoffrey leaned his head on one side, resting his ear on the receiver of the hand-microphone, screwed up one eye, and with the other squinted over the mouthpiece at the sticky blob upon the mirror. "Go on," it seemed to say, "I wouldn't be here, if you hadn't been so fed-up!"

Geoffrey said rather doubtfully, "Thanks a lot, Lois, but I'm not quite sure .... Are you sure that it will be all right?"

"Of course, it will be all right. Everybody's welcome, and Lesley wanted us to look after you while she is away. Come along now. Snap out of it. You'll come? Good. Come to 112A Sunset, on the first floor. It looks like an office, but don't mind that, come right up. First door that you come to - facing the stairs. 112A. Got it? Right, see you soon then. Don't be long. Bye-bye." There was a light "click" and the instrument went dead.

Geoffrey replaced the receiver. Oh, well, anything was better than hanging around here, waiting for a Lesley who wouldn't come, anyway. Even a party. A party? What kind of a party? White tie - black tie? Why the blazes couldn't people say? " Looks like an office"! That didn't sound in the least formal. What in heaven's name was Lois doing running a party in an office? No, that wasn't quite right. In a place that looked like an office. It was probably one of her crazy, impromptu parties. Yes, that was it. Lois had been in an office, when something had happened to make her happy. "Let's celebrate," she would say. "Let's have a party. Right here-in the office. Don't worry," she would say to the Mr. Jones or Mr. Smith, or whatever his name was that occupied the office. "Don't worry. We won't harm your lovely office. You're in this you know -" And she would send the poor bewildered soul scuttling off to help Bill Grant collect the drinks and glasses, and things to eat, while she sat down at the telephone and called all the people she could think of who would be likely to enjoy a crazy party.

He wouldn't change, anyway. If it transpired that it was not, after all, the sort of party he had visualised, and he did find himself precipitated into the midst of a lot of ties, fluttering about like a host of black and white butterflies, then he would just breeze in and tell Lois that he'd, "Just had to come, because she had asked him," have half-a-dozen drinks, and then come home to bed. Half-a-dozen drinks, a smoky room, and the righteous feeling he always had if he left a party when it was in full-swing, induced sleep more surely than any potion that he knew.

2

He cruised slowly down Sunset and found the building he wanted. He was surprised that there were no cars parked outside. He thought that perhaps Lois, knowing that he was alone, had called him first. That might account for the absence of cars. Perhaps he was the first to arrive. That was hardly likely though - he had driven quite slowly and it was not exactly a short distance. He surveyed the entrance to the building. It was an office building right enough. The place was deserted. Nothing surprising in that - there were not many offices that worked as late as this. He thought that there might have been some sign of life, however. Lois' parties were usually full of life. Once again he thought, "I'm probably the first."

He climbed the stairs to the first floor. Facing him was the door of 112A. Painted on a glass panel in the door were the words, "The Beverley Academy of Motion Picture Art." No sounds of gaiety or laughter came from behind the closed door. Rather hesitantly he tapped lightly on the door. He had a feeling that the whole place was lonely and deserted.

There was a shuffling sound inside and a moment later the door opened a little way to disclose a little old woman, who peered up at him with suspicious eyes. Her hair was dirty-grey in colour, and was arranged on her head in a series of loose folds, which threatened at any minute to break adrift from their moorings of hairpins and deluge her face in a cascade of greasy, greying hair. Her lips were thin, and set in a straight, hard line. Her skin was so pock-marked, coarse and uneven as to inspire in Geoffrey a horror somewhat akin to that experienced by Gulliver, who when travelling in Brob-dingnag, viewed at close quarters the skins of the maids of honour in the king's palace at Lorbrulgrud.

She spoke to Geoffrey, revealing teeth so white and even, that they heightened rather than diminished the general unattractiveness of her appearance. "You'll be Mr. Manners, eh?"

Geoffrey nodded his head in assent.

"You're expected. Come right in," she said.

He found himself in an office, the main furnishings of which appeared to be steel filing and record cabinets. In one corner was a desk bearing a covered type-writer, and a telephone switchboard was just inside a small wicket-gate that the old woman held open for him.

She let the gate swing to, and motioned to him to follow her. She moved with her shuffling walk to a door marked "Private," which was set in the wall at the far side of the office. Through this door was another office, luxuriously furnished with a chromium and glass desk, a handsome swivel-chair, a deep pile-carpet, a cocktail cabinet, and on the walls numerous photos of prominent film-actors and actresses. Beyond the desk a part of the wall was screened by a heavy velvet curtain.

The old woman had not given him time to ask what meaning lay behind this silent perambulation into a second unoccupied office. She shuffled over to the velvet curtain, and drew it back to reveal a heavy wooden door.

She tapped on the door with her bony knuckles. Somebody inside called out, "Come in." She pushed open the door for Geoffrey to enter and then pulled the door to behind him.

There was only one other occupant of the room in which he now found himself. A girl. She was reclining in the depths of a luxurious armchair, and was regarding him with a flicker of amusement in her brown eyes.

"Good evening, Mr. Manners," she said. "You seem somewhat surprised to find me here!"

Geoffrey glanced round the room. It was quite small, but everywhere there were signs of a luxuriant opulence. His eyes searched for signs of a forthcoming party. In one corner there was a tiny cocktail-bar and, three high stools with red morocco-leather seats and shining chromium-plated legs. On the tiny bar was a cocktail shaker and an assortment of bottles. But these appeared to be only a part of the normal furnishings of the room, and in no way conveyed any suggestion that they had been placed there in anticipation of the arrival of guests imbued with the party spirit.

He looked again at the girl in the armchair. "Well, a little perhaps," he said, "but I am surprised not to find Miss Lamont here."

Mavis Lee rose from the chair and came towards him. "I trust that you will forgive the little deception. I telephoned you to-night, not Lois Lamont. I'm rather clever with my voice, don't you think?"

"But why on earth . . .?"

She interrupted him. "Because I wanted to see you. Because I thought that perhaps you would not come if I asked you to come here and see *me*. That's why I practised my little deception." She laughed up at him. "Am I forgiven?"

"It all seems rather futile to me," he said. "You are quite correct in your assumption that I would not have come here to meet you - or any other place for that matter - but now that I am here, I presume that you must have some reason . . . something to say to me."

She turned away from him and walked to a small table. Standing with her back towards him she took a cigarette from a box on the table, and for a moment rolled it between her fingers. Then she said, "Yes, I had a reason, but I'm not going to tell you what it is though - at least, not yet." She paused. "And I don't think that there is really anything in particular that I have to say."

She turned and came towards him again. "Have you a light?" she asked, and held the cigarette to her lips.

Geoffrey flicked his lighter, and held the flame to the end of her cigarette. As she stooped her head he was aware of a faint perfume from her shining black hair. It was pleasant and yet tantalising.

"Well, in that event there does not seem to be much point in my staying any longer."

"Scared?" she said, exhaling smoke so that it almost reached his face.

"Scared? Why should I be? I haven't been kidnapped have I?"

"Well, hardly. I mean scared of being here alone ... with me."

"My dear, you misjudge yourself. You wouldn't scare anybody."

"I might," she said.

"Well, have it your own way, but really I have no feeling of trepidation about being here alone with you, and I'm going because ... well, because there doesn't seem to be much point in my staying. Does there?"

"I still think that you're frightened."

"Frightened? What possible reason could there be for me to be frightened?" His voice was sharper, and it had lost something of the patient friendly tone he had used till now.

It was as if a hot red light was reflected in her eyes. "There might be reasons," she said very slowly. Once again he had that strange sense of awareness of her. That slim, vibrant and yet voluptuous body. Tense, eager. Once again that enveloping, persistent femininity.

"There is a possibility that you may be right," he said, " but I can only repeat that I am not aware of them."

He moved towards the door, his voice had recovered its previous friendly tone. "I trust that you have enjoyed your little practical joke, Miss Lee. Frankly, if I may say so, it seems a particularly pointless joke to me!"

She was angry now. "Oh, stop this damned fooling. You know very well why I asked you here like this! You know, and you know that you want to stay. Except that you're scared – scared of me, and what your precious Lesley would say if she knew!"

"I find the constant repetition of your conviction that I am scared rather boring," he said. "Why not let us forget the whole incident? I most freely acknowledge both your beauty and your charm. But I happen to be very much in love with my wife. Under different circumstances," he made a little gesture as if to indicate the inevitability of things as they were, "I should have considered it an honour to be your most devoted and humble admirer."

"If that is the way you feel," she said, "there can be no harm in your staying. If you go like this, you'll always wonder just what it was that I was going to say to you."

He looked at her; she was smiling at him in a friendly sort of way. "Maybe," he said, "but I don't think that it could be important, anyway. Come along, why not say good-bye now, and then, when we meet again, we can just be friends just as if all this hadn't happened."

"Why not?" she said, and held out her hand to him. Then she said, "You came expecting a party, you must at least have a drink. Just one, before you go."

He hesitated a moment, but there was no change in the open friendly expression that her face had assumed when her little burst of anger had faded.

"Just one then," he said, "Scotch, if I may."

"It's over here," she said, and moved over to the little bar. He followed her across the room. She poured out two whiskies. Almost automatically he slid on to one of the high stools.

"Soda?" she enquired. He nodded.

He took a sip at the long drink she had poured for him. He looked round the room. "This is a strange sort of place to be tucked away in an office building," he said.

Mavis seated herself upon one of the two remaining stools and glanced around with every evidence of satisfaction. "Rather nice, don't you think? I find this a most secluded and comfortable hideaway. I can come down here and shut myself right away from all the brawling, and shouting and bally-hoo that goes on out there." She jerked her head in the direction of the street, and presumably towards Hollywood generally. "A town with more suckers to the square yard than any other place on earth. You don't even begin to understand the meaning of 'living up to the Jones's' until you strike this burg. Make it and spend it. Spend it before you make it, if you like, but spend, spend, spend. Everybody must be a success in Hollywood. Go without the groceries but buy yourself a new pair of stockings. Have an overdraft at the bank but have a bigger mansion in Beverley Hills than the next guy! Have a bigger car! Have a yacht! Have everything - the sky's the limit!"

This was a new side of the glamorous Mavis Lee. Geoffrey noticed the hard, almost mercenary, look; the note of contempt in her voice. "Well, I suppose it's fun while it lasts," he said.

"While it lasts. Yes. But how long does it last, for most of them? Hanging on playing bits, when they should have got out years ago. No, not for me, thanks. I'll make mine and get out while the going is good. I'm only interested in this business because there is money in it. Money, that's the thing, Geoffrey. For every dollar I spend I make ten! That office outside, you wondered about that perhaps?"

"A bit," he said.

"It doesn't look much, does it? But it is. The Beverley Academy of Motion Picture Art makes more money for me in a month, than I can make in a year by acting. One day I'll have a sign put up outside and it will read: 'Through these doors have passed the greatest collection of suckers, saps and just plain chumps that the world has ever seen!'"

Something in her voice sent Geoffrey's mind back into the past. His companion was no longer the dazzling, attractive Mavis Lee of the films, it was a somewhat weather-beaten product of Chicago in a loud suit, and highly-polished brown shoes. Above the 'clickety-click, clickety-click,' of the wheels as the train sped westward, he heard a voice saying,". . . the sweetest little racket you ever saw. And do them suckers pay?"

Surely it couldn't be Mavis - Mavis Lee the film actress - who was behind it all? What sort of woman was she? Loving her would be something like keeping a tiger as a house-pet. Beautiful, exciting and . . . dangerous.

Dimly he was aware that she was still talking, " ... I can give you everything. Everything that money, passion and desire could ever mean to any man."

She glanced up at him for a moment. "You're a funny guy," she said," here I am throwing myself at you, and you just .... " She drew a deep breath so that it was almost like a sigh of incredulity. "People just don't do that sort of thing to me. Why should you? I want you - I've wanted you since that first time we met. It hurt like hell for Lesley Travis to have something that I wanted. It's always been like that - at the studio - the parts I want - she gets them. Standing there, all the time, in my way. Getting the things I want, and secretly laughing at me. Oh, you've heard of the rivalry between us - you must have done. Rivalry!" she laughed bitterly. "I hate her!"

She was not looking at him, but had her eyes fixed on the glass which she was twisting between her fingers. "And then as if that was not enough, I want you!" She looked across at him. She saw the hard expression on his face that had not been there before she had spoken about Lesley, and went on hurriedly: "But not because of her. Not just because you're married to Lesley and I want to hurt her." Her voice was earnest, pleading. "Perhaps that's how it started - but not now. I want you, you! I want you more than anything I ever wanted before. I love you - love you! Do you understand?"

He did not look at her, but examined the glowing end of his cigarette. "This is not quite what we agreed you know. We were having a drink after arranging to forget . . . all this."

She said fiercely, "But I can't forget. I love you! Not the clinging, pallid sort of love you get from her, but something warm, passionate, possessive - selfish, spiteful, cruel, if you like, I don't know. But it's real. With me you would be alive - gloriously alive. Together we could do anything – everything! I have all the money that we could ever want. I want you to take me in your arms, I want to see the hunger in your eyes. I want to show you what love - my kind of love - is really like!" She stood before him, her head thrown back. Her lips were parted and she was breathing quickly. Every line of her glorious figure was enhanced by her air of reckless, abandoned surrender. Her eyes laughed challengingly into his. Her whole bearing was a monstrous invitation to the joy of possessing her.

Geoffrey felt the surge of his blood, there was a distant beating in his ears. Dimly he was aware of a knocking on the door. She did not move away from him but looked over his shoulder and called, "Yes? What is it?" The door opened, and the old woman was silhouetted in the opening. Standing behind her was Lesley!

3

Geoffrey thought, "This can't be true. This situation has occurred in every third film since they started making them." Indignant wife bursting in upon faithful husband who has been tricked into a compromising assignation. How did it go in the films? It was usually very exasperating, he remembered. The outraged wife made some eloquent dissertation upon her husband's morals, quite overpowering his feeble attempts to give her the true explanation of his presence, and all the time everybody in the audience was itching to get up and shout, "For Pete's sake, tell her why you're there. Shout her down if you have to - but tell her! Tell her!" But the poor sap wouldn't, he'd just make one or two abortive attempts to get a word in, and by the time he had gathered himself together, his true love had turned on her heel and swept out of his life forever. Or at least for another forty minutes or so of the film. And during those forty minutes he would drink, and let his beard grow, and drink, and let his clothes get tattered, and drink, until one day his soul-mate discovered how dreadfully she had misjudged him, and would then start in upon his regeneration, when the only thing he was really fit for was as a specimen in some hospital laboratory, where they could use his body to discover whether the human internal organs could achieve any degree of immortality as a result of constant immersion in alcohol.

It took only a moment for these thoughts to chase themselves through his brain, and he wondered a little that he could be quite so flippant in the face of what might be a somewhat serious situation. But he hadn't done anything wrong, and he had no feeling of guilt, and so he went forward to meet Lesley and smiled and said, "Why, darling, how wonderful. What are you doing here?"

Lesley was very cool and unruffled. Except for two spots of colour high up on her cheeks, and a somewhat suspicious brightness in her eyes, she was the same beautiful, self-possessed Lesley he knew, and loved so well.

She allowed him to take her hand and draw her towards the bar, where Mavis Lee was still standing.

Lesley acknowledged Mavis with a somewhat casual greeting. Then she turned to Geoffrey and said, "They gave me your 'phone message when I finished work today. I couldn't imagine what it could be that was so urgent .... "

"Just a minute," said Geoffrey, "what message did you say?"

"Why your message! Didn't you 'phone through to say that it was most urgent for you to see me right away, and asking me not to 'phone, but to drive down as soon as I could, and that you would wait for me at your Club?"

"Like hell I did," he replied. "Well, then what happened, Lesley?"

"I couldn't think what on earth it was that had happened, so I jumped into my car and drove like mad. When I got to your club the porter told me that you had given him a message that you were expecting me, but that you had gone to meet somebody at this address. I found my way here, and well ... here I am."

"The porter told you that I gave him a message?" " Yes, he said so quite distinctly."

"Just a minute," he said, and lifted the telephone. He dialled the club number. He made an enquiry and then waited for a few moments. "Hello, Parsons? This is Mr. Manners. You gave a message to Mrs. Manners a little while ago. You said that I asked you to give it to her. . . .?" He took the receiver from his ear and held it away from him. In the stillness of the room they all heard the porter's voice, sounding very minute and metallic.

"Why, yes, Mr. Manners. You remember, about an hour ago, you telephoned to say that ...."

"Oh, I telephoned," Geoffrey interrupted him. "Yes, I remember. Sorry to have troubled you Parsons. No, that's quite all right. Forget it. Thanks very much. Good-bye."

He turned back to Lesley, who was leaning on the bar. "You see, dear, I telephoned my message to the club. Or rather somebody else, whose voice sounded like mine, must have telephoned. The same somebody who telephoned the message to you earlier in the evening. I don't think that it was you Mavis, gifted as you are. I can't quite see you managing that, unless," he smiled, "unless my voice is pitched a good bit higher than it has any right to be. But I suspect that you do know who did do the telephoning."

He turned to Lesley. " You know, Mavis is very clever with her voice. She 'phoned me this evening, and I could have sworn that it was Lois Lamont inviting me here to a party. Oh, it's all rather obvious isn't it, when there is time to talk about it and sift it out. Mavis gets someone to 'phone you and ask you to call at the club for me. Then she 'phones me as Lois, and invites me to a party here. When I say that I'll come, her accomplice 'phones the club and gives them a message supposed to come from me, which she knows will bring you round here. If I hadn't agreed to come, then the message wouldn't have been 'phoned to the club. Then when you arrived there you wouldn't have found me, and for both of us it would have been just one of those little mysteries ,that are never solved."

Mavis lounged across the room and took a cigarette from a box on the table. "It all sounds very simple when you put it like that. Too simple. Do you think that I'd pull a phoney trick like that? Something a schoolboy could see through in five minutes?"

Geoffrey's voice was almost caressing. "Why, of course you would, Mavis. By the time Lesley arrived here you were supposed to be in my arms." He glanced around the room. "On that divan probably, with lipstick smeared all across my face. . . . Then it wouldn't have mattered if it had been obvious, would it? The reason for my being here wouldn't have been important, only the result would have mattered."

Mavis flung her unlighted cigarette into the fireplace. "Oh; don't go on. All right, you win. What if I did do all that you say? Everything I said to you before she got here was true! Everything, do you understand? If she hadn't come bursting in when she did, she would never have taken you away from me! Why, if she had any spirit at all in that little wax-doll make-up of hers, she would .... "

Lesley moved a step nearer. "If I had any spirit at all," she said, "I should do just what I've been longing to do for a very long time."

Geoffrey caught her hand before it had time to connect with Mavis's startled face. He laughed down at her, "Darling, you're full of surprises." He piloted her towards the door. He paused for a moment and looked back at Mavis. "Please give my regards to Mr. Jack Donovan" he said, "Mr. ' Mouth ' Donovan!"

For the second time within a few seconds Mavis was startled out of her habitual calm. "What the hell do you know about that ....?"

In the middle of her enquiry he closed the door.

4

Outside the building Lesley's car was parked behind Geoffrey's. When she was seated behind the wheel he leaned through the open door and said, "Darling, you won't have to make that awful drive back to-night, will you?" She pondered for a moment, and he went on, "Let's go home to-night, and then you can make an early start in the morning. If you do drive back to-night you won't be fit for anything to-morrow, and there is so much that I want to say to you, so much that I don't think should wait until whenever it is that you'll be back again."

"How you can ever expect me to get my contract renewed, when you make me neglect my work like this, I don't know," she said, smiling at him. "In the morning you will have to write a note to teacher explaining why I am late for school!"

He leaned across and kissed her. "Okay, I will.   Look! I'll park my car at the studio to-night and then we can drive home together. Will you follow me down?" She nodded, and he closed the door of her car, and then walked down and slid in behind the wheel of his roadster.

When they were on their way home in Lesley' s car, he said: "You were wonderful to-night."

"I still have one or two questions I should like to ask you," she said.

He put his arm around her. "Darling, if our positions had been reversed, it would not be one or two, but a hundred questions that I should want to ask you! But please, don't ask them now, let's wait until we get home."

She was sitting cross-legged on the bed when he came into the bedroom towelling vigorously at his hair, which was still glistening with water from the shower.

"Washing away your sins?" she asked, with a mischievous grin on her face.

He laughed, and flung the towel at her, but she fell back on the pillows, and it sailed over her and fell harmlessly on the floor. He combed his hair and then came and sat on the side of her bed. "Now for the interrogation," he said. "Go ahead with your questions, dear."

She clasped her hands behind her head, and gazed at the ceiling for a moment or two before she looked at him. "There's only one question really. Everything else all seems very clear to me now. But what I do want to know is, what did Mavis mean when she said, that if I hadn't come bursting in when I did, that I should never have got you away from her again?"

"Oh, she had just started to switch on her famous 'Come-hither' technique, and I suppose she felt that in a little while she would have had me forever captivated and ensnared by her multitudinous and somewhat obvious charms.''

"And would she?"

He leaned over her so that he could look deep into her beautiful grey-blue eyes. "No," he said. "No. That is one thing I know would be impossible even if she had a thousand times the charms of the present Mavis Lee. There is no woman in all the world who could ever make me stop loving you, even for a moment. I'm impression-able enough, and, thank heaven, I can appreciate to the full all the joy and wonderment that a man can experience through the loveliness of women. I like to see beautiful women. Their shining hair, white teeth and scarlet mouths; their pretty dresses, fantastic shoes, the unbelievable daintiness of the things they wear; their soft, sweet, curving slenderness; to me it is all a sort of symphony - a symphony of light, and beauty, and colour, in an otherwise dull and prosaic world. And you, darling, you are to me the very embodiment of all those things. There is nothing worth while that any woman has, or is, that I cannot see in you, only a thousandfold more beautiful, more desirable. Oh, my dear, I think that it would be impossible for you ever to have any true conception of all the joys you bring me, by just being you. Sometimes, when I look at you, there is a twisting pain inside me, because of your loveliness. I will see some part of you, something about you, in a way that I have never seen before, and it will send a new appreciation, a new realisation of your beauty, flooding through me. One time, it may be the slim perfection of your legs; another, it may be your hair, as I stand behind you and see the way it falls on your shoulders; or perhaps your shoes, with their fantastic high-heels, looking so small and forlorn on the floor, where you have discarded them; or your hands - so slim and tiny, inadequate almost they seem, sometimes, when I hold them. The way your teeth glisten when the light catches them; the incredible cobwebby little things that you wear ... all these, and a thousand other things about you. But above and beyond all those things, yet making them all, even the most insignificant, seem so worth while, is the knowledge that you are so real, so honest, so genuine a person.

"Before I met you, my joy in the loveliness of women was something inchoate, undefined. You have given it reality in its most perfect and wonderful form. There is nothing, nothing that I can say, that could convey to you any conception of my gratitude for all that you have given to me. No princess, bestowing her love on the most humble of her admirers, could give more than you have given. And if there should come a time, which God forbid, when your love is no longer mine, then I shall cherish, even beyond the span of time, the memory of the joy that I have known. Once again you would become my dream-Lesley, only this time, a Lesley that I should clothe with the habiliments of reality; surround with memories so sweet, so poignant, to make me, for all time, impregnable against the assaults of a weary mind, an aching body. No, Lesley. After this, come what may, there can be no other woman."

Her eyes were deep wells; infinite. Love, sympathy, tenderness, wonderment; unfathomable depths. She twisted her hands in his damp hair. Her surrender, the things she had given him, they were no longer new - yet always he made it seem so. The triumphant ecstasy of her conquest made her voice tremulous; "Oh, you fool, you fool, you fool. Can I ever, ever stop loving you now?"

The shadow of Mavis Lee trembled, and was gone.

CHAPTER 12

AT the end of August 1939, the dull sullen anticipation **of** approaching war, became almost a certainty. Day after day, the radio would record the steady progress of a Europe marching into insanity. Germany demanded. Germany insisted. Germany would wait no longer. But Poland would not be cowed; would not be overwhelmed with fear of her mighty, vainglorious neighbour. They waited, with their nerves taut, every muscle tense. Waiting for the inevitable conflict.

And with them, their ears perhaps not so fearful; their hearts not so sick, waited Geoffrey and Lesley. Not an obvious waiting, because they would not talk about it, but waiting. Waiting and wondering. Lesley wondering if he would want to go, and determined to stop him. Not, as on that time a year ago, because she saw some new ineffable sweetness about to be snatched from her almost before she had realised the glory of her love; but because in the year that had passed, she had known the deep, wonderful peace his love had brought her; had realised that now he was a thousand times more dear to her.

Geoffrey, wondering if this time there could be any eleventh hour intervention to avoid a horrible, bloody catastrophe; and if not, wondering what Lesley's reaction would be when he told her that this was the one thing on earth that could take him away from her. More than ever he realised that he would have to be in it. The senseless injustice of the German demands; the realisation of the boundless, searing ambition of the new Germany; the constant withdrawals of his own country, the insults that had been heaped upon her. It must stop. There must be some line beyond which his country would not withdraw; there must be some limit to the sacrifice of his country's honour and dignity. Despite all that it would mean to him, he thanked God that there was, as yet, no sign of weakness; of withdrawing, in the face of threats from Germany, the undertakings which had been given to Poland. They would need every ounce of strength and courage, every man, to meet the challenge of this new, drilled, well-armed, German colossus.

But neither of them would give words to their thoughts.

Like children, they clung to these last few remaining hours of happiness. Hoping, hoping that somehow, there would be no need to face this new, horrible, difficulty. They played their parts well in those dark days, laughing and joking when they could; and Lesley was patient with him when he was irritable. On that last day of August, when only a miracle could have saved the peace of the world, Lesley knew that he was worried; dangerously worried.

She said quite gaily, "You spend so much time with that old radio now, that I suppose you will be too tired of it to tune in the 'Galloway Soup-Hour' to-night. I'm to be their guest-star, remember?"

"Of course I do, darling. You'll be wonderful. You're always wonderful. On the screen, on the radio, or just being yourself at home here with me."

She came and sat on the arm of his chair. "I've a much better idea. Why should you stay moping at home here? Why don't you come with me? It will be quite amusing I expect. I should feel much happier knowing that you were there with me. I always have the most awful attack of stage-fright when I see that microphone staring at me, or mike-fright they call it, don't they? If you were there, I could just think, 'All this will be over in a little while, and then my own darling husband can wrap me up, and tuck me into the car, and drive me home, and perhaps, who knows? he may fall in love with me all over again.' Will you come?"

He laughed up at her, and putting his arm around her pulled her down on his knees. "I don't believe you've ever been frightened of a microphone in your life," he said. "But I'd love to come. There is one thing though, on which I am afraid that I shall have to disappoint you. You see it's no good your thinking that I shall ever fall in love with you again." She pouted at him. "I fell in love with you once - a long time ago - when you were a little slip of a thing just out of pigtails ... "

She said: "Really, I'd no idea .... "

"Well, perhaps that is exaggerating a little, but it does seem a long time since the loveliest, sweetest person in all the world came into my life. And when she did, I fell in love with her right away, and I have been very much in love with her ever since." She made herself more comfortable on his lap. "So you see, darling, there really isn't very much chance of my falling in love with you again, as I already love you so much that sometimes .... "

"Darling," she said, "I wish we hadn't to go to that beastly broadcast."

But when they were there, it was quite good fun. Geoffrey sat in a little sound-proof room, with a loud speaker reproducing all the humour and music and gaiety that was proceeding on the stage, and he could look out, through the thick plate-glass window, across the audience who had greeted Lesley with a spontaneous burst of deafening applause. He was so proud of her and the popularity she had achieved.

Sitting there with Mr. Otis Galloway, the proprietor of the O. J. Galloway Soup Company; one of the officials of the radio-station, and an account executive from the advertising agency who had produced the broadcast, he listened to them congratulating each other on their success in getting Lesley to appear on the programme.

Mr. Galloway, a self-made prince of commerce; a down-to-earth business man to his very finger stubs, leaned across to Geoffrey and in a deep rasping voice, grated in his ear, "She's wonderful, Mr. Manners. Wonderful!"

Mr. Galloway was short and round. So round that if he had tucked in his arms and legs he could have rolled around the place with a very minimum of effort, instead of puffing and blowing, as he did when he had to walk. His head, which was really quite normal, looked the size of a tennis ball, set on top of the huge sphere that was his body. But though his head may have looked the size of a tennis ball, the general impression was more akin to that of a round, rosy apple.

"It's wonderful the things they do to-day to sell soup," he confided. "Why, when I started, we just made it, and put it into cans, and then left it to Mrs. Jones to tell Mrs. Smith that the soup tasted good and saved a lot of time!" He settled his massive stomach more comfortably in front of him. "Nowadays, they make up songs about it, and do almost everything, except lay it on to a house like water." He chuckled to himself, and his stomach bounced rhythmically in time with his chuckles. "I like selling things to eat," he said. "Eating and selling things to eat, are two of the good things in life, and God knows we need as many of the good things as we can get in the world to-day."

Not even Mr. Galloway had been immune from the depression that had radiated out over the world from Central Europe. Galloway's Soups sold far beyond the confines of his beloved United States. Indeed, Mr. Galloway had been heard to boast, that there was not a civilised nation on earth, or an uncivilised one for that matter, where his soups had not pandered to the appetite of an epicure; or where the manifold joys that lay in a can of Galloway's Soup, had not been savoured, and brought a new light to the eye, a new spring to the step, and new zest to the difficult job of living.

Mr. Galloway loved food. When he mentioned it there was a new soft cadence in his voice. For a moment there was a dreamy look of anticipation in his eye, and then he said, "You'll have supper with me when this is over, won't you? With Miss Travis? Er ... that is to say, Mrs. Manners, of course."

Geoffrey said, "Thanks a lot, Mr. Galloway, I'd like to come. But Miss Travis – er - my wife that is, did say something about being a little tired and going home. But I've no doubt that you'll be able to persuade her."

As the minutes fled by and they listened to songs, dance numbers, and to Lesley engaged in brilliant repartee with one of America's foremost radio comedians, Geoffrey forgot his fears and his worries and for a little while there was nothing in the world but

Lesley's voice, and the way she looked; and there was no to-morrow.

All too soon the programme neared its end, and Mr. Galloway edged himself out of his chair, as the vocalists in the band ranged themselves round the microphone, and swung into the Galloway Soup Theme Song.

It came drifting through the loud speaker, the words set to the tune of a popular dance number.

"Galloway's soup, Galloway's soup,
Bucks you up, defeats the 'droop.'
Galloway's soup is guaranteed,
Galloway's soup is a meal with speed.
Twenty varieties of the soup that pays,
Now don't forget, it's Galloway's I!"

The tune was a very catchy one, and Geoffrey found himself whistling it, as Lesley came into the room.

Mr. Galloway beamed, and all his ponderous persuasiveness rolled into action. Over Mr. Galloway's shoulder Geoffrey nodded his agreement, and Lesley capitulated without a struggle, taking the arm which Mr. Galloway held out in an old-world manner. Geoffrey followed on behind, still whistling the Galloway Theme Song.

As they passed through the building there was an undercurrent of excitement all around them. People were talking excitedly. Snatches of conversation reached their ears. "It's started I tell you!" "Nothing definite yet, but ... " "They're going to interrupt the programme with a news-flash that ... "

Geoffrey thought, "Well, Nero fiddled while Rome was burning, so I am at least going to have one more good binge before the new conflagration starts!"

Even in the night-club where Mr. Galloway took them, there was an atmosphere of impending sensation, as if everybody was waiting; afraid to hear something unpleasant that they knew must come.

But Lesley and Geoffrey put their own private fears in the background, and Mr. Galloway, magnificent in his rotundity, and despite the fact that when he was engrossed in his food the rest of the world ceased to exist, was a charming host.

It was getting quite late when the last of the champagne was sent bubbling into the glasses. They all began to think of moving. Geoffrey had been humming the tune of Mr. Galloway's theme-song. Mr. Galloway was quite pleased and was beating time with his forefinger. Geoffrey tried hard to remember the words but they completely escaped him. All he could remember was the Mock Turtle's song from *Alice in Wonderland;* the words fitted the tune very well. He began to chant softly :

" Beautiful Soup, so rich and green,
Waiting in a hot tureen!
Who for such dainties would not stoop?
Soup of the evening, beautiful Soup!
Soup of the evening, beautiful Soup!
Beau - ootiful Soo – oop!
Beau - ootiful Soo – oop!
Soo - oop of the e-e-evening,
 Beautiful, beautiful Soup!"

Mr. Galloway beamed. "I like it," he said. "I like it. Did you make it up? I think I could use it."

"Well, hardly," said Geoffrey.

"Then who did?" asked Mr. Galloway. "Is it a friend of yours? Do you know him?"

"Yes, in a way. He was a sort of friend of my childhood days. Lewis Carroll; you remember him, don't you?"

But still Mr. Galloway did not appreciate the twinkle in Geoffrey's eye, neither did he see the amused yet warning look that Lesley flashed in Geoffrey's direction. "Can you persuade him to let me use it?" he asked.

"It would go over big in our programme!"

"Oh, I should think so," said Geoffrey. "The only trouble is, that he would probably insist that you got a Mock Turtle to sing it! "

When they said good-bye, the champagne had transported Mr. Galloway into a Wonderland of his own, and he was still communing with himself, "Mock Turtle? Mock Turtle? What the heck is a Mock Turtle doing singing with a band?"

2

Lesley left for the studio early the following morning.

Very early, before they knew that the blow they both feared so much had fallen.

At dawn Germany's hordes had invaded Poland. Bombs had screamed down on Warsaw. The eagle of Germany had become a vulture, spreading its filthy wings of desolation over Europe. But still there was no news of any declaration of war by England or France. They could not fail now! No country, no nation, could survive, if it failed in so solemn an undertaking. He told himself, again and again, that they must be trying desperately, feverishly, to avert all the horror and suffering that would follow inevitably in the wake of the gods of war, if they were free once more to clank and roar their bloody trail across the earth.

With Britain's declaration delayed, there were curious glances, some whispered words that he could not catch; the very breeze blowing through the windows breathed a taunt: "What the Hell's happened to England?" He could stand it no longer. He saw the people who mattered at World Wide. They must release him from his agreement, he said. England was at war. And when they said that that was not true, he said, not technically perhaps, but morally. The other would follow; it was, after all, only a technicality. Had not Britain ordered immediately a complete mobilisation of her Army, Navy and Air Force? There could be no doubt. But it was such a monstrous thing - even now bombers might be winging their way to London .... They must release him because, well, he would go anyway.

Of course, they would release him. They understood the way he felt. They only hoped that England felt the same. It was hard to understand - this delay. They would be sorry to see him go, but they understood, because all of them, not only Englishmen, wanted to see the end of this bestial Nazi persecutor. It was too early for

America, yet. . . . But there was Britain and France, and the Maginot Line! The Nazi Goliath might have feet of clay. They were untested, these dictatorships, founded, as they were, upon cruelty, privation, persecution and a mass hero-worship that amounted almost to idolatry. Perhaps, after all, it would be a short war, but in any case, when it was over, they would be glad to have him back.

He smiled, and thanked them and said good-bye. When he had gone, their doubts as to England's intentions did not seem quite so important as before.

Lesley telephoned. "Please, please do not do anything until I have seen you," she said. "I shall be home as soon as I can. Promise me." He promised.

3

They sat together and listened to the slow, solemn announcement that the British Prime Minister was making in far-off London. Not even the lilting, wave-like background of atmospherics, could hide the disappointment and tragedy in his voice. But there was no weakness; no appeasement now. The die was cast. He was near the end:" . . . . It is the evil things we shall be fighting against - brute force, bad faith, injustice, oppression and persecution - and against them I am certain that the right will prevail."

Geoffrey was holding Lesley's hand; she stared wide-eyed at the radio. He was aware of a feeling, almost of relief, that all the waiting and sickening apprehension was over. But there was another feeling - one of compassion - for his countrymen, who must be fearful. Not for themselves, but for their children, their families, all that they held dear in life. Were they, even now, glancing apprehensively into the sky of a September morning? Fearful of what they might see and hear?

The menace to his island home was in the air. It must be met and defeated in the air. He could fly a plane - surely that was something? They said that eighteen was the ideal age to fly these new fighter planes. Could that be true, he wondered? Surely the men who had piloted the planes that had won the Schneider Trophy had not been as young as that? And there were other planes - bombers, to hit back. Surely they could find a place for him there? Surely Lesley would understand now? Things were so different; they had both of them known that this must happen. Even though they had not spoken about it, secretly they had known and dreaded its coming.

He said, as lightly as he could, "Well, darling, it's here at last!"

Her reply was slow, the tone bitter. "How I hate the world that can be so unthinking, so cruel."

He put his arm around her shoulders. "Perhaps it will be a better world, after this," he said.

She made a gesture as if to convey the futility of such a hope.

"World Wide have agreed to let me go right away - if I want to," he said, and walked over and switched off the radio.

Lesley said, "Please sit down, Geoffrey. I must talk to you about this." Her voice was quite calm, and she went on as if she was presenting a reasoned argument; an argument that she knew almost by heart.

"My dear, I'm proud that you want to go. If you hadn't, perhaps I should have wanted you to, I don't know. But I do know that I most desperately, selfishly, don't want you to go now! I've thought about it a hundred times - tried to see your point of view. Sometimes I think that I can. But even then, I cannot convince myself that I should be asked to lose you. Ask yourself, is there anything, anything on earth, that you would willingly agree to, that would take me away from you, perhaps for ever? If there is, then maybe, after all, your love is not as strong as mine, because there is nothing that would ever make me agree to let you go. It may be because all this is happening so far away - because it is no direct concern of mine, that I feel as I do. I cannot tell. I only know that patriotism, the sense of right and wrong, weigh very lightly in the balance against my love for you. If you accuse me of being selfish, of being without a true sense of the rightness of things, I will admit it. I am selfish where my love for you is concerned; selfish to the point of heartlessness. It is my life. I do not think that you have ever really understood just how much my life is your life, happy when you are happy, sad when you are sad. You have made me belong to you; life would be a lonely purgatory without you. You have never known loneliness - as I have. Not just a lack of companionship, but loneliness – indescribable - horrible. Like being in a dark cell - cut off from all communion. It would be hard for you to understand how Lesley Travis, famous, sought-after, could be lonely. But fame, popularity - these are not things that matter; a panacea to the pain that is solitariness, perhaps, but no more. To feel alone in one's thoughts, hopes and desires. Not to know the peace that flows from the unity of thought, or of touch, or of emotion. No, I will not willingly go back to that. If your sense of duty is stronger than your love for me, then there is nothing more that I can do. If you go, then I shall know that I have lost you, not just for while this war lasts - but for ever. If you survive you will be lost to me just as surely as if you are killed."

He was appalled by the vehemence of her utterance; the coldness of the tone she used. There was about her an air of finality, of resignation. He had a strange feeling that she intended all this to be something in the nature of an ultimatum.

He said, "But Lesley, surely you cannot, even for a moment, doubt my love for you? Surely you can see this is different? I have never been aware of any conscious sense of patriotism, or of a sense of duty. Perhaps if I were there, in England, I should not feel as I do now. Perhaps it is just the feeling of being here - away from all danger, that makes me feel that my self-respect, and eventually yours, demands that I should go. Won't you say that you understand?"

But she would not look at him, and so he went on: "You must know that being parted from you will be an agony in itself. The very thought of death will be a thousand times more hateful, for death would mean that I should never see you again; never love you again."

She looked at him at last. "Then why risk death? **Why** go, until they send for you? Until they say that they need you?"

"Oh, Lesley. How can I make you understand? Don't you see that I want to go? That I'm not doing anything useful here - nothing to help. After all, it may not be for long. It isn't as if we were the only ones. Why, at this very moment, there must be thousands saying good-bye, and wondering when they will meet again."

"Only because they have to."

He raised his voice a little, "No! Not because they have to! Because they feel that if life is to be worth living there is a job to be done. Because there is something in having a pride in one's country, because ... oh, I don't want to sound melodramatic, but because there is something in patriotism."

"I don't want a patriot - I don't want a hero! I just want you - as you are. What use will you be to me, or to anyone, getting yourself blown to smithereens in some filthy war? A war that we have had no part in making. Why should we suffer the heartache of separation before **we** have to?"

Don't let us argue any more," he said. "I feel that I must go, and in a little while you will feel the same way."

She rose from her chair, and walked to the window.

With her back to him she said, "I do not want you to make any mistake about this Geoffrey. I shall never change in the way I feel. What I am offering you now is a choice between my love and this sense of duty of yours. If you go - then I shall never want you to come back. Perhaps that comes as a shock to you after all that I have said that you mean to me? I will not suffer the agony of separation for nothing. A clean cut, a clean separation now, will hurt no more. At least, I shall not have the anguish and anxiety of forever wondering if you are still alive; of dying a thousand deaths every time there is a report of some new offensive."

He mustered every argument that occurred to him, but nothing he could say would make her change.

She closed her mind to every argument he presented. She told herself again and again that if she was adamant, if she did not depart so much as a fraction from the policy she had decided upon, that he must, in the end, give way.

They were so bitterly in opposition that any possibility of an immediate reconciliation appeared to Geoffrey to be an impossibility. His bewilderment at her coldness and her absolute refusal to negotiate, to discuss any possible alternative, reached its climax when she turned on him and said, "If you go, then I shall divorce you! I hope that will convince you how determined I am."

It was unbelievable that it was Lesley talking like this. It was as if she had slashed him across the face with a whip. She had turned her back on him again, so that she could not see the agony in his eyes. He could not argue any more. When the initial shock had passed; when she had had time to think it over, she would be more herself again - more the old Lesley he had known. She would not say these horrible things. At the moment, there seemed to be nothing more that he could do, so he went away, and left her staring out of the window. But now there was no silver-splashed sea; no star-flecked sky. Everything was dull and grey and dark.

He did not see Lesley at breakfast and learned that she had left the house very early. She did not come back and so he went out and spent the time saying good-bye to the many friends he had made in Hollywood. He was both surprised and gratified to learn how rapidly his stock had appreciated, following Britain's declaration of war.

He arranged accommodation on a plane leaving on the following day. Only to Ronald Rawlings he confided the secret of his trouble with Lesley. It was good to have a friend who was sympathetic, even though he could not be convinced by Ronald's "Cheer up, old boy. Women are the most unpredictable creatures. Lesley will soon come round - you'll see."

Lesley stayed away that night, and in the morning he was in a fever of anxiety to see her before he left.

The small hand-luggage he was taking with him was packed and waiting in the hall. Ronald would be calling to take him to the airport.

He paced nervously from one room to another. He wondered where she could be, the hope that she would return before he had to leave, gradually dying within him. In a few minutes now Ronald would be here. Under other circumstances he would already have been well on his way to the airport. But he had refused to leave until the last possible moment. As it was, Ronald had pointed out that the time he had allowed left no margin to cover any unforeseen delay.

He paused in his restless pacing as his ears caught the sound of a taxi, in low gear, making its way up the little semi-circular drive.

He met Lesley as she came into the hall and went quickly towards her. "Darling," he said, "thank God you've come!"

But she ignored him and walked to the stairs and made her way upwards towards her own room. For a few seconds he stood motionless in the hall, as if the shock of her passing him without recognition had dulled his senses. Then suddenly, he darted to the stairs and bounded up them, taking three stairs in a stride. He reached the door of her room and flung it open. Lesley was taking off her gloves. He tried to keep any semblance of anger from his voice, but the words tumbled out urgently, rapidly, "Lesley, for heaven's sake don't be such a Goddam fool! I shall be leaving in a few moments. For pity's sake say that you forgive me - that you still love me."

There was no change in the cold, almost uninterested, expression on her face.

He said slowly, "At least - you'll say good-bye to me?"

She completed the operation of taking off her gloves, rolled them into a ball, and flung them into a chair.

"There is really no necessity to say good-bye at all," she said.

There was the sound of a car in the drive below; then two sharp notes of an electric horn. He looked across at the window. "There's Ronald," he said.

When he spoke again there was a note of defeat **in** his voice. "There does not seem to be much point in our going over all that again."

The sound of his voice brought an icy hand to clutch at her heart. She had anticipated his defeat, but not a defeat that brought that dull tone of resignation to his voice; that hurt, bewildered look in his eyes. She refused to believe that he was resigned to losing her. He could not deny his love. He must stay!

Again there was the sudden, sharp noise of the car-horn, sounding impatiently.

Never before had she heard his voice so broken; she realised that it was only with a great effort that he controlled it at all.

"Good-bye, Lesley my darling. Forgive me. I have always feared that the wonderment of this past year could never last. Thank you for . . . loving me. I shall love you always. God keep you, sweetheart."

He was at the door; she was numb with a screaming fear that he would not give in to her.

He paused with his hand upon the handle of the door. When he spoke his voice was tentative, shy almost, "In time you may forgive me. Perhaps if I write ...?" She longed to hold out her arms to him; to kiss away that dazed, hurt look;

But this was the crisis. If she weakened now he would be lost to her - perhaps maimed or killed. She steeled herself to keep her voice casual; not to look at him.

"Oh, I shouldn't trouble to write," she said.

As he went through the door she called after him, and a note of hysteria in her voice made it sound almost as if she were laughing. "Yes, do write - your address will be useful - for forwarding the divorce papers!"

The words followed him, hammering into his brain, as he flung down the stairs and out into Ronald's car.

Lesley clutched at some support to steady herself. She felt as if the room was whirling about her. Dimly she was aware of the slamming of a door; the bubble of the car's exhaust as it rolled down the drive. She reached the window just in time to glimpse the car turning out of the gates. Her brain refused to register the thing that she had seen with her own eyes; he had gone!

In the car he had a sudden, urgent impulse to return.

But Ronald was saying, "You've cut it very fine old man, we shall only just make it." And there was that memory of her unbelievable casualness; the words she had flung after him. He could not face that again.

   How swiftly he would have returned to her had he but known of the flood of blinding tears that had come to sweep away the appearance of casualness she had assumed; had he but guessed at the twisting agony of her mind; had he heard but one of the shuddering, choking sobs that threatened to tear her very life away.

4

   At the airport he said to Ronald, "I'll write and let you know how I get on. If there is anything that you can do for Lesley .... "

   "I'll do everything I can," said Ronald, as they shook hands.

   "I know you will, thanks a lot - it makes me feel just a little better about ... everything. You'll write and let me know what happens - about Lesley I mean, won't you?"

   "Sure I will, Geoff."

   "Well, so long, Ronald. Thanks for everything."

   "Good-bye, old boy. Take care of yourself - give those Nazi swine one for me - until I can get things cleared up here and give them one for myself."

   Geoffrey paused on the steps leading into the plane. "Oh, just one thing more. When I write don't let Lesley know my address ... .''

   "Why on earth not?" asked Ronald.

   "I haven't time to explain now, but I don't want her to know - there might be some unpleasant news or documents she might want to send me - if she knew."

   "Well, you know best, I suppose. Okay, Geoff."

   The door was closed; the engines roared into noisy turbulent life; the plane taxied forward. . . .

CHAPTER 13

His return journey across the Atlantic was a crossing very different from the one that had borne him to America. Then he had been eager for a sight of a strange new world; anxious of his ability to undertake a new job in strange surroundings; his pulses quickening with the thought of a possible meeting with Lesley.

Now he had only a dull, depressing sense of loss. Even the thought of returning home held no pleasurable anticipations. True, there had been no attacks upon England - her war with Germany had opened without any spectacular gambit, it was almost stalemate. So that, at times, he almost regretted his impulsiveness. But the news that came from Poland; of the horrible things committed there; of the bombardment of Warsaw; swept aside any doubts which he had had as to the rightness of the step he had taken.

The nights when they travelled with lights obscured, and cut swiftly forward into the eerie blackness; the atmosphere of tense anticipation that prevailed, especially during the hours of darkness, that grew sometimes until it was almost a presentiment of disaster ... until one could feel the ship shudder - hear the deafening explosion.

It was not an atmosphere calculated to raise him from the feeling of depression into which he had fallen.

It was with a sensation of utter relief that he saw at last, in the fading light of a September evening, the roofs and spires of Liverpool.

When, after all the boring formalities, he was allowed to land, he stepped ashore into his first experience of the black-out. It was like entering the house of a friend who was dead, where all the blinds were drawn, and there was only a small, faint light. In the darkness everything seemed hushed. Even the traffic, lamps muffled with paper or rags, appeared to move with less noise than usual. He shivered slightly although the night air was not noticeably cold.

Not until he was inside the Adelphi, with its warmth and brilliant illumination, did he begin to feel human again. Everything here was so secure and established; so - normal.

It was good to sigh and to relax in a deep, comfortable armchair. It was good to have a waiter bring him a large whisky, as if the war were a million miles away. He missed the tinkle of ice in the glass. It was difficult to keep his eyes open. This was not America it was England. Don't go to sleep in the lounge, you idiot! The thing about this hotel, that reminded him of America, was the air-conditioning. It had always made him feel tired - even in America. America - Lesley. Would he always have that empty feeling when he thought of her? He roused himself and poured some soda-water into his whisky. It tasted warm. Perhaps that was because he felt tired. He finished his drink and went to bed. As he switched out the light he saw a printed instruction on the telephone at his bedside. If he wanted service -if he wanted anything, he was to lift the telephone and ask for it. What would they think if he were to ask for Lesley Travis? He wanted her - God, how he wanted her. She had said that he hadn't known what it was like to be lonely - really lonely. Well, she had been right. But he knew now .... "Good-night Lesley, darling."

2

In London, at the Air Ministry, they were sympathetic. but a little doubtful. He was a little old, perhaps. . . .? He could pilot a plane? How many hours? Well, that was good, but still .... He had flown in America? What sort of plane had he handled there? Oh, a Beechcraft! That was good. He had come all the way from America just to volunteer for this? Well, he hadn't wasted much time, anyway. That showed he was keen. They wanted men who were keen and could fly. They would arrange for him to have a medical examination. Would he go back to his job, and wait until he heard from them? Oh, of course he hadn't a job. Would he be staying at this address? Good, then they would get in touch with him there. No, they were sorry, but he would appreciate that these things took time ....

The period of waiting seemed endless. He filled in the time by renewing old friendships. He surprised Sir Highley Nitely, by appearing in the office of that worthy gentleman, when he was busily engaged on the telephone explaining to his wife that it was essential that she should remain evacuated in the country. No, he was not making it an excuse for him to have a good time on his own! The suggestion was most unfair; it hurt him more than he could say. It was her safety alone he was thinking of - just because there had been no bombs up till now, did not mean that there would be no bombs. He was working like a slave. The war had made things very difficult in his business. The woman he had been dining with last night? How the devil did she know about that? Oh, that interfering old busybody! His voice assumed a new dignity. The suspicion was quite unjustified. It had been the wife of one of his most valued clients. The poor woman was terrified of being left alone in London, with all this talk of air-raids. He had done the only decent, and commercially sane thing, in inviting her to dinner. When he had heard that her husband was detained in the country, and would not be back in London until late, he had stepped into the breach, thus cementing still more strongly the bond of friendship with his valued client. Was she attractive! Bah! he hadn't even noticed. There was only one woman in the world who was attractive to Sir Highley. He trailed off into a recitation of endearing compliments.

When he had looked up and seen Geoffrey, there had been a bright light of welcome in his eyes. He had stabbed his forefinger two or three times in the direction of the telephone mouthpiece, and in silence, but with an exaggerated movement of his lips, he had formed the words, "My wife!"

The moment he had set the receiver down in its cradle, he came round the desk with his hand outstretched.

"Well, of all people! I am glad to see you. When did you get to England?" Geoffrey was kept busy answering a hundred questions.

Was his wife with him? No. That was a pity, Sir Highley wanted very much to meet her. She would follow on later perhaps? Geoffrey couldn't say. Of course not, she must be busy, and England wasn't exactly a health resort at the moment! And so it went on, "How was business?" Oh, he couldn't complain really. Of course, there had been a flood of cancellations at first, and things hadn't straightened themselves out yet. It was all a mix-up of, 'Business-as-usual,' 'Not-wasting-money,' and 'keeping-the-brand-name alive.' But things would come out all right in the end, they always did.

Much later, he said that it was a pity that Geoffrey had not warned him of his coming. He had an engagement for dinner. No-o, it was not exactly a business engagement, but it would be most ungallant of him ... Geoffrey said that he would not think of allowing him to break such an important engagement on his account.

He promised Sir Highley that in the near future, he would telephone him so that they might meet again when Sir Highley was not so heavily engaged, and then he went to look for "Laddie" Arthur.

He found her in her office surrounded by a dozen different presentations of a slogan which some enthusiastic Civil Servant imagined would, if displayed in the largest possible size on the largest possible hoardings, serve to bolster-up public morale.

"Laddie " had heard that Geoffrey was with Sir Highley and as he entered the room she came round her desk towards him, her hands outstretched in welcome.

"Why! Hello, you Hollywood buccaneer, it's lovely to see you again."

He took her hands and held her away from him whilst he surveyed her. "I declare that you're lovelier than ever," he said.

She smiled with pleasure. "Come and sit down and tell me all about yourself," she invited.

He glanced at his watch. "It's almost five-thirty," he said.

"Oh, we don't finish at five-thirty any more now. There's a war on, you know!"

His face expressed mock despair. "I'd rather hoped that perhaps you would be able to spend at least a part of the evening with me. Can you?"

She brushed her dark hair away from her eyes and glanced rather disconsolately at the slogan poster-designs spread around the room.

"Yes, of course I can, Geoffrey, but I really must try and select three of these designs to go to the Ministry this evening."

He gave them a quizzical glance. She went on, "Hopeless aren't they? Can you imagine the public wanting drivel like this stuck up in front of them to keep them cheerful? No, of course you can't. But I suppose our amateur publicists have got to have their fling. The 'old-man,' bless his heart, hasn't any patience with them at all. I remember the first time he went along to see them - just after we had been appointed as agents to the Ministry - he came back absolutely bursting with indignation. He'd taken along his usual bulky folder packed with the latest Nitely inspirations and brilliant ideas - which we'd slaved for days to get ready on time - and all they did was to glance at them and tell him that they weren't dignified enough! None of them had ever had anything to do with publicity before, but they promptly sat down and told the 'old man' just how he'd got to do the job. You can imagine how he reacted to that - anyway, he just came back and flung the stuff at me and he hasn't even been near the place since."

She glanced around her again, "This is one of their efforts. A bit difficult to get enthusiastic about, aren't they?"

She surveyed them rapidly in turn. "Well, here goes," she said, and selected three of the designs at random. She put them on one side with a letter and rang the bell for a messenger. The messenger came in as she was putting on her hat. "Get those off right away," she said, moving over to the door with Geoffrey. A moment later she put her head back through the doorway and indicating the remaining designs said, "And put those in the ash-can!"

With the vivacious Miss Arthur as a companion, London in the black-out seemed so very much more cheerful. They walked slowly through the darkened streets between the sand-bagged buildings, and for the first time Geoffrey had the feeling of being home again.

After dinner they danced together and once again the smooth rhythmic movements brought to Geoffrey some cessation of the pain and longing in his heart.

She sensed the disquiet in him and although they talked of his life in America and of Lesley, he did not tell her then of the manner in which they had parted.

It was late when the taxi drew up outside the Kensington flat, but in spite of the lateness of the hour she insisted that he should "Come on up and see Oswald again."

Oswald Whistler, clad in a vermilion dressing-gown appeared sleepy-eyed from his bedroom. In one hand he clutched a calf-bound copy of *The Meditations of Marcus Aurelius*, whilst with the other he scratched himself luxuriously, all the while murmuring, " 'And lice destroyed Democritus; and other lice killed Socrates. What means all this? ' " ·

He greeted Geoffrey with an absent-minded cordiality, as if he had seen him only the night before instead of more than a year ago, and after he had consumed an enormous whisky which he drained off in one gulp, he asked if he might be excused to return to his bed in order that he might resume his perusal of a philosophy which he said he found most comforting in these mad, bewildering days.

Geoffrey rose to go, but "Laddie" said, "Don't go yet. Stay a little while and talk to me some more." He sank back in the deep settee and after she had replenished their glasses, she came and sat beside him.

"You're unhappy, Geoffrey," she said. "What is it?"

And so he told her.

It was a relief to talk to somebody about it, especially somebody that he felt would understand.

When he was silent again she started to speak in her low-pitched attractive voice.

"I don't think that she has stopped loving you," she said. "Women like Lesley Travis don't stop loving a man because he has notions, however quixotic, about honour or duty or things like that.

They stop loving because of other women, or through neglect, or perhaps because the man they once saw as a knight in shining armour turns out to be something very different and second-rate. But, my dear, I do think that you have handled the whole thing rather clumsily, don't you? After all, when you went to Hollywood and married Lesley you did a most unusual thing - I don't mean that you did anything particularly memorable or worth while - but it is certainly unusual to marry a film-star, and knowing you, I should imagine that you have not been prepared to admit the unusualness of things. You have wanted to see Lesley only as a woman - an ordinary woman - without realising how different her life is from that of an ordinary woman. The adulation, the material things of this world which it is so easy for her to possess, must, unless she is something more than human, have had a vast effect upon her. Her ability to obtain and to hold things could seldom, if ever, have been questioned before.

"But Lesley is not like that at all," he said.

"No, don't misunderstand me, I don't mean to convey that I think she is selfish or anything like that, but I don't suppose that she has ever had to worry about losing anything before, and she is still very young and probably very much in love. Can't you understand that she just couldn't bear to think that you could have any feeling that was stronger than your love for her?"

But this was quite different."

"Of course it was, but that is not the point, she wanted your love for her to transcend everything - honour, love of country, your sense of right and wrong, duty, everything. Don't you see, it must have seemed to her that you had a clear choice; to stay and prove your love, or to go away, perhaps for ever. You must appreciate how difficult it must have been for the famous Lesley Travis, who had married you unknown and neither wealthy nor famous, to understand that you should want to leave her - "

"But she must have known. that I didn't want to leave her! "

" Oh, I expect that deep down inside her she knew that, but she would think about it and think about it, until everything became twisted up in her mind and she could only see that you wanted to go away and leave her. If you could have said, 'Darling, I feel that I must go - everything inside me tells me that I should go, but in spite of everything - I can't go away and leave you, because I love you so much,' she would have won. All her fears would have been set at rest and then perhaps in a little while she would have wanted you to go, not because she loved you any less, but because she would have come to see your point of view, have understood that it was not choice but a necessity forced upon you by circumstances that had nothing at all to do with how much you loved her."

He said slowly, his mind in the past: "Lesley said something very much like that when I tried to talk to her about it, but it was impossible to make her understand, I tried, but it was no good. She seemed so determined not to discuss the matter; to give me no alternative but to do as she wished, that I suppose I was unreasonable. Oh, I can see well enough now that I did the very thing that I had always been so very sure that I would never do - allow a misunderstanding to break up something without doing everything possible, without saying everything that I could, to dispose of the difficulty. But perhaps you can understand how I felt when she just would not talk about it, and that horrible feeling I had that I was there hiding safely away from it all, and the way people looked - "

She gave him a warm, friendly smile - she was very fond of this good-looking young man who, despite his air of sophistication had such a decent, and in a way, naive attitude towards her sex. She could imagine what it must be like to feel that this attractive healthy young male belonged to one. To be able to run one's fingers through the dark hair; to feel the lithe strength of those broad shoulders and tapering hips when his arms were holding you; to see admiration in his eyes and perhaps passion kindling; to surrender to the caresses of his clean strong hands - he would be gentle, treating you as if you were something almost too lovely and wonderful to touch; burying his face against you when he tried to tell you of your loveliness. . . .

She moved restlessly against him, and forced her thoughts away from these dangerous channels.

"She'll go on loving you," she said. "Don't blame yourself too much. The fault was not all on your side. Wait a little while before you do anything. Missing you, being without you, will show her more than anything else whether she can let you go out of her life for ever. Whether she loves you or not, to be weak now would spoil everything."

He rose from the settee and walked over to the fireplace, and with his foot stirred the embers of the dying fire.

"If I knew that she still loved me," he said, "I would not want her to worry or to be unhappy because of me."

"But you don't know. You must wait. Lesley gave you a choice of staying with her or of returning to England. There was nothing in between - no alternative. Only Lesley can withdraw that - and she will."

He said, "But she doesn't know where I am, she could not communicate with me even if she wanted to."

"Laddie" moved over towards him. "If she wants to, she will find you. Now for goodness sake give up worrying about it - I'm sure everything will turn out all right in the end."

There was a new bantering note in her voice and he smiled back at her. "I must be an awful bore," he said. "I'm rather fond of you," she said, and then changing her tone, "What about another drink, my dear?"

Geoffrey glanced at the clock. "Good heavens! I'd no idea that it was so late. No, thank you, 'Laddie,' I really must be getting along now. I'll have to walk as it is."

"We can put you up if you like."

"No, I think I had better go." She was very attractive standing there before him.

She saw him to the door. He said: "Thank you for your sympathy and everything. You're the grandest person."   .

She did not say anything; she was standing very close to him. He went on: "I have been very lucky in the people I have met in these last few years and especially lucky in the friends that I have made, but most especially I have been lucky to have you as a friend - a very dear friend."

She thought: "This is unbearable," and then for a brief moment she was in his arms, felt his lips firm and warm. "Good-night, my dear," he said.

"Good-night, darling," she said softly, too softly for him to hear. She heard him going down the stairs. The room was very empty without him.

3

Only the night-porter was in evidence when he arrived back at his hotel, but on the table in his bedroom he found waiting for him, a notice instructing him to attend for his medical examination.

4

They tested his eyes, his heart, his lungs. Asked him questions. Made him walk round chairs until he was dizzy. He became depressed in the conviction that he was bound to fail on something or other. As the conviction grew he became quite unreasonable. He forgot that he was asking to be allowed to handle a machine that cost thousands of pounds; that upon his physical fitness might depend the safety of lives other than his own. He thought, "It's not as if I wanted a life insurance policy - quite the reverse!" He tried to think of all the tests which might cause him to fail. When he had finished walking round and round that chair he had been as dizzy as an inebriated blonde. They were bound to flunk him on that!

When at last, he heard that he had got through, he experienced a sensation something akin to a feeling he had had, long ago, when his headmaster had presented him with the one and only prize which he had managed to acquire during his carefree days at school.

But, if waiting for the notice calling him for his medical examination had seemed an age, then waiting for some further communication from the Air Ministry seemed an eternity.

He went to his cottage, and was welcomed so ecstatically by Bobby, who had grown almost beyond recognition, and with such genuine pleasure and friendship by Elsa Knight, that his heart was warmed.

She swept convention to the wind, and insisted that he should stay.

As they sat together through one of those long evenings, she listened sympathetically whilst he told her of his life with Lesley, and of the tragedy of their parting. She had no feeling of pleasure when she learned of his separation from Lesley. She had, long since, put away any feelings for him, other than those of gratitude and true friendship. She was aware only that he was unhappy, and that it hurt her to see him so. She knew that he was still desperately in love with Lesley, and as she listened to him, she alternated between a desire for revenge upon the woman who had hurt him, and a foolish hope that somehow, something that she could do would be successful in effecting a reconciliation.

She tried hard to make him happy whilst he was at the cottage, and in the main she succeeded. But all the time she knew that he was crying out for the opportunity of some active occupation. This period of waiting with its long hours of idleness, when his thoughts would be with Lesley, was becoming unbearable for him.

But at last, when he had almost despaired of hearing anything, she handed him an official-looking envelope and watched fearfully while he opened it. "Elsa, dear, it's here," he said, waving his instructions to report, and her disappointment because he would have to leave, vanished utterly, when she noticed the new light in his eye, the way he threw back his shoulders, saw, once again, the old, happy, attractive smile, which she had missed so much since his return.

5

On the day that Geoffrey went to London to purchase the uniforms, and clothes, and the hundred and one other things that had been detailed for him on a neat little list, he kept his promise to Sir Highley Nitely and telephoned him of his coming.

At dinner that night Geoffrey told Sir Highley that he was under orders to report for training; and Sir Highley wished him all the luck in the world. It was a regrettable and unfortunate thing, he said, that such a promising career should be interrupted and perhaps ruined, but the war was responsible for a lot of cruel things and a lot of curious things.

"Take advertising and publicity, for instance," said Sir Highley. "Could there be anything more closely allied to propaganda than those two things? And is there anything that this country needs more, at the moment, than intelligent propaganda in the neutral countries, and directed to the German people? Yet what have the Government done? Fiddled with the problem! If I had my way I'd sift through every competent journalist, publicist, advertising and public relations expert in this country and then commandeer the best of the whole bunch. I'd do the same thing with all the people who have inside knowledge of the conditions, aspirations, fears and sympathies of all the different countries, and then I'd lump the whole lot of them together and tell them to get on with the job. If the Government laid down a policy of what they wanted to achieve in any particular country, and, damn it all, when you come to boil it down it can't be more than creating goodwill and assistance for this country, and fostering a dislike for Germany and German methods and instilling in them a determination to resist German aggression, then, knowing your policy and aims, you would have the men who could tell you how they would have to be amended, or strengthened, or changed about, to suit the particular conditions of the country concerned, and then the fellows who have earned their livings appealing to the mass mind could get to work and lick the stuff into shape."

Sir Highley sighed, and selected one of his fat, expensive cigarettes to smoke between courses.

"As it is ... well, perhaps it's early days to criticise what they have done - but, have you seen one of those leaflets that they have been dropping over Germany? What on earth is the good of telling a nation that's all swelled up with its own importance and as jubilant as hell over its regeneration, and has created the largest and best equipped army and air-force in the world, that they are in for the most almighty licking? and just can't win? Why, it's like a weedy kid of ten years old slipping a note through the front-door of some heavy-weight boxing champion and telling him that he's going to get beaten up because in another ten years' time the kid's going to grow into the biggest and toughest proposition that the boxing wallah's ever had to face! No! It won't wash. We shall want something a lot more subtle than that. It was British propaganda that brought about the collapse of the German people from the inside last time, and it's going to be a thousand times more necessary this time, and it's got to be a thousand times more clever."

Sir Highley stubbed out his cigarette - he seldom seemed to smoke more than an inch or so of his cigarettes - and then twinkled a smile at Geoffrey. "Here I go, boring you with my grievances again. You won't want to hear all this, but all the same, I think that you're just as well out of it. It'd make your heart bleed to read and hear of some of the things that are going on!"

He played with his savoury, pushed it on one side, and selected another cigarette.

"By the way, how is Mrs. Manners?" Geoffrey said that she was very well.

"It's a pity that you couldn't have brought her with you," said Sir Highley. "A great pity, but then I suppose that she must be a very busy woman. Oh, that reminds me, I had a letter from Hollywood a few days ago. Let me see, who was it from now? Er ... a Miss Phyllis Peters. Yes, that's it. Said that you had left very hurriedly and asking if I would send on your address, as there were some rather important matters that should be communicated to you."

Geoffrey tried not to display any undue interest. "Did she give any idea what matters they were?" he enquired.

"No," said Sir Highley. "I hadn't got your address, so I replied saying that I hoped to see you in the near future, and would ask you to get in touch with her. By the way - who is she?"

Geoffrey said, as casually as he could, "Oh, one of the secretaries. I did dash off at very short notice, you know. I intended writing and letting the people over there know where they could get in touch with me, but as there is somebody there looking after my affairs, I just haven't troubled."

Sir Highley nodded absent-mindedly as if the whole matter was one of very little importance, and went on talking of other things.

Geoffrey listened, but all the time he was wondering just why Lesley wanted his address, and had asked Phyllis Peters to write to Sir Highley. Had Lesley forgiven him? Or was it the first step towards obtaining her freedom?

CHAPTER 14

GEOFFREY'S days of training restored his confidence in himself; made him feel once more that he was a useful member of the community.

"Forget all that you know, or think that you know, about flying," they said, "except anything that coincides with what we teach you. We don't want individual supermen - the day of the independent 'ace' is over; what we want are pilots who can make a team. Fly together - fight together. For every hour that you will spend flying alone, you will spend hundreds flying in formation; fighting in formation. We want no individual brilliance, no individual heroics, of a nature likely to jeopardize the safety or success of the team .... "

They were long arduous days. Days of lectures, and flying-training, and demonstrations, and of practice with deadly, chattering weapons. But he made a sure and steady progress; a progress designed to convert him, with as little delay as possible, into the quick-thinking brain and nerve-centre of a high-speed, complicated, death-dealing weapon of the skies.

With all his energies directed towards one clear-cut aim; with his mind occupied, he had no time to be despondent. He still thought of Lesley, the memory of her would intrude upon him at the oddest moments, but his thoughts were without bitterness. He no longer chided himself upon his clumsy handling of the whole affair. Lesley had become the symbol of a lovely, fragrant happiness, that might perhaps be achieved again one day far distant in the uncertain future that stretched before him.

Then, just as he was reaching the end of his operational training, he received a letter from Ronald Rawlings. When he saw the postmark, his heart bounded almost as much as if the letter had been from Lesley herself. He read it eagerly. The first part dealt only with one or two matters in connection with his own activities, about which Geoffrey had written to him a short time before. The letter went on: "... I know that the only news that will really interest you, is news of Lesley. You will, I know, appreciate how sorry I am that I have, very little to tell you. I have seen Lesley only once since you left, and she gave me very little opportunity for any long discussion. I am sure there is nobody here who has so much as a suspicion that there is any trouble between you, or that you quarrelled before you left. When I saw her, there were a number of people who enquired about you, and whilst, of course, she was not very communicative in her replies, she said (quite proudly, it seemed to me) that you had gone to England to join the R.A.F., and that she hadn't much news, because it came through so slowly nowadays ....

"When, at last, I did have an opportunity of speaking to her alone, she seemed rather uncertain what to say - as if she was doubtful just what I knew. She was aware that I had seen you off, and thanked me for helping you. It had all been such a terrible rush, she said. She asked me if I had heard from you, and I told her, quite truthfully, that I hadn't. (I was beginning to wonder if I should ever hear from you!) She asked, if I did get a letter from you, whether she might read it. She laughed a little, and said that husbands were notoriously bad correspondents where their wives were concerned, and never thought of giving the really important news.

"It was such a brave deception, that I had not the heart to tell her that I knew.

"When, at last, your letter did arrive I was sorely tempted to take it to her. Only my promise not to disclose your address prevented me. But a promise is a promise, and I have kept my word, although I am sure that in keeping it, I have done you a disservice. I am certain that she still loves you, and that if she could write to you, it would be only to tell you of her love. You can have no idea how difficult, almost impossible, it is, to trace anybody who disappears as suddenly and completely as you did. Why, even at the studio they have no idea what has happened to you - your promised letter advising them of your whereabouts has just failed to materialise! I was rather worried myself, because I had not heard from you, and wrote to the Air Ministry in London asking them if they could put me in touch with you, but they replied saying that unless I could give them something more than your name, they regretted their inability to help. I am sure that Lesley must be frantic to find some way of communicating with you - she is not even certain that you have been successful in getting into the Air Force!

"I do urge you most sincerely to write to her. I am sure that the unpleasant possibilities you feared will not materialise. Her voice and eyes betray her when she speaks of you. I am sure that she has no intention of divorcing you - if she has, then she is a far better actress than I have ever deemed her to be.

"I have been tempted to go to her quite openly and tell her that I know about everything, and ask her what she really feels; what her intentions really are. But somehow I cannot. If I should be wrong, my intrusion would be unforgivable.

"I am afraid that I shall not have another opportunity of seeing Lesley, or of writing to you again, before I leave Hollywood. My long-distance negotiations have been successful, and I am under orders to report to a Cadet Training Unit in Wiltshire. World Wide have been very decent in releasing me from my contract, and I will let you know as soon as I arrive in England in order that we may meet. There have been numerous enquiries about you from your old colleagues, and they wish you well.

"There is just one more item of news about Lesley. I have forgotten to say that she is looking very well, although not perhaps as gay as in the days when you were here. She is still working hard, as usual. There have been one or two rumours, you know how these things get round, that she is becoming 'temperamental' - I find that hard to believe - but as far as I can make out (and you will appreciate the reason that prompted my enquiries) there has been some trouble about the story of her present film. She has apparently been insisting on certain alterations - never a very popular procedure, as you know - although lots of them do it. I suppose it is only because she has always been so amenable in the past that people in her studio should think it worth mentioning at all. I only write this as an afterthought, but it occurs to me that if there is any trouble, it may be because she is worrying about you, and it may prove an additional inducement for you to write to her.

"I apologise for writing at such length, but it has been a long time since you left, and I have tried to deal as fully as possible with the few items of news that I have about Lesley. It should not be long now before we meet, and I hope that when we do, you will be able to tell me that you have written to Lesley, because I know that she still loves you very much. . . . "

Geoffrey read the last line again and again. If only he could be sure that it was true. If only he could be sure that Lesley no longer intended to divorce him; no longer needed his address just to assist her in obtaining a divorce. He supposed that it was all rather cowardly and foolish - this running off and hiding himself away; hoping that if they could not trace him, there could be no divorce. His ideas about divorce were of the haziest especially about divorce in America. Some people in Hollywood had slipped in and out of marriage as easily, and with no greater concern, than he would have displayed in buying a new car. One discontented wife had obtained a divorce because her husband had snored and kept her awake! For all he knew, it might be quite possible for Lesley to get a divorce without him knowing anything about it until he saw it in the papers.

For a long time, following the receipt of Ronald's letter, he could not find the answer to the question which was forever in the forefront of his mind. To write or not? He was exasperated by his own inability to reach a decision. When he remembered Ronald's convictions about Lesley; when he imagined, with almost breathless anticipation, receiving a letter from her - a letter telling him that her love was not dead, a letter redolent with new hope, with new happiness for the future, then he would start to write feverishly. Words of love, expressions of tenderness, explanations, flowing rapidly from his pen. Until a tiny, whispered doubt in his mind would grow in volume until it became a thunder, drowning his hope, his conviction; staying his hand in the very act of writing.

Could Ronald have been mistaken? Was it love that had restrained Lesley from making public the knowledge of their quarrel? Might not her reticence have been prompted more by her pride, her refusal to admit a failure, than by her continued love? Swift to her defence would come all his knowledge of her. Lesley would not do that. She would not hide their failure behind a false face, an assumed love. If she believed that he had failed her so badly that she could no longer love him, if his desertion had wounded her so deeply that her faith in him had gone, then no taunt of failure, no fear of unkind whispered words, would have dissuaded her from taking any action which she felt was best to end a relationship her heart could no longer endorse.

But the damage would have been done. The withering hand of indecision would be upon him again. Slowly he would tear up the pages he had written so eagerly.

In the end, it was a new and potent argument he found to strengthen him in his decision not to write. He was posted for duty with a fighter squadron stationed in Scotland. A knowledge of the insecurity of his future, the doubtful tenure of a new and dangerous life, forced itself upon him. Illogical and twisted arguments assailed him. He had no right to involve Lesley, no right to subject her to the emotional fears and doubts which must be associated with the hazards and dangers of his new life. If he kept silent, if he made no attempt to bring about a reconciliation, then if anything did happen to him .... Well, he could not deny that he hoped that she would have regrets, that she would be sorry, but her grief (yes, he even hoped that she would grieve for him a little) would not be so poignant, so brutal in its sense of loss, as it would be if he succeeded in once again tangling her emotions in the insecure threads of his own life; if he caused her to look forward to a new happiness sometime in the distant future. He used his new decision as a balm to assuage his reawakened, burning desire for her. It was one little thing that he could do as a tribute to his love. Not perhaps a thing of the order of self-sacrifice, which he would willingly have undergone to serve her, but a self-denial which might perhaps be instrumental in sparing her some small torment, something which he could set as a shield between her and the sharpest edge of pain which she might experience if he were to die.

2

In Scotland, when the first strangeness of everything had gone, he fell into a routine of operational duties. There was nothing dull about this routine. Every time he left the ground in his eight-gun Hurricane, he felt that he wanted to shout aloud to relieve the feeling of excitement that surged through him. As the ground fell away below him, his hands would grip hard on the controls; the only physical manifestation of the exhilaration he felt in controlling this deadly, throbbing machine, which nevertheless had more sense of life in it than any other machine he had ever known before. It was ever new, this thrill of speed combined with a sense of power that he had; at a touch of his finger death would stream unchecked from the wings that spread below him. Eight little innocuous holes in the forward edges of the tapering wings; eight holes, at the mouth of each would flicker fitfully myriads of little wicked, spiteful flames, dancing as if in unholy glee at the stream of hard, biting metal that spouted from the centre of each one. Eight individual streams of death, converging into one devastating, annihilating vortex of destruction. Eight rods of steel to break the wings and beat the life from the vultures who had prostituted man's conquest of the air.

And at last his guns chattered in earnest. A Dornier on reconnaissance blundered into their patrol on the east coast of Scotland.

As the black pencil of a fuselage came within his gun-sights there was a blood-lust within him that he could never have imagined; his blood had a fiery heat as it sped frantically before the pounding of his heart; the palms of his hands were wet with excitement. In those few seconds he saw his bullets biting and tearing great holes in the Dornier. There was no pity, only a triumph, a desire to kill, that constricted his lungs. He must turn, swoop and slash this carrion again. This clumsy, blundering pace would not wing them to safety; had they the winged speed of Mercury it could no longer have borne them to security. He swung easily into position, above and behind them. Stab! Stab! Stab! They were firing at him! He laughed. He had forgotten all about that! It was his turn again now. A longer burst this time. The Dornier was falling away. What was wrong? How could it survive? Ah! Now it was down - rushing, falling. Why don't you get out, you fools? Don't you know that you're lost? Still no sign. Oh, it would be like the cunning of the Hun - diving almost to sea-level and then flattening out! No escape that way, by God! Down behind them. Another burst. Down, down, death screaming in the rushing wind. The sea was hurtling towards them now, it looked hard, like a rippled bed of concrete. He must pull out now. But no, wait! Fear must not deprive him of this victory! Now! Now! No further you fool! He eased back. The Dornier sped on, on into a blinding cascade of spume, smoke and disintegrating destruction. He circled round. No sign of living thing - nothing. "Poor devils! Would there be some German Lesley, waiting, waiting?" Rejoin formation. "What would Lesley's feelings have been - if it had been his turn?" Resume patrol.

3

The memory of that solitary victory could not appease he urgent desire he felt for action, or his impatience that they were not called upon when the German hordes poured irresistibly over the low countries. The collapse of France! The fantastic and tragic, yet brilliant and heroic, epic of Dunkirk. Days when his colleagues of the air brought their heroism and self-sacrifice to a common pool of bravery and self-abnegation. To be isolated here! To have missed all that! It was quite impossible to understand. There were many hard words in the mess.

And then, one day in that unbelievably lovely summer, his squadron was moved near London. The tempo of his life was changed. There was a sense of urgency in the air. A reshuffling of the squadrons that had been so sorely depleted over France and Holland and Belgium.

There was a great deal to be done. Regular patrols to be flown, and sudden urgent sorties as German aircraft made more frequent and daring appearances over England.

But for all this, it was still a time of waiting; these things were no more than the little gusts and flurries that presaged the coming storm. There was still time to rest and seek relaxation; times when he had a few hours to himself to seek distraction.

It was on one such afternoon early in August that he decided to while away a few hours in going to see one of the films that he had watched in the making at the World Wide studios. It was being shown in the market town near the aerodrome, and he thought that it would be interesting to see how it had turned out. There would be memories for him in the film. Not just memories of the studios and of the people in the studio, but memories recalled by the recollection of incidents of those days, memories of happy days with Lesley ....

He walked through the gates and down the road towards the little row of villas where the single-decker 'bus stopped to pick up passengers for the town.

Everything was very quiet and peaceful, and as he walked slowly down the road his thoughts were far away. He was scarcely aware of the ambulance parked in the kerb. It was one of those stout, well-built American ambulances, and on the side was painted the flags of the United States and of Britain.

He was halted in his tracks when a voice, which he recognised as familiar, but could not place, said: "Hello, stranger!"

He looked round quickly, but it was difficult to see through the windshield of the ambulance. He walked back a few paces and looked into the driving compartment.

A girl in khaki uniform was sitting behind the wheel, regarding him with an amused expression in her eyes.

"Good heavens;" he exclaimed. "Mavis Lee! What on earth are you doing here?"

"Oh, just waiting," she said.

He made a little gesture of impatience. "No, I mean what are you doing here - in England, in that uniform, and driving this ambulance?"

"Doing my little bit to help," she told him. And then asked: "Surprised?"

"What do you think?" he said, and she laughed. A deep, gurgling, friendly laugh that made him suddenly aware again of her dark, vibrant beauty.

There was a new air about her - a purposefulness that had not been there when he had last seen her. The uniform seemed somehow to have suppressed the old overwhelming atmosphere of sex; to have eradicated the flamboyance of her attraction.

She was, if anything, even more beautiful in this new dark quiet way.

"Why don't you get in and talk to me?" she asked.

"Or do you still regard me as a loose and evil woman?" He opened the door and climbed in beside her. "Well, this is the biggest surprise I've had since I left Hollywood," he said.

"I heard that you'd gone to join the R.A.F.," she said, "and I wondered if I might possibly run into you."

"How long have you been over here?" he enquired.

"Oh, about three months. When I left the States we had hopes of going to France, but ... " She shrugged her shoulders, "I think that it will be a long time before I shall see France again!"

"I just can't get over it," he said. "You, of all people - driving an ambulance! What about all those old ideas of yours? You know, dollars being the only thing that matters - and that sort of thing?"

He said this laughingly, but there was no laughter in her response. She spoke very quietly.

"After you had gone there was some trouble - in connection with that Academy of mine. There was a girl - only a kid really - who came to us with a wad of money and in the end we had it all. She was quite hopeless, screen possibilities were nil, but we kidded her along until we had everything. Then, when there were no more pickings, we tried to get rid of her. But she just hung around, saying that she just had to get something - must get some money somehow. We offered to pay her fare home just to get her out of the way, but she refused to go. So then we told her that she was the worst kind of a flop and wouldn't make anything in Hollywood if she stayed there until she was a hundred. She went away after that. The next thing I heard about her was a report in the paper that she had poisoned herself. Apparently she had stolen the money - the money that we had taken - and just couldn't go back. I killed that kid." She paused, and he could see that she was under the stress of a strong emotion. She went on, "Yes, I killed her as surely as if I had forced her to take the poison myself .... "

There was a catch in her voice and she just sat there staring through the windscreen. He did not say anything because he sensed that it was a relief for her to talk to someone about it. She sighed, "That made me see the whole thing for what it really was - a dirty, filthy, cheap racket. I took every cent we had and bought a fleet of these ambulances. You can see it on the side if you care to look - 'Presented by the Beverley Academy of California." Sometimes I think it is the only thing that spoils the ambulances. You know that I'd always been able to hide my association with the Academy - there had always been someone to front for me - so that I was not associated with the gift in any way. But I did manage to arrange for a provision to be made in regard to the nominations for certain drivers. Actually, there was only one nomination that I was interested in, and so - well, here I am!"

He leaned across and took her hand. "Good for you," he said. " I always knew that the hard mercenary person you tried so hard to be, wasn't the real you."

"Oh, do you really think so?" she asked. "Do you think that these," she indicated the ambulance in which they were sitting, "that these will do something to make up for all the disappointments and suffering that I have caused in the past?"

"I think it is a pretty wonderful thing you have done, Mavis. You've made a big sacrifice in giving up everything, and ... "

He was interrupted by the thin wailing note of a siren that rose and fell in a melancholy yet urgent warning.

They jumped from the ambulance, and above the noise of the siren they heard the throbbing note of aircraft high above them. Suddenly there was the shattering noise of powerful engines roaring into life on the aerodrome, and then plane after plane took off and climbed feverishly upwards and away.

The little black planes droning overhead circled in line and then dived down. Their speed was terrific - they rushed downwards growing larger and larger, making a tearing rushing scream like the tortured cries of a fiend in agony.

There was no time to run to shelter. "Down!" bawled Geoffrey. "Dive bombers!"

He fell flat in the roadway and rolled under the ambulance, dragging Mavis with him.

The screaming reached an unbearable crescendo - nerve-tearing, sickening. It was interspersed with dull, heavy thuds. Then the very roadway beneath them heaved and shuddered. Again and again. Bomb splinters screamed by, their whining noise broken by the chattering noise of machine-gun fire and the heavier less rapid reports of quick-firing anti-aircraft guns.

Several of the diving aircraft overshot their target and their bombs screamed on to burst squarely upon the little row of villas. Great clouds of plaster dust rose in the air, obliterating everything. It surged up the road, choking. It was in their eyes, their nostrils, their throats; dry, rasping. There was a discordant echoing of unrelated noises, yet each separate noise was one of destruction. The groaning and tearing of timber; the shriek of flying metal; the woolly noise of crumbling and disintegrating bricks and mortar; and still there was the noise of the scream of diving planes, the rush of falling bombs, explosions, the crackle of fire taking hold of old dry wood. Through all this they heard, or thought that they heard, the thin faint cries of human voices, bewildered, terrified. . . .

Then they were aware that the thunder of explosions, the scream and roar of planes had ceased. They crawled out from under the ambulance. They were streaked from head to foot with grey, dirty dust. In the ambulance there were several ugly jagged holes. They were unharmed.

The confusion was indescribable. In the soft earth were torn large gaping craters; grey, dust covered debris was scattered everywhere around them. Where, a few short minutes before, had stood a row of neat little villas was now only a flattened expanse of rubble. Nothing was standing. It was as if a giant hand had swept them down and had then smoothed over the destruction it had caused, levelling everything. Scarcely a thing was recognisable. Beyond a few piles of bricks, a twisted remnant of a baby-carriage, the end of an iron bedstead, there was nothing remaining of those once happy little cottages, or of their furnishings, or of the people who had lived in them. Over everything was that awful disfiguring pall of grey dust. Camouflaging, hiding .... It still swirled lazily in the air, settling slowly. At the end of the rubble flames were rushing from a broken gas-pipe, and nearby the fire licked hungrily along pieces of dry, torn wood. There was no sign of movement among all this devastation.

Then there were people rushing towards the ruined area clawing at the planks and rubble - searching. . . . Geoffrey and, Mavis saw all this as they ran, half-dazed, towards the destruction.

In the air Geoffrey had seen fighters diving on the bombers; had seen one bomber hurtling down in smoke and flames; as he ran he had shouted filthy words at it.

Already there was someone in charge. Giving hurried directions; indicating the piles of rubble that should be moved first.

Already they had discovered some poor, shattered bodies, as grey and unrecognisable under their pall of dust as the debris from which they had been lifted.

"Get that ambulance," they called to Mavis, and she turned and ran back towards it.

High above, Geoffrey heard the beating, pulsing note of more German aircraft. He paused in dragging away what had once been a shining enamelled bath, and looked up. Above him the aircraft were coming on, flying in broken formation; British fighters were diving and weaving among them. First one German plane and then another broke away, trying to escape. But others came on. Then once more the bombs screamed down. It was not so terrifying as the first attack. This time it was a high-level attack - to follow up the devastation of the dive-bombers. This time the aim was poor, with the fighters among them they were anxious to jettison their bombs and escape to safety.

Many of the bombs fell wide of the aerodrome, hundreds of yards away in the open fields.

The rescue work went on. Mavis had reached the ambulance and now it was bumping towards them, over the bomb-torn, debris-strewn roadway.

More bombs! The same rushing, whistling scream. They flung themselves down; pressing into the rubble of the ruined houses. Geoffrey raised his head and looked at the ambulance. It was still bumping slowly forward. Then there was a blinding, searing flash; a deafening, ear-splitting explosion.

The blast flung the ambulance through the air as if it had been a toy. It crashed bonnet first into the hedge at the side of the road, for a moment balanced drunkenly on the radiator, and then toppled over on to its side.

Great clods of earth and stones were falling on and around him as Geoffrey struggled to his feet and stumbled towards the wrecked ambulance. He was unhurt and yet somehow he had to force his legs to work. His feet felt like heavy leaden weights that had to be dragged forward.

His anguish, his exertion in dragging himself along, his frustration at his slow progress, made his breath come in short, sobbing gasps.

At last he was there. The ambulance was torn and battered. It was lying on its side where it had fallen; he climbed up and pulled feverishly at the door. It was bent inwards and jammed tight. He peered through the shattered safety glass in the door. He could see Mavis huddled grotesquely over the steering wheel. The wheel was pressing into her chest and the tunic of her uniform was soaked with blood-the blood was running down the steering column. He strained every muscle wrenching at the door, but it would not move. The window was too small for him to get through. He looked round to see if there was anyone who could help him to open the door, but everyone was pulling at the debris of the houses, or attending to others who had been hurt. In the roadway he saw a broken spade. The steel was bright and shining under the dust, and there was still about a foot of the wooden handle sticking jagged and splintered from the blade.

He seized it and rushed back to the ambulance. He forced the blade down between the edge of the door and the bodywork. Then he put all his weight on the short broken handle and levered. The door would not move. He put his knee on the handle and pushed with all his strength. The splintered wood drove sharp splinters into his knee and he felt the blood warm upon his leg. Slowly the door was forced open; he made a gap of about two inches at the top. But now the spade was flat against the body and he could not get a leverage. He flung the spade away and clawed fiercely at the door. The metal was torn with splinters and twisted into sharp jagged edges.

He strained until the muscles in his back shrieked in protest. His hands were torn and lacerated by the sharp metal, but slowly the door was wrenched open.

He lowered himself through the doorway, careful to avoid disturbing Mavis. He placed one foot on the steering column and with the other found a hold on the broken back of the driving compartment. He reached down and slid his hands beneath her armpits. Very gently he raised her and slowly lifted her up through the doorway.

He saw that her chest had been crushed and smashed on the steering wheel, and there surged through him a wave of pity and burning anger. In that moment he loved her. It was not that his love for Lesley was weakened or was lost. This love he felt, but did not understand, was something different - something quite apart. It was gratitude for the help she had given so unselfishly to his beleaguered country; the magnitude of her sacrifice; ineffable pity for her young body so cruelly broken. All these and other emotions combined within him to produce one desperate emotion; he would have done anything, suffered any agony, to have made her well again; he would willingly have given his life to save her.

Holding that small, limp, shattered body there was within him an agony of pain.

Then, wonderfully, she opened her eyes. Deep in their dark loveliness, down beyond the film of pain, he saw a growing look of puzzled wonder, like the look in the eyes of a child that wakes frightened in its sleep. She tried to speak but a thin trickle of blood ran from her mouth.

There were others to help him now, and very gently they lifted her down and laid her on some blankets which they spread at the roadside.

Geoffrey was on his knees beside her. Until the doctor came there was little that they could do.

She looked up at him and there was the faint shadow of a smile upon her lips.

He fumbled for his handkerchief and very gently wiped the blood from her mouth.

Slowly and with great difficulty she said, "Hold me, Geoffrey. Hold me close." He cradled her head in his arm and with his free hand smoothed the hair away from her forehead.

Tears welled into her eyes and ran down; tracing pitiful little lines in the dust on her face.

"It hurts so much," she said.

There was an awful sickness inside him, but he tried to force a smile and whispered, "Don't try to talk, Mavis. The doctor will be here in a moment .... "But she shook her head and his voice died away.

"There isn't much time," she said, and her voice was very faint. There was blood on her lips again and he wiped it away.

When she spoke again he had to bend his head close to her lips to catch her words.

"You don't despise me any more?"

"No! No, of course not. Of course not."

He wanted so much to help her, it was agony not to :e able to do anything. He heard himself whispering, "I love you, Mavis." The words sprang to his lips unbidden, he had not willed himself to speak them. Then he saw a faint dawn of happiness upon her face and he was glad.

"Truly?"

"I love you," he said again. It was impossible not to believe him.

"Will you kiss me?"

He kissed her warm, soft lips and for a moment she was very still in his arms. Then he felt the soft touch of her lashes against his face as she opened her eyes. He raised his head a little and looked down at her. Her eyes were very tender and he heard her whisper, "Darling." Then there was a gush of blood from her mouth, her body jerked convulsively, and her head fell back loosely on his arm.

Very tenderly he lowered her head; softly he closed the lids over her dark eyes. Blindly he moved away. There was the salt taste of blood upon his lips. With the back of one of his dirty, lacerated hands he tried to dash the tears from his unseeing eyes.

4

That attack upon the aerodrome and upon other aerodromes, heralded the opening of the Battle of Britain. His life went mad. There was no time to be tired; no time to think. Taking off in his Hurricane. Landing. refuelling; replenishing ammunition. Taking off again. Fighting; tearing; slashing. Wave-after wave of German planes. Feeling hopeless because there were always so many of them. Feeling triumphant because the sky was clear of them. Feeling sick, and feeling happy. Blasting, and being blasted at. Sad at the loss of old comrades; welcoming new ones.

Soaring, a speck in an infinity of space, he was conscious of a rhythm in his comings and goings in this illimitable vastness; in his fighting and flying and efforts to destroy. He seemed part of some mighty, spacious cosmic rhythm. Kill and destroy. Kill and destroy. A growing sense of mastery and conquest; a confidence of winning. Destruction and destruction. With paperboys marking up the number of planes destroyed as if it had been a Test Match. Three certain victories to his credit - and that one in Scotland. That made four - not bad.

The hollow voice of his radio telephone said: "Bridle calling Dragon Leader - Bridle calling Dragon Leader. Bandits approaching from the south-east." They wheeled in perfect formation. "Heights are now 15 ,000 to 20,000." He said aloud, "Right you bastards, this'll be my fifth!" His radio said: "Over to you - over."

Replying: "Your message received and understood." They were climbing hard now. He turned on the oxygen.

There they were, masses of them! As many as the day before and the day before that. Surely they could not face these losses for much longer. They were clearer now - Heinkels protected by fighters. Looking like a long line of dragonflies surrounded by swarms of tiny, dancing gnats. Never mind about the fighters! Into them and smash up that proud formation of Heinkels. Aah! This one should have the honour of being his fifth. All new and shiny looking. A short life and not even a merry one!

Closer, closer. Now! His sights right on the one he had selected as his prey. A steady pressure on the firing button - guns chattering. Hard to see if that burst was effective - too many planes about. Don't lose him. Again! A longer burst this time. That's got him! A plume of white smoke from the port engine . . . bits flying off now!

Hell! What was that? Those shuddering bangs? Great gashing holes appearing in his own starboard wing! Sweeping in towards him! Quick as thought moving inwards to the fuselage - and to him! God! Cannon shell from a Messerschmitt 109 on his tail. Machine gun bullets tearing his Hurricane now - he must do something. A blinding flash! Everything was black - he could not see. What was the matter with his head? It hurt. It hurt. Don't go under now! What was this wet sticky stuff on his hands and face? Blood? Yes, his blood - making the control column all slippery. He was too tired to do any more - just lay back and rest. No! No! That would be the end. Weave. Weave. Must report that he was in trouble - pull the radio lever to transmit. If only he could find it; if only there wasn't so much blood about everywhere; if only he could see - just for a moment. This was the end then. Had those others felt like this? Would Lesley know? Would she be sorry for him? Perhaps this was the best way after all. He was diving fast now - he could feel it. If only he could see - just that one moment of vision. Oh, it didn't matter. He was dreamy and tired, and his head hurt - it would soon be over now. Just one final almighty crash! No! Not that. Don't be a fool - just one more effort. Reach up and slide back that cockpit cover. Get out! Get out, somehow. Ah, that was better - cooler now. He felt wet all over. Was it sweat or blood? Still falling. God! he'd crashed. It wasn't so bad after all.

Impenetrable blackness rushed in upon him.

CHAPTER 15

1

ON the main road between London and Epping is a narrow side-turning that leads through a part of Epping Forest where the trees grow close together, and the undergrowth and bushes are thick and tangled, as one might expect them to be in forestland. It is one of the small parts remaining of that wide green belt, that has escaped being reduced, by the excursions of succeeding generations of Londoners, into something that had more the appearance of commonland or parkland than a forest.

It is a pleasant and peaceful path to follow, through the close-growing overhanging trees, until suddenly, it emerges from the forest into a narrow high-hedged road. There, quiet and secluded, with red-tiled roof and white-washed walls, is a small inn, known to the local inhabitants as the Fox, and to the casual visitor as the Fox and Duck, where one can obtain in an old dull pewter can, a pint of golden bitter or, should your fancy run the way of the more popular local taste, a pint of "old-and mild."

On this glorious August day there were no casual visitors at the Fox and Duck. Grouped outside the entrance to the Public Bar, were four locals and mine host. Four pints of old-and-mild stood neglected on the well-scoured wooden table outside the inn. Five pair of eyes were gazing with wrapt attention at a myriad of white smoky trails that turned and twisted in the blue vault above them. Shortly after they had assembled for the midday refresher, the mournful, wailing note of the Epping air-raid siren had drifted over forest and field into the bar of the Fox. A few moments later they had heard the dim pulsing note of aircraft and gathering up their beer had adjourned outside, accompanied by the proprietor, to watch the show.

"Only a measly eleven of the bastards down yesterday," said Jim, who was still damp with sweat from his work in the fields.

"Ay, but they'll be gettin' more to-day, from the looks o' things," replied old Tom, who was over seventy and didn't think much of this new-fangled way of fighting a war miles up in the skies.

"Eleven won't stop them, they got plenty more," said a thin young man, who was also a farm-worker, and was in the way of being the pessimist of the party .

"No, but there were a hundred and fifty-three a little while ago, and another hundred and fifty to-day, and to-morrow, and the day after that, will though," interposed a road patrol of one of the motoring organisations who had just ridden up on his bicycle, and joined the little group.

"There's one in trouble!" said the proprietor, as one of the feathery tracings started a steep downward dive.

"Can't tell by that," said the thin youth.

They went on watching. "Yes it is! You can see the plane now - look! There's black smoke coming out of it now!"

"There's another! Look - over there! Didn't see it at first looking at that other one. Blimey, it's all over the shop. It's only a small one - a fighter. Might be one of ours, Look! What's that?"

In the sky appeared a small white speck, gradually growing larger, until it looked like a daisy flung high against the bright blue vault of the sky.

"He's baled out!" said the proprietor.

"Yes, and what little wind there is will drift him this way," replied the road patrol.

Slowly the parachute descended until they could see the body suspended from it.

"It'll be down about two fields from here," said the road patrol and reached for his bicycle.

"I'll come with you," said the thin youth, who also had a bicycle propped outside the inn.

Together they set off cycling down the narrow road. In about a quarter of a mile they threw down their bicycles and clambered through the hedge. The parachute was almost down.

"Coming down in the next field," panted the thin youth. They set off running across the field. As they reached the next hedge, they saw the parachute jerk and then settle down slowly like a deflated balloon. The hedge was very thick and it took them a few moments to find a way through.

"There he is!" they shouted together.

They ran towards the parachute which was now spread out on the ground like a big tumbled white sheet. When they saw the man stretched on the ground they both felt sick. His face was covered with blood; blood had run down his face on to his clothes and soaked in; on his forehead was a long searing cut, blood was still seeping out.

"He's a goner - one of ours too. Poor devil!" exclaimed the thin youth, his face twisted in an expression blending pity and revulsion.

"Don't talk so bloody silly," said the road patrol, "give me a hand here!"

They unhitched the harness. The patrol loosened the clothes at the airman's neck, and wiped some of the blood from his face. He cradled the dark head in his arm, and made a hurried examination.

"He's only knocked out," he said, "get off and get an ambulance as quick as you can." He was already unrolling his first aid kit. The thin youth hared across the field towards his bicycle. When he had gone the patrol said softly, "You'll be all right, laddie. Right enough, anyway, to have another go at those dirty swine!" Tenderly he cleaned away the blood on the young man's face, and staunched the ugly wound in his forehead. Not until he heard the urgent sound of the gong on the ambulance, as it swept down the little country road, did he take away his arm which supported the head with its dark waving hair.

Then he stood up so that they could see where he was.

2

Geoffrey awakened in the hospital with a splitting headache. It was worse than the worst hang-over he had ever known. He was rather surprised, when he opened his eyes, that he did not wonder where he was, or what had happened to him. He knew right away that he was in a hospital, and he had a vivid recollection of those last few horrible moments in the plane. Those moments when he had been diving headlong towards the earth were very clear, but he had only a misty, confused recollection of clambering out, and of his parachute opening above him. After that his mind was a blank. It must have been when the parachute had opened out and had broken his headlong fall with a violent jerk that he had lost consciousness.

Cautiously he moved his arms and legs; they seemed all right, anyway. He put his hand to his head and pressed lightly upon the bandages which swathed his forehead, where the pain was greatest. The sudden agony that followed his pressure made him bite on his lip to stop calling out. As the fierce pain died away he sighed with relief; the dull, throbbing, aching pain which still went on was easily bearable after the shooting agony he had known a moment before. He opened his eyes again and saw a nurse smiling down at him.

"Hallo," she said, " so you're awake at last? You've just had your longest sleep for a good many weeks now." She laughed. "In fact, I expect it is the longest sleep you ever had - two days and two nights without waking!"

"Two days ...?" he echoed incredulously. "Yes, and two nights," she said.

He attempted a thin whistle of amazement, but his lips were too parched and dry.

" Is this serious·?" he asked, 'pointing to his forehead. "No," she said, shaking her head, "you are one of the lucky ones. Another" - she measured a tiny distance between her thumb and forefinger - "and well ... " she shrugged her shoulders.

"Well, thank the Lord for that. Is there anything else - anywhere?" he asked.

"No, just your head," she said. "The bullet must have hit your plane and then glanced off and cut right across your forehead. It's made a nasty deep cut, and, of course, the bone is pretty badly bruised, but in a few days you'll be as right as rain again."

"Well, that's good news, anyway. The way my head feels I thought that it must have a hole in it large enough for me to put my hand in!"

"Oh, I expect that you'll have a nasty headache for quite a little while," she said, smiling at him sympathetically. "Now I must go and let the doctor know that you're awake, and then when he's seen you I expect he'll want you to go off to sleep again."·

"Sleep again! Good heavens, you've just told me that I've been asleep for two days and nights already - you can't want me to go to sleep again after all that?"

" 'Fraid so," she said, "you see, in a minute or two you'll think it is quite a good idea yourself."

When she had gone to fetch the doctor he was surprised to find that he was glad to close his eyes again, and when the door opened and. the doctor came in he was quite drowsy.

He waited until the doctor had finished his examination and then. said, "How long ...?"

"My questions first please," said the doctor, with a smile. "How are you feeling now?"

"Oh, I feel fine - head aches a bit, but otherwise okay."

"No pain directly behind the eyes, or in the ears?"

"No. Just in the front here." He pointed to his forehead. "It feels as if a little devil were sitting up on my head banging away with a hammer!"

Then, as an afterthought, he added: "And I feel darned thirsty."

The doctor motioned to the nurse, and she poured some water into a glass and held it for him.

Whilst he was drinking the doctor said, "Well, I suppose that you were going to ask me how long you will have to stay here?"

Geoffrey nodded,

"Oh, in three or four weeks we should have you up and around again."

"Three or four weeks!" exploded Geoffrey, and tried to raise his head from the pillow. It felt as if a gigantic mallet had descended violently upon his skull; he sank back gasping at the sudden black shrieking pain.

He was faintly aware of the doctor saying, "Now don't get excited. Just take it easy and relax. You'll be more comfortable here, and we can't afford to have anything happening to you fellows now, you know."

"Okay, doctor, you win," he said, and closed his eyes. He felt very tired again.

He roused himself for a moment and said, "How are things going, doctor? You know ... "

"Wonderful. Eighty-eight yesterday and sixty-two the day before - your day. They've confirmed the one that you got. Two of your squadron saw you get it, and it crashed not far from here." ·

Geoffrey was elated; but all the same he could not keep his eyes open a moment longer. When his eyes were closed it was as if he was staring into a great void, a void that was a soft reddish brown in colour; in the distance there was a small flaming spot that came rapidly towards him, growing and growing until he could see that it was a flaming figure five. It came on and on - triumphant. ... Then he fell asleep.

He was awakened by the small capable hand of the nurse shaking his shoulder. "Come along," she said, "you can't sleep all the time, you know. I did say go to sleep, but after all .... "

She was setting another pillow behind him as she spoke, and then he realised that she had lifted his shoulders, and that his head was off the pillow and that there had not been that sudden awful rush of pain. There was a throbbing in his head, but it was no worse than an ordinary headache; his forehead felt hard and stiff but the painful burning sensation had gone.

"There - that's better," she said. "You'll have to eat now - to get your strength back, you know."

Suddenly he was aware that he was ravenously hungry.

3

At the end of his first week in hospital he was able to sit up in a chair, and at the end of a fortnight he was allowed to sit in the garden. His wound healed rapidly and he felt quite fit again; except for one thing.

Sometimes, when he was sitting quietly in the sunshine, a squadron of British fighting planes would roar overhead. If they were flying low he would find the roar and whine of their engines almost unbearable. He would feel the blood mounting to his head and throbbing in his wound, and there would be a roaring noise in his ears that continued long after the planes disappeared into the far distance. When he looked at his hands he would be horrified to find them shaking and unsteady. He mentioned his distress to the doctors, and they told him not to worry, and said that a nervous reaction was not at all unusual after the experience he had undergone.

During the succeeding two weeks he was anxious to be away, but although his forehead no longer needed treatment, and it was healing rapidly, and when the bandages were removed it showed only as a red, angry scar, the doctor still kept him under close observation. His nervous attacks became less frequent and affected him less violently, but the periods when he found that his nerves were still far from being under complete control, left him with a feeling of intense frustration and annoyance.

The nurse whom he had first seen when he had recovered consciousness in the hospital, continued to attend to his needs. She was young, and, he discovered, somewhat romantically inclined. One day, when he was sitting in the garden lazily enjoying the sun and thinking that it was, after all, rather pleasant to be able to sit and rest and think and just do nothing, without feeling that one was shirking a job that had to be done, his nurse turned to him and surprised him by saying, "When they brought you in here, you kept on muttering, 'Lesley. Lesley.' Lots of people that are brought in here murmur somebody's name when they are ill or have had a shock or an injury, but it seemed unusual for you to be murmuring a man's name - if you see what I mean. And then once or twice you would say, 'Lesley, darling ... ' and I must confess that for a while I was quite mystified. When I saw your name it seemed to remind me of something, but I couldn't exactly place what it was. Something in this paper I am reading has almost brought it back to me. There is something in here about Lesley Travis the film-star - weren't you married to her in Hollywood?" She said this last part almost breathlessly, as if she was afraid that he might deny it and disappoint her.

He smiled that old winning smile of his and said, "Yes, as a matter of fact, we were. But that was a long time ago. I haven't seen her for nearly a year now."

"Gosh, isn't that wonderful," she said, as if it was all too good to be true. What a story it would be to tell her girl friends.

"Tell me, is she as wonderful off the screen as she is on?" she enquired.

"More wonderful if anything," he replied. "But how on earth did you remember about me after all this time?"

Suddenly a new thought flashed into his mind; he glanced hurriedly at the paper she was holding. Perhaps it was something about Lesley's divorce - perhaps his own name was mentioned in the report - that would account for his nurse remembering ....

He heard her saying, "Oh, it wasn't difficult really. You see I'm one of her greatest 'fans' and I read everything I can about her. Naturally I read all about her marriage, and when I saw this bit in the paper about her latest film, well, it all just came back to me. See?"

"May I?" he asked, and held out his hand for the paper. It was a critique of Lesley's latest film that had just been released in the West End of London. He started to read it, but gave it up in the face of the interruptions of a dozen questions that came tumbling from the lips of his young nurse.

She wanted to know all about Hollywood and Hollywood people, and she was so sincere, and so obviously regarded Lesley as quite one of the most wonderful people in this world, that for the rest of the afternoon he told her about film-studios, and related some of his experiences in the film-city, and answered the questions that bubbled forth incessantly.

When at last it was time for them to go indoors she said, "Oh, I wish that you weren't going away from here for ages and ages - oh,

I don't mean that! I mean - perhaps if you were going to be here for a long time *she* would come here to see you! I'd love just to meet her."

Geoffrey laughed good-naturedly. "I'm afraid that there wouldn't be much chance of her getting to England now, however long I stayed here. But I'll promise you one thing, my dear, if ever Lesley Travis does come to England to see me, I'll make a special point of bringing her to meet you."

"Oh, would you really?"

"Of course - it would be the very least I could do after you have been so kind to me. But don't forget, Miss Hopkins - if she comes to England, and I am afraid that it is a very big 'if' indeed."

When he reached the privacy of his own room, he read the critique of Lesley's film. It was being screened at the Colossal - the very cinema where he had seen that other film in which Lesley had starred. It seemed so very, very long ago.

The critic had been generous in his praises: " ... Lesley Travis reaches new heights in her career, and sets a new standard for emotional acting upon the screen ... it is a long time since I have been so enthralled by acting so sincere, so real, as to make me forget everything but the film I was watching - in fact, to forget that it was a film. It will make you forget, for a little while, the troubled days through which we are now passing, and help you to remember despite all the hatred, horror and brutality which strikes at us to-day, that there are in this world such things as love, tenderness and decency .... "

4

They allowed him to leave the hospital at the end of the fourth week. There were two doctors to give him a final and exhaustive examination, and in the end they pronounced him quite well again, except that he needed rest - lots of rest. For the next two months they said, he must go away somewhere and rest; somewhere that was quiet, and that he must do nothing but just rest and laze about.

He rebelled a little at that. "Two months, doctor? Why, that's almost a lifetime in these days! I just can't stay grounded for as long as that!"

The doctor was sympathetic but adamant. "Sorry, old man, but there it is. Two months is the very minimum I'm afraid. If you take it easily and really rest - not go dashing about having a good time - then perhaps at the end of that time we shall be able to say that you are fit to fly again, but certainly not before then."

Geoffrey grinned a little ruefully. "Well, if that's the way it is, there's not much I can do about it, is there, doctor? Anyway, thanks a million for all that you have done for me, you've fixed the old napper as good as new and I'm eternally grateful to you."

He shook hands with both of them, but when he reached the door he paused and said, "I'll be so lazy and get so much sleep during the next few weeks that I'm willing to bet you a level fiver that I'll be back on the job again within a month!"

His doctor laughed good-naturedly, "I won't take your money," he said, "but whatever happens come and have dinner with me one evening and if you're right I'll stand you a bottle of the best - if you lose then the beer will be on you."

"You're on," said Geoffrey, and the door closed behind him.

When he had gone his doctor turned to his younger colleague, "That was the easiest fiver I'll ever have the chance of making," he said. "Damned bad luck, but he won't be flying again in two months - or in two years for that matter. Anyway, he won't if I'm correct in the way I see things, and I think that I am."

"But two years?" ventured his colleague. "I know that his nerves are a bit shot, but after all, he's fit enough, and when he's had a chance to rest .... "

"Oh, yes. He'll be fit enough for most things, but he's had a nasty experience - that crack on the head wasn't everything. . . . " He shook his head. " I should think that his nerves have been under a strain for a long time. There's something on his mind." They were moving towards the door. "Then all this on top of it ... No, I'm afraid that it's going to be a long time. But he seems a bright kind of fellow, sort of capable, I don't suppose that they'll have any difficulty in finding something really useful for him to do."

5

When Geoffrey left the hospital, he knew that the first thing that he wanted to do was to see Lesley's new film. But all the same he did not hurry straight to the Colossal Cinema. He went slowly, anticipating his coming pleasure, like a schoolboy storing up a very special treat.

He caught a fussy old steam train to Liverpool Street Station, and then went by Underground to Marble Arch, just so that he could have the pleasure of walking down Park Lane to Piccadilly, and then right along that busy thoroughfare until he reached the Circus.

He took deep breaths of London air and felt that he was home once again. The red 'buses and squat taxis were like old friends; if only Lesley were here then everything would be perfect, despite the wailing sirens and the uncertainty of everything. The sun and the pavement were hot; the grass in the park looked dry and dusty; there was a smell of petrol exhaust, and sometimes, when he passed the entrance to an hotel, a smell of food and perfume and cigar smoke, all blending together. He loved it; loved the smell, and noise, and bustle, and pretty women, and all the people in uniform. It was his city and he loved it. He loved it even more than usual to-day because it seemed that he had been away from it for so long, and because he knew, that if he was to get well again so that he could get back, then he would have to leave London with its noise and bustle and find somewhere quiet where he could relax. But before that he would have just one more lunch in London - where should he go? The Ivy? Yes, that was a good idea. Then he would go to Lesley's film and then have dinner at. . . . Now where should he have dinner? Well, there was no hurry about that. He could decide when he had seen the film.

He reached Piccadilly Circus and waited for the traffic-lights to change, in order that he might cross in comparative safety. He had always objected to crossing the Circus by the subway - there were so many exits, and although they were all clearly marked, somehow he always seemed to come up at the wrong place.

He circled round, passing Regent Street and Shaftesbury Avenue, and then walked on towards Leicester Square. He stopped outside the Colossal and looked at the "stills" from the film which were exhibited outside. Lesley was as lovely as ever. Then he read the time-sheet and glanced at his watch. Lesley's film was due to start at 2.45 and it was now 12.30. Ample time for him to lunch at leisure and return unhurried to the cinema. He bought a paper and walked on.

At twenty minutes to three he bought his ticket. How well he remembered the luxury of the Colossal, with its soft carpets laid on the softest of sponge rubber; the elegance; the tasteful decorations.

He saw the last few minutes of a film portraying an attack by Nazi airmen on some unarmed fishing trawlers. It was so exciting and true to life that he was sorry that he had not come earlier. He thought that perhaps he could wait and see it through again, and decided that he would, unless this meant that he would have to sit through an interlude of music on the "mighty organ."

And then all he could think was, "Oh, Lesley, Lesley. How wonderful you are!" She was there, almost real and alive; lovely, vivacious. At first he was unable to follow the film for watching her; listening to her voice. It seemed so normal, so right, to hear her talking again, to see once again all those little mannerisms. Gradually he found himself becoming interested in the story of the film. In this part she was so much in character with herself -the real Lesley Travis. She had George Bernard as her leading man - in the film she called him Geoffrey -strange that this film name should be the same as his own. It made little things that she said seem somehow personal. He had only to close his eyes for a moment and to hear her speak his name, for them to be back together again - back in those happy carefree days.

But in a little while there was something that jarred upon him. Lesley was listening to a declaration of love from George Bernard, but it was not this that stirred something within him; gave him a feeling of disquiet. Lesley and her screen-lover had ridden together into the hills, and had dismounted near a lovely cascading waterfall. This had been Indian country George Bernard explained - the Indians had had a legend about this waterfall. Lovers who plighted their love within sound of its tumbling waters would be forever favoured by the great god of the Dancing Water. If they should be parted, and one should come to the Dancing Water (that name again!) and speak, then their words, even though they had to travel around the world, would be carried, swift and sure as an arrow to the heart of the absent lover.

They had been too much in love to laugh at this old legend. Lesley had said that if ever he had gone from her, and that she needed him, then she would come again to the waterfall and speak to him within the sound of the Dancing Water.

"The Dancing Water." It was uncanny that the name that had meant so much to him should be in the film - had it been in the original script he wondered? That name, and his own name, together in this film with Lesley. She must have known. Was this her way of laughing at him? Hurting him? No, there had been nothing in the film to suggest that - nothing. It was coincidence that was all.

He brought his mind back to the film. They were married and for a time they were ideally happy. Then, gradually, came misunderstandings, and finally a terrible quarrel, and she was left alone. There was nothing brilliant in the story, but many successful films had been founded on a similar formula. It was the quality of the acting that would make this film an outstanding success. Lesley was magnificent - her portrayal of the grief and loneliness that engulfed her when her husband had gone, tore at his very heart. At last she went again to the Dancing Water and spoke softly - her voice barely audible above the noise of the turbulent water.

The camera moved in to a close-up; now her voice was soft and clear. It was a most unusual technique. It was almost as if she was looking at the audience - speaking to them.

"Oh, Geoffrey. Geoffrey, my darling. Am I mad to hope that you will hear me and understand? I was foolish, cruel, to let you go unhappy and alone. But I have suffered heartache and loneliness beyond all imagining."

Geoffrey moved uncomfortably, his face was burning. It was as if Lesley was speaking to him of private things, speaking to him in front of all these people. Oh, this was unbearable! But no one had moved, or looked at him. Of course they hadn't. Nobody knew him here. All around him was only a quiet rapt attention on the screen. He cursed himself for his foolishness. His thoughts had taken but a fleeting moment, but he had missed a little of what she had said.

Again he had that strange feeling that of all the people in the theatre she was speaking only to him. He heard the voice that he knew and loved so well saying: "I have tried so hard to find you. And now at last I am here saying that I love you, that I have always loved you. Asking you to forgive me and come back to me. Oh, Geoffrey, Geoffrey dearest, I am here - here at the Dancing Water - waiting for you!"

At last realisation burst upon him, crashing and flooding over him in a deluge that left him shaken and breathless. Lesley was speaking to him; this was the way she had found to tell him - to declare her love again! He wanted to jump up and shout aloud; to dance and cheer, but he could not move, it was as if he was paralysed in his seat.

He heard Lesley saying, " ... every day I shall wait for you - at the Dancing Water - until you come to me."

His mind reeled. Lesley was in England - in England waiting for him - at the cottage, at their very own "Dancing Water."

Suddenly he came alive again. By good fortune he was at the end of the row, but as he leaped into the gangway there were many angry curious glances thrown in his direction. He started up the sloping gangway and then remembered his respirator and tin-hat which he had left under the seat. Cursing he retraced his steps and fumbled for them.

"Quiet," said an angry voice nearby.

"Sorry," muttered Geoffrey, and fled.

Outside the theatre he paused for a moment, bewildered. He must get to the cottage without delay. Train? No, that was hopeless. Sitting in a carriage, waiting, waiting, doing nothing while the train meandered slowly to its destination. That would drive him mad.

Thank goodness he had kept his car licensed. He hailed a taxi and said, "Fisher's Garage - quick as you can!

As he sat on the edge of the seat in the taxi he suddenly wondered whether he would have enough petrol for the journey. He worked it out. He had kept the car at Fisher's garage since he had been moved near to London. It had been useful for running about in London, especially in these days when taxis were so hard to get. He had put the whole of his August ration in the tank - there hadn't been much time for him to use the car in those hectic days! Then he had been in hospital for a month and his September ration was untouched. Yes, he could manage all right. Driving the car would at least be something to relieve this agony of apprehension from which he was suffering.

"Fisher's garage, sir," said the taxi-driver.

Geoffrey gave him half-a-crown and dashed into the garage; it was not quite five o'clock.

"Hallo, sir," said the garage attendant, "we'd almost given you up. Haven't seen you for weeks. Suppose they've been keeping you pretty busy, eh?"

"Busy enough, anyway, Jim," replied Geoffrey. "Look old man, I've got to get going right away. Is the old bus okay to go?"

"Sure she is. Battery, tyres, oil - everything's first class. It'll take me a few minutes to get it out though, As you haven't been using her, we've parked her right at the back - out of the way. I'll start shifting 'em now."

"I'll give you a hand," said Geoffrey.

It seemed an age before he was at last able to jump into the driving seat of his own car. He switched on the ignition; the engine pulsed to life at the first touch of the starter button.

Geoffrey fumbled for his petrol ration book. "Put my month's ration in the tank Jim, will you?" he said, and waited impatiently while the needle of the electric delivery pump swung slowly round.

He gave Jim the petrol coupons and a pound note. "Thanks Jim, keep the change," he said, and let in the clutch.

He fumed at every traffic-light and cursed at the traffic. It seemed an eternity before he was clear of London and the open road stretched invitingly before him. He opened up the car and swept up to an effortless sixty. It was a Buick drop-head coupe, 1938 vintage, that he had picked up for a song shortly after he had returned to England. Since his sojourn in America he had developed a liking for American cars.

The rush of the wind and the steady throb of the engine was music in his ears. The road was wide and straight and there was little traffic; he increased his pressure upon the accelerator pedal. The needle crept round to seventy.

The noise of the tyres on the road, the rushing wind, and the hum of the engine, combined to make a rhythmic sound that beat upon his ears and repeated over and over again: "Lesley's waiting. Lesley's waiting." It was too wonderful to be true. Lesley waiting for him! Lesley waiting at the cottage. His heart filled with happiness - a happiness that was akin to pain.

Suddenly he shivered, as if the wind was cold. Supposing she was not there! Supposing she had planned to come and something had happened to prevent her? Perhaps she had been refused permission to come to England. He might after all have misunderstood - perhaps it had not been a message for him in the film. . . . Oh, but that was impossible! Everything had been so clear. Yes. Yes. Yes. Lesley would be there. She must be there!

The miles fled by, as fast as his racing thoughts.

They might try to stop him getting to the cottage. It was in a defence area. But he would get through. He had a good story. He was convalescent - on sick-leave - the cottage was his home; his only home now .... Yes, he would manage all right.

The sun was near to setting and the red glow was reflected on his windscreen; the miles clicked up on the recorder. He drove fast, reducing speed only through the villages and built-up areas.

The last lap - not long now! His hands were gripping the wheel so that his knuckles showed white and tense; it seemed that he was urging the car forward by the very intensity of his own impatient desire.

Saltern village! Just a few moments now - and then?

He swung the car on to the gravel road. Slowly now - passing the little cottage where Elsa Knight had lived with Bobby before he had gone away. The cottage was dark and silent now. Round the bend, the tyres slithering noisily on the loose gravel. The cottage at last! There it was, lovely in the fading light of approaching dusk. It was difficult for him to see clearly through the dusty windscreen. Someone - a woman in a light summer dress - was running to the gate. She must have heard the noise of the car on the road.

He braked, and was out of the car almost before it was at a standstill. She was running towards him now! Oh, God! This was too much. His heart sang in a delirium of ecstasy. In his arms, sobbing and laughing all together, was Lesley, Lesley, Lesley!

He held her close against his pounding heart, showering kisses upon her. They could not speak; this emotion was too strong for words.

At length he murmured, "Lesley darling, at last," but she could only look up at him, tears brimming in her lovely grey-blue eyes, her lips trembling, and shake her head as if she could not believe he was really and truly there, holding her in his arms.

And so for long minutes he held her trembling body until she was calm again, and his own heart pounded less frantically.

At last, and very gently, she released herself from his encircling arms, and held him away from her. "Geoffrey, my husband. You look so grand." With her finger-tips she touched lightly upon the silver wings upon his breast. "I'm so proud of you; so humble before you. I love you so very, very much."

He made a movement as if to take her in his arms again, but very gently she held him away.

She said: "Darling, have you forgiven me. . . .?"

"There was never anything to forgive. I have loved you every minute - every second - since that first evening so long ago. I have never stopped loving you - not even for a moment. . . . " She no longer resisted him as he swept her into his arms.

Then she said, "Elsa will wonder what on earth has happened. We must go in now." She linked her arm in his and drew him towards the gate.

"Elsa has been wonderful to me. She told me everything that she knew, and that you still . . . cared for me. But it has seemed so long waiting for you. You got my . . . my message?"

"Just a few hours ago, darling. I came right here. It was wonderful of you .... "

The door of the cottage closed behind them.

6

The morning dew was still upon the grass as Bobby tumbled in the garden, impatient for the appearance of his Uncle Geoff - for stories of Hurricanes and Spitfires.

In the kitchen the whole week's bacon ration sizzled enticingly in the pan, as Elsa prepared breakfast. She thought, "Thank God they are together again - that he is happy again .... "

In the bedroom the early morning sun streamed in through the window, there was the soft splashing sound of the waves on the beach, a few gulls were sending their shrill mewing cries in little brittle bursts of sound. Lesley swept the fair hair from her eyes, and looked down at Geoffrey at her side. He was sleeping, with his dark hair all tumbled on the pillow. She saw where the bullet from the Messerschmitt had traced a livid furrow across his brow; death's own sign of death defeated.

Her eyes filled with tears, "O thank You, God," she said. "Thank You for sending him back to me."

THE END

Printed in Great Britain
by Amazon